M000309182

Souls Harbor is a work of fiction.

And similarities to any living individual or events, real or imagined are purely coincidental.

Any unauthorized use of some or all of this book is strictly prohibited without expressed

written consent.

A note from the author:

Hello dear reader,

First of all, let me thank you for opening up my work. I hope you enjoy reading it. This book took me all of 2019 to write, edit, and put forth to you. That might seem quick to some, and like a long time to others, but for me, it felt like a long time. I won't pretend that I'll enthrall you like the masters, but I am a simple man and I write simply. The thing that captivates me most is the human spirit and its ability to adapt to even the harshest of conditions and situations.

In this book there are several such conditions that may seem severe to some, but the sad reality is that things like these happen every day. The flipside of the human spirit's ability to endure and adapt, is the level of depravity and cruelty that we humans are capable of, especially towards each other.

If you read this book and are entertained, moved, and touched in some way, then good. I have done my job. The truth of the matter is that our lives are complicated beyond the ability of a stranger to understand, so a little kindness and love, or just being there for someone, will go a long way.

PROLOUGE

"What was that?" Cara asked aloud, the car horn still blaring in her ears as she staggered along the narrow roadside on the edge of town.

"Shut up!" said a loud, angry voice from the darkness of her mind.

"Please just stop!" The pleading scream sounded like her voice.

"What's wrong with you?" asked the old woman, her coarse voice dripping with venom.

"Nothing." Cara squinted, the sunlight hurting her eyes. "Nothing."

"Retard!" Silence followed the young boy's voice.

"I'm not a retard."

"Crazy Cara." The boy's voice was always teasing and vile. In many ways, his was the worst of the people who talked to her.

"I'm not crazy!" Cara pushed her palms against her temples to quiet the voices. The oversized flannel shirt she wore flapped in the wind of another passing car.

"Crazy, Crazy, Craaaazy!" the boy said.

"Crazy ass bitch!" the old woman said.

"I just need to find them."

An old man laughed. "You need a lot of things. For starters a straitjacket!"

"Please stop." The mousy voice came from deep in her memory.

"Mama help me. Please." Cara rubbed her eyes and wiped her hands on her dirty jeans.

The old woman cackled. "Well, mama's dead now!"

"Please let me alone…" More a whine than anything else.

Everyone else in her head ignored her almost as much as they ignored the quiet, small voice that was nice to her—the one from the little black girl who came to her sometimes when the others were being so loud.

The sound of chains rattling thundered through her head like a battleship dropping anchor. She cringed and covered her head with her hands as she stumbled through the wild grasses alongside the road.

"Mama's dead. You're the mama now," the old man said. "Don't you remember?" A chorus of laughter echoed through Cara's head. "You remember the fire, don't you?"

As she tripped over one of the innumerable anthills that lined the road, Cara's body waivered, and she almost lost her balance. The jolt as her body reacted snatched her back from within herself, if only momentarily.

That and the car horn booming in her ears as it sped by in a gray blur, its driver screaming out the open passenger window. She didn't know what he said, but she knew they were angry words. Angry words from an angry man. That she was used to.

She watched it tear down the road, its muffler roaring as loud as the horn. Her gaze followed it through a curtain of hair **that had fallen across her face** until it reached the intersection of the road she was on and another road. The car braked hard and disappeared around the corner.

"I don't like him," her mind said.

"You don't like anybody," she replied aloud.

"I like you," the old woman said sarcastically.

"Then why are you always trying to kill me?"

The voices had no answer.

Cara pushed her hair, more just dirty than dirty blonde, out of her face and looked down at the ants swarming out of the hill she'd disturbed. For a long time, she stared at them, allowing their movements to blur her vision and give her a sense of falling from a great height. It was like being close to a waterfall, hearing nothing but the white noise of the water.

Falling, only hearing the wind roar as she fell through it. Wind, white noise. Nothing else. Eventually, you wouldn't even hear the wind. It turned into silence, drowning out everything else. Everybody else.

She stared for a long while, oblivious to the cars that passed a few feet from her. Some people shouted out the window, and one even tossed an empty Mountain Dew bottle at her. The teenagers in the car laughed despite the bottle missing her.

"Nasty bastards." She spat on the ant hill before stomping it again.

Turning from the road, she began to make her way down a small embankment. The spring growth of kudzoo was turning into a ravenous assault on the hillside. One of the vines wrapped around her ankle. She lost her footing and tumbled once, then regained an unsteady balance. As she reached the bottom of the hill, she unzipped her filthy, oversized jeans, pushed them to her ankles, squatted, and urinated.

Above her on the road, another car's horn blared.

"That's five points!" one of the men said. "I just saw Crazy Cara pissing."

If every southern town had a designated "town crazy," then Cara was Souls Harbor's. So much so that some people kept a running tally for when they saw her. No one really knew who she was or ever tried to find out. The young kids couldn't remember a time when she hadn't been there, but the older ones, the ones around her own age of twenty, might have remembered if they ever took a notion to. They might remember the little girl she'd once been before her world slipped into the dark place.

They might remember a little girl with blond hair and bright blue eyes or that she'd ridden the school bus with them or that she was in their class. They might have remembered who she was if they took the time to remember. But they didn't remember, and most days neither did she.

The people who didn't harass her drove past with little more than a pitiful glance, assuming her to be another drug-addled homeless person they didn't know and didn't want to know. As with a lot of small towns, Souls Harbor had grown. Not everybody knew everybody, and most people were fine with that. There were some people you didn't want to know.

In Souls Harbor, the Cara sighting scale was simple: One point was a plain Cara sighting. Two if she was talking to herself. Three if she was in the city limits. Four if she was outside the city limits. Five if she was using the bathroom. And finally, the coup de grâs, six if you could tell if 'the drapes matched the carpet'. No one ever claimed a six except Tommy Bream. He walked into Tanks just before closing time, looking like he'd been in a fight, and proclaimed that he'd just gotten a six and that Crazy Cara was "au naturel." Nobody asked many questions. Tommy was a mean drunk, and he was already loaded when he'd walked into the place. It was just Crazy Cara anyway.

ONE

Evelyn closed her suitcase, took one last look around the bedroom of her tiny apartment, and sighed. She didn't want to leave, but she knew it was better this way after what happened. Taking in a deep breath, she fought back the wave of emotions threatening to consume her. She was running away, and she knew it, but it couldn't be helped. There were some things that look better from a distance and just now, her life at the University of North Central Alabama was one of them.

Months of guilt were weighing on her and she needed a break. She felt like a different person- a person she didn't like. Her grades were suffering, her friends were worried about her, and her personal life felt forced. She was slowly becoming consumed by her own mind, her own thoughts, and she simply couldn't take it anymore.

Aaron leaned against the door frame, his eyes falling on the young, athletic woman in the process of packing her suitcase. Even in such a miserable moment, she was a vision of beauty. Things had changed between them. There was a distance that hadn't been there before. Her usual, carefree spirit was pensive and solemn. She was barely the Eve he knew and loved.

In the months they'd dated, he'd never given much thought to the fact that they came from different races; different cultures, but lately he'd began to wonder if the change in her was somehow related to those differences. Admittedly, she was the first woman of color that he'd ever been with, but it seemed unlikely. He was grasping at straws to try and figure it out before she left, so maybe he could change her mind.

"That should just about do it," he said.

Evelyn startled, then turned with a hand on her chest. "Oh my God! You scared me. I thought you were still downstairs."

Looking at him, she felt her heart lift a little. She'd never seriously considered marrying a man of a different race before, but if things were different, if things hadn't worked out the way they had, she could see herself with him for a very long time. Maybe even forever.

Growing up as a tall, gangly girl was bad enough, but growing up as a tall, gangly, black girl with way too much hair in a small town named Souls Harbor in rural Alabama was, as they say, "a whole 'nother story". Nestled in the woods of west central Alabama along the banks of the Black Warrior River, Souls Harbor's only major exports were coal, timber, and people who never look back. It wasn't a perfect place to grow up but being from a small town had imprinted several characteristics deep within her psyche. Truth, honesty, and loyalty were three that had been hammered into her by her parents, by her preacher, and by every adult that was in her life.

She'd managed to break all three in one fail swoop and had been for months now.

"Eve, You okay?" Aaron asked as he pushed off the door frame and walked into the room.

"Thanks. I'm okay, just spaced for a minute there," she said with a sigh, avoiding his gaze. That was happening a lot lately. Her mind would just dump information on her, reminding her how much she'd hurt the people who loved her most, even if they didn't know it yet. She didn't have the strength to look at him anymore.

Looking at Aaron Deavours, the corners of her mouth gave way to a sad smile. Theirs was a whirlwind romance, almost magical. Her girlfriends were all jealous, not only because he was tall, smart, and handsome but also because he was kind and gentle and always treated her with respect. He cherished her, and it showed, leaving her convinced he was one of the few remaining good guys left in the world. Aaron was a happy soul that loved to make her laugh; what her mother would call "good people".

Looking at him, she remembered how enamored he was with her skin every time they made love. He always took his time and caressed her body, watching his fingers trail over her features with quiet adoration that transcended the usual sexual interactions she had in the past. It was as if he was creating a topographical map of her body in his mind. He didn't even mind when, occasionally, she'd be so relaxed that she fell asleep.

"I had the most beautiful woman in the world in my bed all night, naked. What's to be mad about?" he said after the first time she'd nodded off on him. The sincerity in his eyes told her he meant it and she knew she'd never forget the way he looked at her.

"You still with us?" Aaron asked.

"Yeah. I'm still here," she answered with another sigh.

"Was that a smile?" he asked as he put his hands on the curve of her hips, pulling her close. "Those have been rare lately. What cha thinking about?"

Evelyn forced a smile for his sake. "I don't know. Nothing. Everything." She shrugged and slid her hands around his stout waist. She was tall at five-seven, but he was taller by six inches and her head fell perfectly on his chest, allowing him to rest his chin on the top of her head as he enveloped her in a tight embrace. Taking in a deep breath, she consumed his smell as a slight moan escaped her. She could stay right here forever. His natural, slightly rugged smell blended perfectly with the lightly scented cologne he wore. It was the smell of a man who loved her, and she'd never forget it.

"Well, I like seeing you smile, even if it does hurt my ego just a little that you're doing it just before you walk out of my life, maybe forever," he said, adding a dramatic flair to the last two words.

"What'd you do with the money?" she asked.

"What money?" he said, playing along with the joke.

"The money yo' mama gave you for acting classes." They shared a laugh then he leaned in and kissed her.

She moaned lightly through the kiss. "I'm going to miss that when I'm home."

"Me too," he agreed heartily. "What about a little fun before you go?" He pulled her tightly to his chest and slid his hands down to her butt, pulling it close, hoping she could feel the beginnings of his erection. "Three, four minutes, tops. It'll be over before you know it," he joked.

"Stop," she told him with a laugh, slapping his chest playfully.

"You know you could just stay…" he said, trailing off as he watched the light flicker from her deep brown eyes.

"Babe," she began, almost pleadingly. "I just can't. We've been through this already. It's just something I have to do for a while." She felt him tense and slid her hands up his body to the sides of his face. "Look at me."

Aaron did as she asked. He hadn't meant to broach the subject again, but it sprung out in one final plea. The last few weeks were hard, but somewhere in the back of his mind, he always thought she'd change her mind. Now that she was packed and loaded, it was all so final.

"You know how I feel about you. There's just something I have to work through, and I cannot do it here. I can't even explain it to myself. It's just…" she struggled for the words, fighting back tears as she looked

10

into his sad, green eyes. "It's just something I gotta do. Plus, I need to see my folks anyway. Two birds, one stone."

"I know," he relented, wrapping her in his arms tightly again. He sighed as he held her, quickly wiping a tear from the corner of his eye.

Being in Aaron's arms was second only to being in her fathers' in the level of joy it brought her. He was tall and strong, yet gentle when she wanted him to be. He was her third lover, first man of a different race, and she felt safe and loved in his arms; protected. That was exactly what she wanted right now, to feel safe. Her resolution to leave and go back home faltered in his embrace. Her desire for time and space faded. Her body ached to be beneath him; to feel him; to smell him close to her. She loved him and he loved her, she was sure of it. She knew he loved her. It showed in everything he said and did when they were together.

But that was all a fantasy and she knew it. She couldn't spend the rest of her life hiding out in her apartment in the arms of a sexy man, as wonderful as that sounded. It was what she wanted, but it wasn't what she needed.

Especially after what happened over Christmas break.

Aaron Devours flopped down onto the sofa in his apartment with a sigh. He suddenly felt heavy. Not fat, not tired, just heavy. Like the world was pushing down on him.

"She gone?"

Aaron looked at his friend and roommate of four years. Kevin was dressed in dirty grey sweatpants and a tee shirt with the saying 'Haters gonna hate- taters gonna potate' and a picture of a smiling potato wearing sunglasses. It was one of those shirts you had to search for in the dark recess of the internet, and it suited his roommate to a tee.

"Yep," he answered with a heavy sigh.

"You going to be okay?" Kevin asked sympathetically, lowering the leg rest of the second-hand leather recliner and shutting off the baseball game on television.

Aaron sighed again and nodded his head. "I'm sure I will be. I mean, no one ever thought it would last forever anyway. Right?"

"Dude, I'm no expert in sentiments of the heart. You know that."

Aaron nodded. "Who doesn't? To be honest, I don't know how you even get dates anymore."

The friends shared a laugh, but it faded quickly. Aaron wasn't in the mood to hear about his roommate's exploits. He'd seen, heard about, and actually heard too many of them to count already. Though he and Kevin were as close as brothers, they were different in a great many ways. He made good grades; Kevin barely skimmed by. He partied; Kevin *lived* to party. He'd been with a few women; Kevin literally charmed the pants off at least twenty women in the time he'd known him.

"Don't hate the playa…," Kevin bragged, flashing his broad smile and perfect, white teeth as he flattened the front of his shirt for Aaron to read.

"I think I'm going to take a shower." Aaron stood, ran a hand through his thick, black hair, and started for the bathroom only to be stopped by Kevin swiveling in his chair and extending a leg in his path.

"Hold on, buddy. I'm here, man. Talk to me. You okay?"

Aaron threw his hands into the air and let them drop to his side. "I don't know. I've been telling myself for weeks that I was fine with all

12

this; that it was no big deal, but I don't know now. Now that she's actually gone, I just don't know."

"Look at me." Kevin said as he stood and grabbed Aaron's shoulders. "Not to get all mushy and stuff but know that it's okay. It's okay that you didn't want her to leave. It's okay that you love her, whatever that means."

"C'mon, man. Shit." Aaron pulled away from his friend and went into the bathroom. "I need a shower." He was running the water for the shower when Kevin came into the bathroom.

"I'm sorry. Really. I know it sucks. I've seen you two. I know how y'all were. Hell, we had you two pegged for love and marriage, two kids, a dog, living in the suburbs with a white picket fence. All that shit, man. Y'all were like that black and white cookie they sell at the mall. It was kind of a private joke."

"Hope everyone had a good laugh." Aaron pulled his tee shirt over his head. Turning his back to Kevin he slid out of his jeans and stepped into the shower.

"Not like that, man. Hell, most of us are jealous of you two."

"Were. Y'all were jealous. Not much to be jealous about now."

"Anyway." Kevin looked at himself in the mirror, raking his blonde hair back from his face. With his strong jaw line and deep, blue eyes, he'd always known he was handsome. Since he was a little boy, he heard it from everyone. "What a handsome boy you are." "In a few years, he'll be beating the girls off with a stick." Even as a teenager, he'd caught the attention of a few of the younger teachers in school. Nothing physical ever happened, but he charmed a little extra credit on more than one occasion.

13

"Did she at least come out and tell you why she was leaving?" Kevin asked tentatively.

"No," Aaron replied flatly. "Does it really matter?"

"It might help you to know if it was something you did or if there was someone else."

"That's not it." Aaron poked his head out the shower, holding back the curtain in a tight fist. "And there is no one else."

"Okay, okay. Sorry," Kevin said, holding his hands in front of him defensively. Aaron shook his head and returned to the shower.

"So, she didn't say anything at all?"

"Just the same stuff she's been saying. That she 'needed to work things out' and that there were some 'things to work through', stuff like that."

"What does that even mean?" Kevin asked. Her rubbed his face with both hands. He didn't like being in the position he found himself in.

"Haven't got a freaking clue, man."

"Maybe it's something personal. Woman stuff, maybe?"

"That would be a best-case scenario, actually."

"So, what is the deal? She gone for good, she coming back, or what?

"I don't know." Aaron insisted. "I've told you she's been distant for a while, since Christmas really. She didn't say she wanted to break up, just that she had stuff to work through."

Kevin tensed. "Christmas? That long?" he asked nervously. "She's seemed the same to me."

"Like you would notice."

"Okay, then." Kevin ran a hand through his hair with a sigh. "There's nothing you can do then except let her work through her own crap. You never know what's going on in a chick's head, man."

"You do realize this isn't helping?"

"I know. I told you I'm bad at this stuff." Kevin stepped in front of the toilet and began to urinate. "Why don't we go out tonight?"

"I can't. I need to study."

"I can't. I need to study," Kevin mocked in a girly voice. He finished peeing and flushed. In his regular voice he continued, "C'mon. A few beers at Chubby's, play some pool or something. Maybe find someone to help you feel better?"

"She's barely off campus and you want me hooking up with some drunk skank?" Aaron asked, the irritation evident in his voice. "And nobody said it was over. She just needed some space."

"Okay then, whatever you say, just a few beers. Hang out. I don't know." Kevin awaited a reply, but none came from behind the shower curtain. "You know you're not going to be able to study at all anyway. Probably mope around here all night, jack off to a picture of her, and cry yourself to sleep."

"Screw you, asshole."

"Okay then. At least a few beers might help you sleep better."

Inside the shower, the water went off, and a hand reached out for a towel. "That might not be a bad idea. The last thing I want to do right now is study."

Aaron stepped out of the shower and wrapped the towel around his waist. He looked at his best friend, smiled, and shook his head.

"Thanks, man, even if you are an ass."

"What? Was I wrong?" Kevin asked.

"Probably not," Aaron admitted. "Thanks anyway."

"For what?"

"I don't know. Just being there all these years."

"Wow, estrogen much?" Kevin laughed. "Is this night going to turn into a Lifetime movie?"

"You gotta always be jerk?"

Kevin held up an invisible microphone. "Tonight, on a very special episode of 'College Life', will Aaron finally get his period like all the other girls?"

"You really are an asshole. Do you know that?" Aaron pushed his friend playfully.

"Oh. PG thirteen already. I like where this is going."

"Do me a favor? No matter what happens, please don't let me get drunk and call Eve. Nobody wants a drunk crying in their ear at two in the morning."

"I can't make any promises, but I do willingly accept the assignment, General." Kevin snapped to attention and saluted his friend. "Look, don't drive yourself crazy trying to figure this crap out, man. Just let it be. Go home, relax and try to forget about it."

"That's easy for you to say."

"Maybe so, but if you stress over this and pick at it, it will only make it worse. Maybe you don't wanna know what it is. Maybe it's nothing. There's really no way to find out anyway."

"I guess," Aaron sighed.

"One word of advice, let it go."

16

"That's three words, genius."

"Not the way I say it," Kevin said with a grin. "Letitgo."

TWO

The anonymity of the interstate gave Evelyn time to think, but that wasn't what she wanted to do. It was the reason she'd given Aaron. It was the reason she wasn't spending a leisurely summer practically living with him while he worked on his summer classes. It was why she wasn't spending long nights lying in bed with him after making love, naked, and talking about anything and everything. Time to figure things out was what she had, but it was the last thing she wanted.

This trip home, she knew, was not like any of the other times. She was going to come clean to her parents, cry, hide, probably cry some more, and hope. Hope. Hope springs eternal. It was about all she could cling to now.

Her parents, like so many others, had moved to Souls Harbor in hopes of her father finding work with one of the underground coal mines in the area, if he was lucky, or one of the timber companies, if less so. Souls Harbor was a working town with lots of opportunity and good schools. That was all they needed to know.

"We've got to get out of these backwoods and find a place where we can have a chance," she remembered her father recounting with his ever-optimistic smile. "And what better place is there than a town called Souls Harbor?"

"That's right. And if ever some souls needed harboring, was us," her mother agreed with a hearty laugh.

Fredrick Jackson and Martha Ruth Robbins grew up next-door neighbors and had been in love since they could remember. Holven Heights was a quiet neighborhood. There never seemed to be many problems- not major ones anyway. School wasn't a priority to their own parents, not as much as surviving the rural Alabama landscape and the natural difficulties of life. There always seemed to be more chores than hours in the day, not leaving much time to get into any trouble. It was a simple fact of life that many of the events that garnered national attention barely made a ripple through their tiny neighborhood. Most of the other parents were just like theirs, glad to have a job and able to provide what they could for their family. The Heights, as everyone called it, was a mixed neighborhood where both blacks and whites alike tried their best to stave off the ever-present, and very real, specter of hunger and poverty. It was just a fact of life to them. It was just the way it was. Some folks got a better lot in life, some folks didn't. But there was always hope. Hope was the only thing that ever really thrived in the Heights.

Growing up in such conditions left an indelible mark on them both. They learned the value of a good education by not having one themselves. It was too late for them, but not their babies. They were determined that their children weren't ever going to live hand to mouth. Their children would be educated. Their children would be somebody or at least have a chance to be somebody.

Due to complications during delivery, the Jacksons were only blessed with one baby girl. Evelyn Beatrice Jackson, named after both their mothers, became the culmination of their life's work. She became the embodiment of their love for each other; of the hope that they clung to; and they became the wellspring of her strength. They were the one safe place she could always count on in a scary, unpredictable world. Her soul was in a storm and she needed a safe harbor in which to hide. Her mother's words echoed in her mind.

"If ever a soul needed harboring it's mine," she whispered aloud, shaking her head.

The sound of Rihanna's "Only girl in the world" suddenly filled her car, startling Evelyn out of the whirlwind of thoughts as she drove southward on Interstate sixty-five. She looked at the darkened radio screen, then at the phone on the seat next to her and her heart began to race.

The message was from Aaron, she knew, the song was the alert for his texts and calls. Picking up the phone hesitantly, as if he already knew her secret, she swiped the screen and looked at the message.

"Miss you already. Let me know when you make it home safe. <3."

"Miss you too," she said to the empty car as she typed the message and included a row of hearts. She did love him, there was no doubt about that. Every ounce of her body loved him. That's why her soul ached so bad. Whether or not he would love her for much longer was the question. How could she have been so foolish?

Dropping the phone back onto the seat, she felt her walls beginning to break down. The past few months had been hell. Studying for finals with a tornado raging in her mind took its toll, and it was a daily struggle just to keep herself together.

She put a hand over her mouth, hoping to maintain composure, breathing deeply as the first tear welled in the corner of her eye, swelled, and escaped. Streaking down her cheek, it slipped beneath one manicured nail, and disappeared behind her fingers.

"You're not doing this now, Evelyn," she told herself, determined to fight off the wave of emotions rising into her throat. "You've gotta hold it together," she demanded angrily as another tear escaped each eye and sprinted down her smooth cheek. "Dammit!" The tears were coming now in groups, the dam was breaking. It was happening now and there was nothing she could do to stop it. The waves of pain and guilt washed over her once again, pouring from her eyes as tears. This time, she didn't have to be strong. She didn't have anyone to hide from.

Steering her Silver Toyota Corolla onto an exit ramp, she navigated through bleary eyes and pulled to the far end of the parking lot. Putting the car into park, she tried to absorb the force of the tidal wave that washed over her, but it was too late. Her body wracked by sobs, she finally allowed herself to cry like she'd needed to for what felt like an eternity.

"Oh my God," she cried, wrapping her arms around herself. "Why? Why? Why?" But no answers came, only tears and pain. It was happening. She was having a good-old ugly cry in a gas station parking lot. Admittedly, not the ideal spot, but she knew she needed it. Her mind was a bomb about to explode. She had to let it all out.

She found a small, travel-sized pack of tissues in her center console. She was not a graceful crier, and the small collection of tissue was seriously overmatched. Ripping open the pack, she gripped them in one fist and clutched her hands against of her face as another round of gut-wrenching sobs fought their way up from the pit of her stomach.

Raising her head from the steering wheel as the sobs began to subside, Evelyn noticed a man standing next to her car. Startled, she jumped back from the window. He was in his mid-sixties and had a worried look on his face. Wearing a blue windbreaker and a head full of silver hair, he bent, looking at her through the window.

"Shit," she muttered to herself as she quickly cleaned her face as best she could, trying to make herself presentable.

The old man smiled, gave her a quick wave to say he wasn't a murdering rapist, made the motion of rolling down a window. She heard him ask if she was okay and she nodded, wishing he'd go away. He didn't.

Hitting the button to roll down the window, she breathed deeply, praying she wouldn't have a hitch in her voice like she always got as a child after a good cry.

"H-Hello," she said, forcing a smile as she continued to clean her face. Shit.

"Missy? Are you okay?" he asked.

"Y-yeah," she said and cleared her throat. "Yes, sir. I'm fine. Thank you."

"It's just that you looked quite upset."

"I know. T-thank you. I'm fine. Really I am."

"Me and the missus," he pointed to the red ford pickup truck parked diagonally across two spaces behind him, "We noticed you over here and the whole time I was filling up, we saw you was crying something fierce. She wanted me to come check on you; to see if you was alright. I told her it weren't none of our business."

"Thank you, really," Evelyn assured him just as his "missus" joined them. Evelyn shook her head. Things were going from bad to worse.

"I'm so sorry, sweetie. I hope we didn't disturb you. I told Jack here that every girl needs a good cry now and again."

"Apparently so," Evelyn replied flatly, eager for them to leave. She blotted more tears from her cheeks.

"Is it a man?" the missus asked, bending at the waist to look at her. "I'm sure it is. They really can put us through the wringer sometimes, don't they?"

"Just stop it, hun. She said she's okay. No need to pry."

"I'm just saying. Am I right?" The missus leaned in closer, her hair a fresh color of red, which looked anything but natural, wrapped neatly in a scarf. It was an odd color that almost matched the paint on her wrinkled smokers' lips perfectly. The scent of cheap cigarettes floated in through her open window.

"Of sorts," Evelyn agreed. "But look, thanks for checking on me. It really was nice of you, but I've gotta get back on the road. I've got a long way to go. Thank you very much." She started to roll up the window, but the woman held out a purple box of tissues. The old woman's eyes begged her to take them.

Evelyn stopped the window, took the box of tissues, then rolled the window up, giving them a smile and wave.

"Oh my God!" she sighed, backing out of the space. Allowing herself a slight laugh at the situation, she flipped down the sun visor and opened the vanity mirror.

Evelyn looked at herself and groaned. "No wonder they checked on you," she told herself. She was a mess. Her mascara was smeared on her cheeks, her lipstick was smudged, and some of her hair had even managed to escape the clip that held it back in a tight knot low on her head. A good cry never hurt anyone, provided you don't have an audience when you do it.

After filling up with her father's credit card, she pointed her car south on Interstate sixty-five south and headed home. Switching on the radio, the sound of "Only Girl in the World" filled her car again.

"Really?" she asked, shaking her head. She switched channels and settled into her seat. Home was less than two hours away, but it felt like a million miles.

Cara stumbled out of the woods and stopped on the edge of the clearing. Darkness was already falling in the thick scope of woods behind her, but here in the open, the last vestiges of the day cast an odd glow over the only home she'd ever known. It never looked very friendly and welcoming to her, but the years of neglect gave it a menacing look that sent a shudder down her spine.

Very little semblance of the home it had once been remained. What yellow paint hadn't already peeled away and fallen off hung to the old pine boards in clumps, dirty patch of color on the weathered, gray siding. Gone also were most of the flowers that needed tending. The bright yellow flowers that came up every year in bunches had already come and gone and soon the wild roses would bloom to take some of the sorrow from the place, but they too were fleeting. Everything else had been choked out by weeds or simply died off with the lack of care.

Scanning the area to make sure she had no 'visitors', Cara swept her eyes across the yard and found the usual landscape pockmarked by countless holes, but no people. There was no rhyme or reason to the holes she'd dug, except that they were rarely more than a foot apart. The cavities in the rich, dark earth swept in a wave all the way to the tree line, past where her rope swing once hung, across the garden patch her family had once tended, to where the trees stood in the growing darkness. Every hole and fresh dirt around it stood as a testament to her failure. Every hole she dug, with the exception of two, had yielded only dirt and lies.

Satisfied that it was safe, Cara began making her way through the yard. With the ease of a ballet dancer but not the grace, she hopped and picked her way through the minefield of holes with a precision that could only come from experience. Many of the cavities, some only inches apart, were knee deep, some less than six inches. Crossing the yard in the quickly fading light would have been near impossible for anyone else, but she spanned the distance in seconds, landing nimbly next to a set of rickety wooden steps.

Climbing them to the top, she froze, staring at the box sitting by her front door. Turning quickly, her eyes found a collection of footprints in the muddy ground in front of the house. They lead to the overgrown track that had once been a driveway. There were two sets. One coming in and the other going out. Good.

Turning back to the box, she stared at it suspiciously. Her stomach, less mistrusting, growled hungrily, already knew what it contained. It looked like every other box that had been left on her porch. It was same size as the others, and it had SOULS HARBOR FOOD BANK handwritten on it with a red marker.

Finally, satisfied it was ok, she hefted the box with ease and carried it through the open door. The house was full of shadows, making her skin crawl. She hated the house, but she had nowhere else to go. They'd offered to take her to a hospital once, where she could be looked after, but she refused. They just wanted to lock her up in a cage and look at her; to point and laugh at Crazy Cara. That is until late at night after all the nurses went home, then the doctors would come by to see her and have their way with her. They wanted to do stuff to her, dirty stuff, just like all the other men.

Shoving the box onto the table in the kitchen, she turned to run from the gloom that enveloped her, but her stomach growled again, begging her to eat. Reaching into the box blindly, her hand found something round and cool then something wrapped in plastic. Clutching these to her chest, she raced through the open back door and sprang from the porch, clearing all three of the broken steps.

Outside, her mind slowly calmed. It was fully dark now, but she didn't mind. She could see good in the dark, but they couldn't see her. Not most of the time anyway. The darkness was a good place to hide, even if it was lonelier there.

Sitting down on the stump cedar tree, felled long ago by her father, she took her first bite of food of the day. The cool, sweet juice of an apple exploded inside her mouth. She smiled, wiping the juice from her chin with the back of her hand.

"Do they know I like apples?" she asked the darkness in a quiet voice, swinging one foot back and forth casually. She thought for a minute about the box of food. They came every so often, but she rarely saw anyone leave it. Maybe it was the lady from the State that came by that time after mama died. The one with the big butt that her daddy talked about so much.

"No," she said, reconsidering. That lady stopped coming when he touched her butt that one day and tried to kiss her. Later, a man came by. He was dressed up with a suit and tie. He argued with her daddy, not knowing she was listening from outside the kitchen window. It wasn't too many days after that when another man showed up. Maybe he was a preacher or something? She couldn't remember. He and daddy didn't argue, but they did talk for a long time. So long that she fell asleep outside the window and only awakened when daddy threw a bucket of water in her face after the man left. He thought it was funny, dashing the water in her face, but she didn't. She didn't think it was funny one damned bit.

Cara's eyes went to the very window she'd fallen asleep beneath. Clenching her teeth, she thought about that day, and that night. That night, the man with the suit and tie came back, but he didn't have his suit on. He wanted her to sit on his lap, but she didn't want to. Daddy said she had to, or they'd send her away. That sounded just fine to her, but he made her do it anyway. After a while, the man wanted to talk to her alone. Daddy said to talk to the man, and he walked out of the house.

It turned out that the man wanted to do more than talk.

"You bastard!" she screamed and threw what was left of her apple at the window. It passed through one of the glassless panes and bounced around inside the kitchen with a series of hollow thuds.

Her eyes narrowed, staring at the reflection of the rising moon in one of the dirty panes still clinging desperately to the frame. The moon was full that night so long ago, giving her just enough light to see the blood as she washed herself after the man left. The moon, blood, tears, and that sticky stuff all men left on her, all over her hands as she straddled the washtub on the back porch frantically trying to wash the shame away while her father sat on the couch and drank whiskey straight from the bottle.

The voices started again, and they sounded mad.

"I tell you what, your mama sure can cook. That's why I'm getting so fat in my old age."

Fredrick Jackson, Freddy to his friends, lead his family out of the kitchen and into the living room. The home he'd bought and paid for wasn't big or fancy, but it was a wonderful place to raise a family, better than any other place he'd lived.

Evelyn followed, then came her mother, Martha Ruth, holding two cups of coffee.

"You sure you don't want anything else to drink, sweetheart?" she asked Evelyn.

"Just the coffee is fine," Freddy said with a grin as he slid into his recliner.

"I was talking to Evie," she quipped.

"I should have known, with the sweetheart and all," Freddy threw in with a grin.

27

"I got 'cho coffee. You want anything else, get it yerself."

Freddy laughed and took the cup from his wife. They were a bit old fashioned and they both knew it, but as they would let anyone know, 'It was how we was raised'.

"You two crack me up. You know it's the twenty-first century," Evelyn laughed.

"Well sweetheart, we're old and set in our ways, I guess," her mother informed her. "Besides, a little spirit of servitude keeps even the proudest of us humble." Freddy spent twenty years treating their daughter like a queen, and her mother had spent the same time keeping her daughter grounded.

"I guess so." Evelyn relaxed into the couch and crossed her legs at the knee, still smiling. It was good to be home. Walking into her parents' house was like being wrapped in a warm blanket. Being hugged and fawned over by her parents was heaven. An only child, coming after years of trying, she'd been given every opportunity her parents could afford, and some they couldn't. Her mother's struggles with the pregnancy and labor, as well as her subsequent issues, assured she always would be an only child and she reaped the benefits.

"Eve baby," her father began, "How's things with you and this fella you been seeing?"

Cringing internally, Evelyn forced a smile. "Uh, same as always, I guess. It's college. We're both busy with classes and all that stuff. You know, study, study, study."

"Uh huh," her mother said, casting a suspicious eye at Evelyn.

"What?" she asked innocently. She hadn't made it a secret that she and Aaron were sleeping together or that he was her third lover, but she didn't make any formal announcements about it either. It was always better to just skirt the subject.

Martha shook her head and sipped her coffee as she feigned interest in the television, on which her father was scrolling through the channels.

"He still treating you good?" Her father asked.

"Always."

"So, if I check your car tomorrow the oil change sticker will be up to date? Taking care of someone doesn't mean just all that lovie dovie stuff, you know."

"I know, dad. First, he doesn't have to 'take care of me'. I can take care of myself. I am twenty years old; you know." The truth was that her car was way past the oil change date and mileage, but he didn't need to know that.

"I know," he answered with a smile, happy to see her tenacity hadn't faded. He knew she could take care of herself because he taught her how to take care of herself. "I know, baby doll."

"Mama, I loved those pork chops. You are the best cook in the world. It's been a while since I had a home-cooked meal," Evelyn said, hoping to change the subject.

"Thank you, baby. You didn't eat much."

"Well, you're comparing me to dad," she laughed. "He could eat more than anybody I know."

"If your mama cooked it, I probably could," he agreed, throwing his wife a wink.

"Have you lost weight? You look like you lost weight. You know black girls don't look as good skinny as those white girls do."

"Ain't nobody looks good skinny," Freddy laughed.

29

"I'm fine, mother," Evelyn said, evading what felt like a jab at the fact that she was dating a white guy. Her mother couldn't seem to wrap her mind around why she dated a white man. Her father, however, was glad although he'd never admit it. All her life, he warned about getting trapped by some no good "brother" and being stuck in a cycle of want and poverty. Of course, he was mostly talking about her high school boyfriend, Trae Colvin. It was a careful minefield that she learned to tiptoe through with a surgeons' deftness.

"Anybody else say 'have you lost weight?' and it's a compliment," Evelyn went on, "But if you're a black girl and your mother says it, it's like you committed a crime."

Ruth shook her head as Evelyn and her father laughed. "Just concerned."

"No, really. I'm fine, mama. If anything, I've put on a few pounds studying for finals."

"How'd it go? Straight A's?" her dad asked hopefully, his eyebrows raised slightly as he stared at her over his coffee cup.

"I doubt that. This has been a tough semester. I mean, I did good, I think, but probably not straight A's. "

"How's the GPA?" Ruth asked.

"If I did like I think I did, I'll probably start in the spring with a three point seven, maybe a three point six."

"Three point six?" her mother asked with wide eyes. "That won't get you into the PsyD program."

"That's not bad, mom, but like I said it was a really tough semester." Evelyn sank into the couch cushions as an unwelcome quiet settled over them. It was a tough semester. Since Christmas, her mind was on things they didn't even know about; life altering things that made it hard to study. Knowing what she knew, Evelyn considered a three point six a not so small victory.

"And it would get me in, by the way," she added.

"Oh, she'll be fine," her father finally said, a strained smile on his face as he spared her a quick glance. "She's smarter than all of us put together. She'll get things sorted out and show us all."

"I hope so," Martha replied, never taking her eyes off the television.

"I will," Evelyn said, deflated. Things were off to a roaring start.

Evelyn awoke in her old bedroom after a fitful night's sleep. Being home hadn't been the distraction she'd hoped for, mostly because the looming conversation she had to have with her father felt like a piece of bread stuck in her throat. She knew he would be angry at her. That, she could deal with. What she feared the most was the disappointment in his eyes. The talk would hurt him, and that was what would break her heart more than it already was.

Pushing the thought out of her mind, she sat up and swung her legs over the side of the bed. The walls of her old room were still the pale lavender that she and her mom painted them her junior year in high school. The thought of growing up in this home brought a smile to her lips. It wasn't perfect, but it was close.

Across the room, hanging off the mirror above her desk right where she'd left it, was the Summa Cum Laude sash she'd gotten for being in the top five percent in GPA in her class. She wore it in the picture taken with her parents at her high school graduation. In the picture, everyone was smiling proudly on the grass of the football stadium, her smile biggest of them all. Her younger self, sure and confident, had everything all figured out. What a fool she'd been.

31

They were all there, all her high school awards. Her Key Club pins hung in a shadow box with a picture of her and two of her best friends: Stephanie Hallers and Shakira (Kiera) Walters. Her SGA vice president certificate, her home coming queen pictures, her Solitarian's speech.

Shaking her head, Evelyn got up and headed for the bathroom. After using the facilities, she looked at herself in the mirror. The insecurities that resurfaced with her memories of high school, however small, left her feeling pensive.

She cupped her breasts, braless beneath the tee shirt. They were very nice, she thought. Aaron also thought they were nice, she told herself. Lifting her shirt, she looked at her flat, toned stomach. She'd learned a lot of things in college but going to the gym and keeping in shape was near the top. Many of her friends were still struggling to lose the "freshmen fifteen" and had even added to them. Her black friends managed to pull it off better than the white girls just as her mother had said, but she preferred to keep them off altogether.

Turning slightly and stretching onto the tips of her toes, she looked at her butt. Clad in a pair of comfortable cotton panties, her butt stood firm and athletic. Giving her hips a little wiggle, she watched it jiggle slightly. Not bad. Contrary to what she'd told her mother, she had lost a couple of pounds, but it didn't seem to bother Aaron.

Walking back into the bedroom, her thoughts were drawn to Aaron and his fascination with her body. Admittedly, she was his first woman of color, but he was simply mesmerized with her body. Their love making sessions would last for hours with him caressing and touching, kissing and loving every inch of her body. He truly did make her feel like she was the only girl in the world when they made love, and really, anytime they were together.

He was always touching her, not in a sexual way, but making sure their bodies were in contact. Once, when she asked him about it, he'd admitted that he wasn't always aware that he was doing it and offered to be more diligent about not doing it so much. No, she'd told him. Don't ever stop, please. He was the best man she'd ever been with, and the only man that had ever touched her that way.

Sighing, she went to her chest of drawers and dug out an old pair of sweatpants from high school. After pulling them on, she slipped her feet into a pair of pink Vans and looked at the bedside table to the clock that had awakened her every day of high school. 7:21 a.m. If things were the same as they always were, and things change slowly in the Jackson household, this early on a Saturday morning, her mom would still be sleeping, and her dad would be "piddlin" in his shop. She knew it was now or never. If she kept putting it off, she'd never do it. It was like taking off a band aid. You knew it would hurt, but best to get it over with quickly.

Armed with two cups of coffee, Evelyn steeled herself against the incoming tide of emotions she was sure to face and marched across their small back yard to her fathers' shop. It was a small ten by fifteen feet wooden kit building he'd picked up at one of the lumber stores in town. It was his happy place, if he had one, and Evelyn hoped breaking the news to him here would help in some way.

"Thought you might like a fresh cup," she said, standing in the open doorway. Her father was near the back of the building cranking on a vice affixed to his cluttered worktable. He looked up and smiled at his daughter, his face lighting up with genuine happiness to see her.

"I surely would, baby."

"Just the way you like it," she said, delivering the cup.

"Hot, strong, and black," he said with a laugh.

"I take mine sweet, with a little cream."

"We still talking about coffee?" he asked with a laugh as he pulled a rag from his back pocket and wiped the dust off one the chairs for her. It was a tall counter chair, black faux leather, with a ring around the bottom to rest your feet on. Smiling as he watched her climb into the seat, he wondered if she knew how much he loved her? How much she meant to him?

"What 'cha working on?" she asked

"Just piddlin," he said as he went back to the vice. "You're up early."

"I didn't rest well. Woke up early. I been laying there a while."

Looking up from his work, he asked if everything was okay before going back to work sharpening the lawn mower blade with a hand file.

"I guess," she shrugged.

"What's botherin' you?"

"I don't know."

"Well, baby, something is. I ain't blind nor stupid."

"What do you mean?" she asked. Holding her cup in the palms of both hands, she took a sip.

"I seen the puffy eyes when you got home, like you been crying," holding his hand up to stop any protest she was about to make he looked at her. "You already said it was a 'tough semester', not that the 'classes were hard' like you always do."

"It has been a hard semester, dad," she sighed. "I just..." She trailed off, staring at the coffee in her cup.

Freddy Jackson walked to his daughter, wiping his hands on the same rag he'd cleaned her chair with. He cupped her face in his right hand and caressed her cheek with his thumb.

"Baby doll, you are the world to me. You know that. You're smart, funny, beautiful, talented and just about anything else I could come up with. You've already done better than me and your mama ever did. You're more determined and stronger than anybody I know. And I love you to the moon and back." He looked at her and sighed. "So, tell me what's eating at you. I can feel it. Something ain't right."

"Oh daddy," she began, fighting back tears. "Things couldn't be wronger." She sat her cup down, knowing that she wouldn't be able to hold back the tears.

"Wronger?" he asked with a smile, hoping to bring some levity to the situation and ease his precious daughter's pain. "All that money on college, and you up in here saying 'wronger'?"

"Dad," she began. "I messed up. Big time. Twice." The tears began to flow as her father wrapped his strong arms around her shoulders and hugged her to him. He held his only child and let her cry against his chest while his heart ached for her. Eve had always been a good child, a smart child, and rarely gave them any trouble growing up. In her teenage years, there were a few minor bouts of rebellion, but nothing that gave him much pause. But this was bad, he could feel it in his daughters' sobs, and he silently prayed for the strength and wisdom to guide her through it.

After allowing her time to cry, he put his hands on her shoulders and gently pushed her away from his chest. His hands, rough and calloused from years of hard work, cradled her face gently as he could while his thumbs brushed back the tears still rolling down her cheeks.

"I'm sorry, daddy. I'm so sorry," she sobbed.

"Baby," he began, shushing her, "You ain't gotta be sorry for nothing. We all human, and we all mess up. You the one who been suffering with this. I'll help you anyway I can." The thought that she was pregnant slowly began to rise in the back of his mind as a knot slowly began to form in his stomach.

Wiping her eyes with the heels of her hands like a child, she shook her head as she accepted the rag her father offered. She blew her nose, folded it, wiped her eyes, and handed it back to her father.

"It kinda smells like grease." Evelyn sniffled and took a deep breath to regain her composure as she watched her father grab a clean roll of shop towels and return to her side.

"Here you go, baby."

"Daddy, I'm gonna start talking. Please let me get through this, okay? If I have to stop, I don't think I'll be able to finish."

"Okay, baby, whatever you need," he told her as he pulled the matching stool up to hers and took her hand in his.

Evelyn took in another deep breath and exhaled slowly. "You remember when I was home at Christmas?" Freddy nodded, but said nothing. "When I went to that party with Kiera?"

"I think so."

"Well, a lot of people were there, from high school, I mean. We all got to talking and laughing and having a good time. And we were drinking." She paused to see if her father would interrupt, but he only nodded solemnly.

"I guess we all stayed late and were pretty far gone, so at some point, we all decided to just spend the night. That way, no one was driving drunk, you know."

"That's smart," Freddy agreed, nodding.

"Well, like I said, we were all talking about the old days, if you could call them that since we've only been out of high school three years now. Really, two and a half at the time."

"Eve," her father said flatly. She sometimes rambled when she was nervous and hesitant to get to the subject.

"Anyway, we were all nostalgic, I guess. Cutting up bitch- ugh, girls we didn't like back then and all that. Bragging about our exploits and what not. Just junk really, but it was fun. Everyone was having a good time and laughing."

"Eve," her father began, his voice stern but in a loving, fatherly way. "It's not a Christmas party that's got you so upset or the fact that you all drank too much. Now is it?"

"No," she sighed. "Daddy, Trae was there…."

Freddy Jackson's jaw clenched tightly, containing anything he might have said. Trae Colvin was Eve's high school boyfriend and, in his opinion, a good-for-nothing piece of trash. They had several fights about his lack of respect for not only Eve, but them as well. He was ill-mannered and lazy; he was a wanna-be thug. It was a joyous day in the Jackson house when Eve went to college, leaving that piece of baggage behind.

"And?" was all Freddy Jackson could manage without showing his anger.

"Well, he was all sweet and nice. We got to talking and you know…" Evelyn's voice trailed off as her gaze dropped to her hands, ashamed. She knew her father would be exploding with anger on the inside and hoped it would stay there.

Freddy sighed heavily again as he rubbed his face hard. Beginning on both sides of his nose then working up to his eyes before finally ending with his forehead. He groaned through his hands before dropping them to his lap and looking at his daughter.

"Okay," he began slowly. "Okay. That's not the end of the world. You messed up; had a relapse. It's no big deal, except maybe to that white boy you been seeing. Does he know?"

Evelyn shook her head as tears began to flow again. "It was a mistake, daddy. Just one stupid mistake. I was drinking too much, and he was nice, and we were all having fun and it just happened. I don't even know how it got to that point, but it did."

"Good to know it was a one-time thing."

"It was daddy. I can see now what y'all were telling me about him back in high school. I mean, he's no good I know that, but..." she trailed off again and blew her nose. "How could I have been so stupid?"

"Baby, look, you're young. Young people do stupid stuff. That's why God gives you parents."

"I know it was dumb. I'm so ashamed of myself."

Taking his daughters hands in his, Freddy looked into her puffy, tear-stained eyes and smiled. "That might not be a bad thing. Means you got morals. But you know it was a mistake and maybe learned a good lesson from all this." Honestly, he was relieved that she wasn't pregnant with Aaron's baby. "Do the white boy know about Trae?

"He has a name, daddy. Aaron. And no, he doesn't know about anything."

"Do you want Aaron to know?"

"No. I wish it never happened, but he deserves to know. He's a wonderful guy, daddy. He's kind, gentle, very respectful to me. He treats me like a lady." She wiped tears away with the shop towel clutched in her hand. "He values me, daddy."

Watching his daughter's face light up when she talked about him in the midst of the turmoil she was going through told Freddy Jackson that his little girl was in love with this man. This white guy. Aaron. There was no doubt about it.

"Baby girl," he sighed. "You went and stepped in it good. Something like this will either send a man running or it won't. Either way, as a man, I can't say I'd blame him. If he cares about you like you care about him, it will be hard on him. Just know that when a man gets knocked down to his knees, even he don't know how he'll react."

"I know," she said sadly. "My heart aches for him. For us, daddy."

Freddy hugged his daughter and stroked her hair. It was a tight spot, but not one that she couldn't recover from. She's young, he told himself. Either way, she will recover.

"Daddy," she said, her voice muffled against his shoulder. "There's something else."

Freddy's heart sank, and he drew back from his daughter and looked into her eyes. The anguish was back.

"Afterwards, Trae just got up to leave. I cussed him out and told him to never speak to me again. I was just an easy target, I guess. He was probably proud of himself for bagging a college girl. He probably told himself 'I still got it.'"

"Well, he is a piece of crap, so probably."

Evelyn drew in a deep breath as she ran her hands over her hair and clasped them behind her head. Looking at the ceiling, she exhaled slowly.

"I got pregnant." The words seemed to echo in the silence that filled the small shop. She held her gaze toward the ceiling, too afraid, too ashamed, to even look at her father until after what felt like an eternity. He gently took her hands and lowered them to her lap.

When she finally mustered the strength to look at her father, his eyes had tears in the edges and her heart broke all over again. "I'm so sorry, daddy."

His gaze dropped to his own hands as he absently picked at an untrimmed thumb nail. It was his worst fear come to fruition. The one thing he'd preached and harped on since she'd turned thirteen had happened. The one thing he'd prayed against every night had come to pass.

"Does he know?" he asked quietly. "Trae?" the name came out of his mouth like venom.

"No. Nobody does."

"Well, everybody will soon find out."

"No, they won't, daddy." She pushed the towel into her eyes, hoping not to have to see her father's face. "I should have gotten my period two weeks later, when I was back at school. When I didn't, I went to a doctor in Huntsville."

"And they told you that you was pregnant?"

"She did. We talked a long time about me being in school, my age, the situation. She gave me some options."

Freddy Jackson looked up from his now ragged thumbnail. "Options?"

"Yes, options," she said, the shop towel still pressed to her eyes. "I laid there on that cold table alone, daddy, and I thought about Trae, about Aaron, about school, my future. I thought about you and mom. I thought, and I cried all alone."

Freddy's heart sank as he thought about his baby girl being cold and alone, heartbroken and scared. "You could've called."

"No, daddy, I couldn't. Not for something like this." Evelyn paused to blow her nose and wipe each eye with the blue shop towel. She wadded it up, tossed it away, and tore another off the roll beside her. "I had a decision to make," she whimpered as a fresh wave of tears rolled down her cheeks.

"They sent me home since I was so upset. I told Aaron I was sick. He wanted to come over and take care of me." She gave her father a wry smile and shook her head. "See what kinda guy he is? Anyway, they said if I wanted to schedule a 'procedure' that I probably should bring someone with me to drive me home."

Freddy stood, needing to move around just for the sense that he was doing something, thought better of it, and returned to his seat. He rubbed Eve's shoulder. Now it was her turn to pick at her fingernails. Not knowing what else to do or what to say, he just sat in silence and rubbed her shoulder while his mind raced down a hundred paths at once.

"I knew I couldn't ask one of my girlfriends. Girls are mean, you know, and we like to gossip. I really had no one to turn to so I talked to a guy named Kevin. He's Aaron's roommate and best friend. It was a crappy thing to do to him, but we'd always gotten along well enough. I always thought he was a shallow jerk about women, but as it turned out, he didn't ask any questions. He drove me there, waited in the parking lot, and drove me home. All he ever asked after he'd made sure I was settled was if I was going to be okay? We never spoke of it again."

"Oh baby, I don't even know what to say," Freddy told her, tears welling in the corners of his eyes.

"Say you still love me, and that you'll forgive me," Evelyn said through her tears.

41

Freddy lifted her chin until their eyes met. "Baby, there ain't nothing in this whole world you could ever do that would make me stop loving you. Nothing. And before you even begin to worry about anyone else' forgiveness, you gotta forgive yourself."

"I don't know if I can," she sobbed as her father pulled her to him and clutched her in a tight embrace. As he felt his only child sob uncontrollably against his chest, Freddy suddenly felt woefully inadequate as a parent. When the tears spilled from his own eyes, he wasn't sure if it was for the situation or the fact that his baby girl had had to go through it alone.

Freddy Jackson clenched his teeth as he held his only child. That damned Trae Colvin, he thought as the name burned inside his mind like a branding iron. He suddenly wanted to kill a man more than he had ever wanted to in his whole life.

THREE

Propped on pillows, Evelyn lay in her bed, scrolling through her phone. She'd been stalking some of her old friends on social media to see what they had been up to. Rachel Medders had gotten into the University of Alabama, a school that her family couldn't afford. She already knew that Kiera Walters got into a very good nursing school but was taking a year off to help her family financially. Brenda Anderson went to Northwestern, went off to college, and apparently hadn't been back home since. A few of the people from high school had gotten married and had babies, some just got married, and two people simply had babies. Nothing earth-shattering.

After her talk with her dad this morning, she retreated to her bedroom, emotionally and physically exhausted, to lay down. She slept, off and on, all day and into the evening, waking only twice to pee and once when her dad brought in a ham and cheese sandwich, chips, and a can of Coke. She was awake but pretended to be asleep when her mother checked on her.

She woke up around ten, hearing her parents not-so-hushed whispered conversation as they lay in bed across the hall. She could only hear snippets of conversation, but enough to know she disappointed her parents more than she ever thought possible. Their voices ranged from shock to sadness to embarrassment. From anger to sorrow as her father recounted the story for her mother. She'd heard the word "God" several times, "future" a lot, and even "spoiled" once spat angrily by her mother. It was all nothing new to her. She called herself far worse in her own thoughts.

Covering her head with a pillow to shut out anymore of the private conversation taking place across the hall, she finally cried herself to sleep again, for the third time in one day.

When her phone vibrated in her hand, she looked at the time. It was after one in the morning. Che clicked on the text icon and found Aaron's message. Her heart began to beat faster and a sad smile crept across her lips. She missed him so bad. God, what a fool she had been.

"You up?"

She typed back "I am," but her thumb hesitated over the send button. She stopped denying how deeply she loved him months ago and if not for the whole situation with Trae, she would be entertaining dreams of marrying him. Now she just hoped they wouldn't be breaking up; that he wouldn't hate her. Her thumb pressed the "send" button, and she settled into the pillows, watching the screen on her phone.

"Finished finals this morning."

"Good," she whispered as she typed the message. "What cha doin?"

"Not much. Lying in bed wishing u were here."

"I'm doin the same thing."

"You ok?" he asked.

"I'm ok," she lied. She was everything but ok. Unburdening herself to her dad had helped, but she still had to tell him and that scared the hell out of her.

"Miss u."

Evelyn closed her eyes as she felt tears begin to well in them. "Miss u 2." Aaron replied with a smiley face, then there was a long pause that allowed her to compose herself.

"I know you've been bothered lately," popped onto her screen. Then, "but whatever it is, we can work through it." There was a slight delay, then "together," showed up.

Evelyn didn't know how to respond. Could they? Would they? Would his tune change when he found out what was bothering her? Could she handle it if he walked away? Could she if he didn't? What if he loved her enough to forgive her? In a strange way, that might be worse than breaking up. Just the fact that she'd betrayed him, and he didn't even know about it yet hurt her heart.

"You're the best. I love you."

"LU2," he responded. "I'm here if u need me. I can come visit you there??"

Evelyn sighed. Having Aaron here would be awesome- under any other circumstances. Having everyone she loved together would be wonderful. But right now, she knew she couldn't look at him without feeling the shame of betrayal. On top of the tension between she and her parents that would be unbearable.

"Think I'll be back in a few more days," she replied, deflecting the question.

"M&D want me to go with to beach next week."

Evelyn remembered Aaron's mom and dad had planned a beach trip for two weeks after school was out. It was supposed to be when she met his parents.

"I remember," she answered, pursing her lips as she stared at the screen.

"I don't have to go. Prolly lame trip. Could come there??"

Evelyn shook her head. "Not right now. Sorry." The "ok" that popped up on her screen looked sad to her. Shaking her head, she closed her eyes then drew in a deep breath, determined not to cry again.

"Love you, babe."

"Doesn't feel like it," he responded.

"I know, sweetie. I'm so sorry." Tears escaped her eyes and ran down her face. "I love you so much," she said as she typed the message, then she added, "You deserve a better woman than me."

Without a delay, his response flashed onto her screen. "There isn't a better woman in the world. You're my Eve."

Dropping the phone to the bed between her legs, she shoved her hands over her hair hard, clasping her fingers behind her head as a flood of conflicting emotions washed over her. Love and shame, guilt and pride, fear and hope. How could he ever forgive her? How could her secret not destroy them? Did she even deserve to be forgiven? What right did she have to even hope for it?

Feeling the phone vibrate again, she picked it up and looked at his response. "NOTHING else matters. Nothing." Wiping a tear from the screen, she stared at the message. How could he love her so much? It didn't make any sense, but then again, doing the things she did made even less sense. Apparently, things didn't have to make sense to happen. Sometimes they just happened.

Leaning back on the park bench, Evelyn turned her face to the warm sunshine and closed her eyes. Dressed casually in a blue and grey raglan shirt and black leggings, she finally began to relax. The mood in her parent's house was thick with judgement. Her father had checked on her early before leaving for work. She'd pretended to be asleep, but he kissed her forehead and told her he loved her anyway.

Her mother, unusually quiet, asked if she wanted breakfast, but she refused politely. While the subject didn't come up, Evelyn knew she was upset, and understandably so. Once, she'd caught her mother staring at her, her face a mixture of anger and disappointment, mostly, things just felt awkward and uncomfortable as they danced around the subject until, finally, Evelyn just needed to get away. She didn't want to be with anyone. Not her friends, not her parents, not even Aaron. She just wanted a reprieve from the weight that had been burdening her for months. She told her mom she was going out, grabbed her keys, and left, hoping a little distance might be what everyone needed. It was exactly what she needed.

Pulling the tortoise shell sunglasses off the top of her head, her hair pulled back in a tight ponytail, she looked around. It was a beautiful Sunday morning, but the park was quiet and still. That was perfectly fine with her.

The park was larger than she remembered, with a nice mix of equipment and open grassy places to play. From where she sat, she could see a big, plastic playground set and not far from that was what looked to be a splash pad, not yet up and running for the summer. An asphalt walking path meandered through large shade trees sporting late spring growth. Following its progress, she noticed several green metal benches like the one she was on and a few water fountains, one of which had a bowl near the ground so people could water their dogs as well as themselves.

Taking in a deep breath of fresh air, she was thankful to have grown up here. Everyone got along pretty well. She experienced an occasional spat of racism or two growing up, but nothing serious. Her father had explained it perfectly at the time: "There are ignorant folks everywhere." But, while she had been called a racial slur a few times in her life, her own parents weren't overjoyed about her dating a white guy either.

She imagined her father talking to his black friends. "I hear Evie got married," they'd say. "Yeah, but to a white guy," her father would reply. "A white guy?" his friends would ask in unison. "Yes, but he's really good to her," her father would answer, and everyone would nod in consolation.

Laughing at herself, Evelyn took in a deep breath and exhaled slowly. Being a psychology major, she'd always been interested in people's interactions and the physiological happenings behind them. Most people weren't aware how much their genetic make-up and environmental markers factored into every decision they made, even the mundane daily reactions to other people. Everyone had tiny little "uglies" inside that they tried to keep hidden. Everyone.

She spent a long time analyzing herself and her current situation. Sleeping with Trae was obviously a yearning for the simpler times of high school. Trae was a basketball and baseball star in and one of the most coveted guys in school. All the black girls and many of the white girls wanted to be with him, but she had won. When they walked down the halls of Souls Harbor High, they both drew envious looks. A high school version of a power couple, they strutted around like a king and queen. The world was their oyster and she'd loved every minute of it.

Now, in college, there was a certain detachment, a focus on a small group of friends. She wasn't famous, most girls didn't bother to give her a second look, much less be jealous of her. It was the real world and very far from the sheltered life she'd once had.

Clinically speaking, all the talk about high school on the night in question had sent her hippocampus into overdrive, flooding her body with emotional memories of a simpler time, then sent the messages to her amygdala, triggering an emotional response to the presence of Trae in the group. Coupled with the amount of alcohol suppressing the logic offered by her frontal lobe, she was doomed to sleep with her ex. It wasn't a new happenstance. It happened so many times that it was practically a cliché.

But things weren't that simple, and she knew it. Aaron had also taken a few psychology classes and he would know the clinical definition too. Somehow, she didn't think it would suffice. She'd cheated on him, gotten pregnant, and gotten rid of the baby. There was nothing in her textbooks to help her explain that to the man she loved, and there was nothing in them to tell him to forgive her for it.

"You're thinking too much," she told herself as she slid her phone from the waistband of her leggings. Holding it in her hand, she considered texting Aaron, but decided against it. She sighed, stretched one arm along the back of the bench, and turned her face skyward again. A few small puffy clouds gently floated in the deep blue heavens. In the distance an airplane, barely visible, left a white contrail as it headed off to its far away destination.

Cara pressed her chest against the rough bark of a giant hickory tree and peered cautiously across the wide, grassy lawn before her. This was always a nice place to come, especially at this time of year. The lush new grass was a good place to lay and lose herself in the blueness of the sky above her. Sometimes she could see shapes in the clouds. Sometimes, if an airplane passed high overhead, she'd make up stories about where it was going and who was onboard. On days like this it was mostly her own voice that she heard in her head. Days like this were few and far between lately though.

Beyond the expanse of grass was the park itself. There was a jungle gym where kids would come and play. It was always fun to sit on the grass, far enough away as to not draw attention to herself, and close her eyes, listening to the children. Their laughs rang in her ears like a joyful chorus. The innocence of their laughter calmed her mind; one of the few things that brought her happiness.

The park had changed over the years. The splash pad was only a few years old, but it brought great joy to the kids. Their laughs and squeals of delight sang to her ears. They had also added a long, hard, black path like a tiny road where people walked their dogs, jogged, and pushed babies in strollers. The water from the fountains was always cold and clear, almost sweet. Several swing sets were scattered about along with picnic tables and barbeque grills, anchored in concrete. Being so early in the summer, the park was practically deserted. Cara saw a man on the path jogging in a blue outfit with two white stripes on the leg. He was older, had those things in his ears and paid little attention to anything else as he trudged along the path, working up a sweat.

Sweeping her eyes along the path she noticed a woman sitting in the sun on one of the benches. She was black, about her age, and looked to be asleep. Staring at the woman, something stirred in her mind. She couldn't put her finger on it, but there was something. A strong urge to get a closer look at this woman slowly began to build.

Working her way along the tree line, her eyes glued to the woman, Cara began to close the distance cautiously. The woman lifted her phone, slid her fingers back and forth across it, then sat it down beside her on the bench. People never went anywhere without those things. What was the attraction? she wondered. Who could look at that thing for so long?

The woman on the bench turned and looked in the direction of a car horn then settled back against the bench again. What was she doing? There was no stroller and no baby? Was she waiting for someone? Maybe that's why she was looking at her phone. People did that a lot when they were waiting on someone. Whoever she was meeting was lucky, because she was beautiful.

Her long, black hair was tied back very neatly, and hung over the back of the bench like a shimmering waterfall as she rested her head on the slats of the bench. It wasn't curly like most of the black people she saw, and it bounced and swayed around every time she moved.

A hand absently went to her own tangled, dirty mop of hair as she stared at the beautiful young black woman on the bench. What was it about this woman that was making her risk such an approach? A slight tickle in her mind began to form, telling her she knew her. But from where? When? She'd been at her home or in the woods her whole life, supposedly home schooled until she was sixteen. After that her father had dropped the pretense of even that. She didn't know anyone in this town. There was no other family; no friends. There had been her parents, then after her mother died there was her dad, then he died, and it was just her.

Pausing briefly in the shadow of a towering oak, Cara cautiously made her way toward the girl, always careful to keep one of the large tree trunks that lined the path between her and the woman on the bench. Working her way from tree to tree, Cara stopped about twenty feet from the girl and stared at her.

Her beauty was even more breathtaking as she neared. Her smooth, black hair shone in the sun, framing the gentle features of her face. A pair of pink lips, sat in a pool of smooth, clear, light brown skin. She looked like a woman in a magazine, or on the television she sometimes watched through people's windows. There was a casual elegance to the girl that drew her like a moth to a flame.

But it wasn't her beauty that called Cara to come closer. There was a knowing; a sense that she needed to meet this woman. There was a kindness in her face, a genuineness that she wanted to touch. Did she know her? If she did, from where?

"Get outta here, you freak!" The suddenness and violence of the man's voice startled both women, drawing a gasp from Evelyn as she relaxed on the bench, her face to the sun with her eyes closed.

Cara stopped, suddenly becoming aware that she'd left the safety of her perch behind the tree and now stood ten feet from the park bench, her hand outstretched toward the woman. Evelyn sprung to her feet, knocking her phone to the ground as she spun to see what the man was pointing at. For an instant the world around them faded away and the two women's eyes locked in a stare.

The jogger in the blue athletic suit was busy pulling his ear buds from his ears. He'd made the circuit and had happened to come upon the scene, somehow unseen or unheard by Cara's ever cautious senses.

"Get on now!" He bellowed again, waving his hand at Cara. "Git!"

"What the hell's wrong with you?" Evelyn asked as she picked her phone up from the ground, checking to see if the screen was broken. Satisfied that it wasn't, she turned her attention to the man. Her hands went to her hips as she awaited an answer.

"She was sneaking up on you, ma'am," the jogger said, defending himself. "It's just Cara, she's a freaking nutcase."

"How about you calm down!" Evelyn ordered as her eyes swept from him to the woman as she slowly edged backwards. "Are you okay?"

Cara held her hands out, showing Evelyn her palms. Confused and afraid, her voice failed her. She stuttered out a few incoherent sounds but said nothing. Evelyn shot the man another stern look then took a step toward Cara, her own hand extended.

The woman wore dirty, loose-fitting jeans and the equally dirty man's collared shirt, also too big for her. Her hair hung in unwashed strings from her head, leaving Evelyn to guess that she was homeless. But there was something else. What was it?

"Are you okay?" Evelyn asked, concerned as she pulled her sunglasses off. "You hungry?"

Cara's eyes darted back and forth between the woman and the man, who had resigned himself to a spectator's role. Slowly she began to back away, drawing herself together as if she wanted to disappear. Pausing to give the woman one last look Cara spun on the heels of her ragged sneakers and sprinted towards the woods. Towards safety.

"What the hell is your problem?" Evelyn asked the man as she watched the woman race across the wide lawn, putting distance between them with surprising speed.

"Me?" The man asked incredulously. "I probably saved you from getting robbed or hurt. Maybe even killed."

"Cool your jets, Lancelot. I really don't think that's what was going on here." Evelyn swept her eyes across the grassy lawn, looking for the girl. She had disappeared.

"Lady, that was Crazy Cara. She's a nutcase."

"So, you've already said," Evelyn replied, shaking her head. "Looks to me like she was a homeless person about to simply ask someone for help."

"She ain't no homeless person. She lives out on Tuck Smith road in a run-down shack. And she's nuttier than squirrel shit."

Evelyn looked at the man and again shook her head. "She's a human being."

"You must not be from around here," he began, putting his left ear bud back into his ear. "Cause if you were, you'd know exactly who that was." He stabbed the air in her direction for emphasis.

"I'll have you know I've lived here all my life, mister."

"Well, if that's so you should know better." The man poked his right ear bud in and jogged away, leaving Evelyn staring toward the wood line where the woman had disappeared. There was no sign of her.

She thought about walking down to the edge of the forest, but decided against it, and sat back down on the bench, stealing one more look in the direction the girl had gone. So much for a peaceful morning at the park.

"Do you know that there are eighty-seven registered homeless people in Souls Harbor, according to the last census?" Evelyn asked her parents across the supper table, hoping to break the awkward silence. "That seems odd for such a small town."

"If they're homeless how do you know they live here?" Her dad asked with a grin.

"You know what I mean," Evelyn answered, unamused.

"I guess that's probably normal. Lots of homeless people all across the country." Her dad forked more greens into his mouth and shrugged.

"We do lots of stuff for them at church," Martha told her as she sliced the piece of ham on her plate. "Especially in the wintertime."

"Well, I met one of them today, I think," Evelyn said.

"You think you met a homeless person, or you met a person that you think might be homeless?" Her mother asked, her tone borderline condescending.

"I met a woman who looked homeless, but some guy said she lived out on Truck Smith road."

"Tuck Smith road," her father corrected. "It's out past where that old sex store was on Turner street, near the edge of town."

Martha shook her head. "Nasty folks."

"Who? Homeless people?" Evelyn asked.

"No," Martha snapped. "Them folks going to that store, buying all sorts of that stuff. Dirty movies and all that stuff. All sorts of immoral folks around here."

"Not enough to keep 'em in business," Freddy added.

"Thank the Lord for that."

Evelyn felt like her mother's eyes were burning a hole in her, but she refused to look up and find out. It was all part of the process. The backhanded comments and thinly veiled judgements would continue until Evelyn finally had enough, blew up, and they talked through things. This time, however, there was the added bitterness of the fact that her daughter had gone to her father first, and not her.

"Whatever," Evelyn dismissed. "She looked homeless."

"What do homeless people look like?" Her mother asked.

"I don't know. Dirty, old, clothes that don't fit, hair a mess."

"Maybe she didn't get to the salon today," her mother quipped as she stood and carried her plate into the kitchen.

Evelyn sighed frustratedly, looking to her father for help. "I guess she hates me now," she whispered.

"No, she doesn't," her father answered in a hushed tone. "She's upset, and understandably so. She just gone take some time to process this. Hell, baby doll, I ain't even wrapped my head around this yet and you all up in here talking about a homeless person. What's up with that?"

"I don't know." Evelyn pouted as she moved the greens around on her plate. All afternoon her curiosity about the interaction at the park had been a pleasant distraction from her thoughts. "I just don't want to spend my every waking moment talking about this. It's bad enough that it's always there, in the back of my mind."

"Let me tell you something, sweetheart," her mother began as she reentered the dining room. "This here is the real world. The real world has homeless people in it. You do what you can, but that's all you can do."

"But surely there must be some place she can go, someone that can help."

"Baby, some folks make bad decisions in life no matter how much you help 'em."

This time Evelyn did see the disappointment and scorn in her mother's eyes, and it hurt. Propping her elbow on the table and rubbing her forehead she absorbed the blow. In what was probably a normal dynamic between mothers and daughters, her mother had rarely held back when Evelyn needed correction. She rarely minced words and always, always, drove her point home with fearless accuracy.

"Okay," her father interrupted. "Let's not turn on each other now. We're family and we all love one another. Let's all remember that." His wife and daughter had had some epic fights through the years, some of them lasting for weeks. Mama had won all of them.

"Fine. Whatever." Evelyn stood from her chair and threw her napkin onto the table. "I'm going to my room."

"You can't hide in there forever," Martha said as her daughter stormed past her.

"I don't wanna hide forever," Evelyn griped as she started down the hall. "Just till I go back to school."

Freddy looked at his wife as the sound of a door being slammed echoed through the house. "That wasn't very productive."

Martha shrugged and picked up Evelyn's plate. "Truth hurts sometimes, Freddy. Now don't it?"

"I guess it does," he sighed as he looked down at the food left on his plate and shook his head. "I guess it does, Martha, but sometimes it hurts too much to bear."

"Come off it, Freddy. You always take up for her."

"What can I say? She's my baby girl."

"Well, your baby girl got her tail in a bad way, now didn't she. Ain't enough pettin' in the world to change that."

"That's right, she did. It's not something we can change, no matter how much we beat her up about it."

Martha stared at her husband for a moment then turned silently and went back into the kitchen. "She was raised better than that and you know it."

Evelyn stomped across her room and flopped down on the bed angrily. Sometimes her mother was just plain mean. Was it too much to ask for one night with a calm, normal dinner where they didn't have to talk about what a slut she was? How immoral she was? How Ghetto she was? Clenching her fist, she punched a pillow on her bed.

It took almost an hour before Evelyn grew bored pouting and allowing herself to wallow in self-pity. Forcing herself off the bed, she took a long hot shower. Toweling off, she found herself hoping she'd used all the hot water so her mother couldn't have any. It was petty and childish, she knew, but it would be a small victory.

Dressed in her usual sleeping attire of an oversized tee shirt and a pair of panties, she went to her closet. She'd been tugging on a mental thread earlier, before her mother's mean-spirited attack, and she wanted to continue. She hefted a box of books from the top shelf and carried it to her bed.

Something the man at the park had said had stuck in her mind. The implication was that the girl had lived in Souls Harbor a long time. It was doubtful because, as best she could judge given her appearance, the girl didn't look much older than she was. How could she not have noticed a person like that? How could she not have seen her through all those years?

Bypassing her junior and senior years, Evelyn went straight to her sophomore yearbook and pulled it out of the box. If the girl lived here, she surely went to school here. Some of their school years had to have overlapped. If she went to school in Souls Harbor, there was a chance she was in one of these books. Souls Harbor only had one high school and one junior high. Today, there were two elementary schools, but there used to be only one.

By the time Aaron called, Evelyn had lost most of her gusto for discovering the woman in her yearbook. She'd gone through year by year, class by class and looked for anyone that might be her. In the beginning she had seen a few forgotten faces, and remembered a few fun times, but they quickly faded into drudgery with each unsuccessful page.

"Hi there, sweets," he said when she answered the phone.

"Hi handsome," she answered as a smile broke out on her face.

"Can you talk?" He asked.

"Sure. I'm just sitting in my room, or rather laying on my bed," she teased.

"I like the sound of that. Wish I was there with you."

"I wish you were too," she began as she laid back against the pillows. "But you may not. Mom's being assy."

Aaron chuckled. "Assy" was a word he and Eve used when people were being "unpleasant".

"Well, I'd put up with assy to be with you."

"Aw. You're so sweet. It's good to hear a friendly voice."

"Look, I'm just going to put this out there," he began, "I don't wanna pressure you, but whatever you've been stressed about, if it has anything to do with me, I'm sorry."

"Honey, baby, it's nothing to do with you. Well, I guess it does, but it's not because of you or anything you've done. Please don't think that. You're perfect." Evelyn wiped a tear from her cheek as her heart sank. I'm so tired of crying, she thought with a heavy sigh.

"Well, as far as I'm concerned, let's just forget it. If it's something you feel like you need to tell me, then don't. I love you, sweets, that's all I need to know."

She could hear the genuine sadness in his voice and wanted nothing more than to say that she was on her way and to run to him, fall into his arms and stay there forever. But how long would it be before her secret ruined them? What about their future? Could she do that? Could she just put this behind her and move on? Aaron was offering her an attractive out, but she already knew she couldn't live with the guilt.

"I wish it was that easy, sweetie. It's me. It's something I have to get through."

"But you are coming back? Right?" He asked, his voice faltering.

"There is nowhere in the whole world I'd rather be right now than in your arms. To be lying next to you, feeling you next to me."

"Good," he sighed, relieved. "I just, I didn't know."

A wave of guilt swept over her. Here she was, the one who had screwed up, and it was HIM worried about losing HER. Closing her eyes, she scolded herself. She hadn't really given a lot of thought to how things would affect him, whether he knew the whole truth or not.

"Can I ask you something?" Evelyn twirled a lock of her hair nervously around her right index finger, biting her lower lip as she awaited his answer.

"Anything."

"Am I a bad person?"

Aaron laughed. "Well no," he said with authority. "You are kind and sweet and smart and funny, not to mention beautiful and you have a smoking hot body."

Evelyn smiled. "Thank you." He always made her feel better. "But do you think I'm bougie?"

"What?" He asked with a laugh. "No, I don't. Well, I've never really known what people mean when they say that, exactly."

"Do I act like I'm better than I am?"

"I don't think so. You're pretty awesome, so…"

"Do you think I'm spoiled? That I'm high maintenance?"

This time there was a pause on the other end of the line.

"As far as spoiled, no. I've seen you work your but off this year. You haven't asked for any special help or favors. You even work part time at the bookstore, and that's a lot with our class load. So, spoiled? No."

"What about high maintenance?"

"That's harder. I mean, you get your hair done, you like your fingernails done. You like to dress nice. Is that high maintenance? If it

60

is, it's never looked better. You're hot, sweets, all hot girls are high maintenance. It's a cross we lucky guys who date y'all have to bear."

"Oh, bless your hearts," she teased. "That's the price you have to pay to ride the golden chariot."

"And worth every cent. Look, I don't think you are high maintenance, or spoiled or anything. I think you're my Eve and I'm in love with you."

Evelyn's heart soared. She knew that he loved her but hearing him say so with such conviction filled her with joy. His adamant declaration of his love for her, and the possible out that he'd given her elevated her mood somewhere close to giddy.

"If I were there you'd be in for a long night, mister," she flirted, lowering her voice to a sexy, throatier octave that she thought of as her bedroom voice.

Aaron moaned into the phone. "If only. After finals and not seeing you for a month I- "

"It's hardly been three days," she interrupted.

"Well, it feels like a month," he laughed.

"I know, sweetie," Evelyn began as she slid her legs beneath the covers and stretched out in the twin bed. Her foot pushed gently against the second-grade yearbook that she was about to begin searching when Aaron had called. It teetered on the bed and fell open on the floor, drawing only a quick glance from Evelyn.

"Maybe I can help a little," she teased as a smile slid across her face. "Where are you?"

"I'm in bed. Kevin is out partying."

"That's good, because all I've got on is a t-shirt and panties."

Aaron sighed heavily into the phone. "Which ones?"

"The little coral colored ones with the tiny bow in the front."

"Oh man, maybe I'll have a long night after all," he said hopefully.

"Maybe we both will," she promised with a naughty chuckle.

FOUR

Cara sat up, clutching the sleeping bag around her, and looked at the remains of her fire. A thin tail of smoke snaked from the bed of grey embers and drifted lazily toward the morning sky. She grabbed a handful of dry branches from the pile she had amassed next to her campsite and tossed them onto the ashes. A long, steady blow on them rewarded her with a face full of smoke before the flames leapt to life and began devouring the twigs.

Warming her hands, she sat by the fire and stared into the flames. The day would be warm, but she needed a little heat after a night spent under the stars. The morning was cool, and a heavy dampness hung in the air, leaving everything covered in a light film of moisture.

Her mind crawled groggily toward her interaction with the woman at the park. What was it about her that had drawn her out in the open like that? Why did she feel the need to be close to her? No one had ever made her feel that way before. Most people were mean and yelled at her, like the running man had. But not her. The girl had reached out to her.

Who was that woman? She wondered as the flames began to dance higher. There was something about her. Something about her eyes. Deep brown and faceted with golden shards that seemed to pierce her. Those eyes. Had she seen them before? It was like the woman could see her, the real her. Not this shell of a woman she'd become. It was like she could see the woman that she herself wanted to be.

A man's laugh, mean and harsh, echoed through her head suddenly, causing her to flinch.

"Shut up you retard!" he screamed.

"No!" Cara spat. "No!" She wanted to think about the girl some more.

"She saw the real you, girl. The crazy you."

"Yeah," a ragged feminine voice chimed in. "You are what you are. Nothing could ever change that."

Shaking her head Cara kicked her way out of her sleeping bag like it was full of snakes. She backed away from the fire on her hands and knees, occasionally raising a hand as it to shield herself from a blow that never came.

"Please stop," she begged.

"Look at that raggedy mop of hair!" The woman told her. "Burn it!"

"Burn it off, you stupid retard!" The old man added. "And that ugly face too. Burn it!"

"You'll look better," the boy chimed in, laughing. "Ugly ass freak!"

"No. Please don't make me," Caroline begged, still backing away from the fire. They were strong and she could feel the want to obey them begin to creep into her mind when her backside struck something firm.

Turning, she grabbed the old wood railing on the back steps of her house and hauled herself up from the cold, damp ground. The wood groaned under her weight, but it held as she steadied herself. Staring at the fire, the desire to touch it slowly began to grow.

"No," she whispered desperately, looking around for help that she knew wouldn't be there. "Please." A hand was suddenly at her mouth and she began viciously chewing on her thumbnail as she continued to search the back yard. Finally, steady enough to stand on her own two bare feet, she sprinted the short distance across the back yard and threw herself onto two small, well- kept mounds of earth. The voices suddenly stopped, and she started to cry. She could feel herself sinking into the usual hopeless fog that always seemed to envelope her. Its presence was so constant and so pervasive that it almost felt like an old friend.

Almost.

Evelyn stretched and yawned, a smile spreading across her face before she opened her eyes. She had slept better than she had in weeks and awoke with the sense that a huge weight had been lifted from her shoulders. Certainly, her conversation with Aaron had helped.

They had talked deep into the night, flirting, laughing, talking dirty to one another. With his amazing command of phrases Aaron had made her feel like he was right beside her, touching her; caressing her skin. Her hand followed his desires as he led her on a tour of her own body; as he moved across her warm, brown skin from a hundred miles away.

Afterwards, they had talked for hours, discussing anything and everything. Everything that is except the reason she'd left in the first place. Her parents, his parents, school, the weather, summer plans, they discussed it all in an amiable, easy flowing conversation that began to rebuild her sense of self, brick by brick. Somewhere along the way she'd realized that her mistakes were beginning to define her to herself. They were consuming who she was and dulling her senses of everything around her. The oftentimes overpowering guilt and shame was reshaping her psyche and forcing it down a dark road she didn't want to travel.

Eventually, unable to hold her eyes open despite wanting desperately to, she had faded into a peaceful sleep with Aaron's voice telling her that he'd love her until the day he died. At least she thought that's what he'd said. Maybe she'd dreamed it. Either way it was a wonderful way to end a tumultuous day.

"Oh, good. You're up." Martha's sharp tone was a splash of cold water in the face to Evelyn's mood, drop kicking Aaron completely out of her mind.

"I'm up, mama," she groaned.

"I know," Martha said again as she crossed the room and sat on the foot of her daughter's bed. "We need to talk."

Evelyn drew in a deep breath and exhaled slowly, puffing her cheeks out. "I know, but can I pee first?" she asked as she slid from beneath the covers and walked to the bathroom.

"Maybe brush your teeth while you're in there," Martha told her through the closed door. "And put some clothes on."

Standing at the kitchen sink, still smarting from her talk with her mother, Evelyn stared out the window as she worked on finishing the second half of her ham and cheese sandwich. Their talk had hit all the "church" points of contrition, repentance, and forgiveness, the dangers of immorality, and the sanctity of life. Having been raised in church, mostly by her mother's hand, she'd already crucified herself with all these topics, as well as honesty, trust, and faithfulness. While this was all new to her mother, she had had nearly five months to punish herself.

Remaining mostly quiet and agreeing with her mother, she had gotten through it with surprisingly few tears, owning the fact that she had disappointed them, and herself. She calmly explained the thoughts that had plagued her as best she could, and in the end they had hugged tightly and her mother had even apologized for putting so much pressure on her, blaming some of it on the fact that she was a young, African-American woman and had to work harder; had to be pushed harder.

"We don't expect much from you, Evie" she said to the window, mocking her mother's voice. "Just perfection." She sighed angrily. No longer hungry, she threw the remainder of the sandwich down the garbage disposal and switched it on.

"What was that?" Her mother asked as she passed through the kitchen with a basket of dirty laundry.

"Nothing," Evelyn lied, switching off the disposal and washing her hands. "Can I throw some things in there?"

"Full load," her mother told her through the open laundry room door. "But feel free to do your own load later."

Evelyn screwed her face up, mimicking her mother. "Feel free to do your own load later."

"What was that, baby?" Her mother asked, poking her head out the doorway. "I got the dryer going and I can't hear a thing in here."

"I said I'd do a load later," Evelyn lied.

"Okay. You got any plans for today?"

"Not really. Chill, I guess. Why?

"I thought we could maybe go shopping or something. Hang out like we used to do. Get something to eat."

I thought you couldn't hear a thing from in there, Evelyn thought. "Yeah, that'll be cool."

"Okay, baby. Let me get this laundry going and do something with this nappy head and I'll be ready."

"Say about an hour then?" Evelyn asked, hiding a smirk with her hand. She heard her mother mumble something under her breath, then she appeared in the doorway with a basket of clean clothes. "Because I need a shower," she added hastily.

"Go take a shower. I'll fold these clothes and still be ready before you, Miss Priss."

"Dynamite don't go off by itself, mama. Somebody's gotta light the fuse," Evelyn sassed as she headed for her room.

"You just take a shower and keep that fuse where it is," Martha called after her daughter. "Damn lit fuses is what got you into this mess to start with," she mumbled to herself as she carried the basket on her hip. These kids, she thought with a heavy sigh.

"You know something?" Martha Jackson asked her daughter as she brought her Toyota Camry to a stop at a traffic light. "You was born on the first day of spring."

"I know mom," Evelyn laughed. "It's my birthday."

"Your father, bless his heart, wanted to name you 'Spring'."

"What?" Evelyn asked. "Really? Tell me you're kidding."

"He did." Martha laughed herself. "I told him not no, but hell no." She shook her head. "Naming my baby girl Spring? What was he thinking?"

"Well, for that, I truly do thank you, Mama." Evelyn shook her head as they rolled through the intersection. "Spring Jackson," she mused. It sounded like a stripper name, one who specialized in G-strings made of vines and daisies for pasties.

"Sometimes, baby, men just don't think. They can't help it though, they just men."

"Maybe so. But I'm glad you vetoed that one." Evelyn turned her attention to the city scape passing by her window. A lot of things had changed in Souls Harbor, but a lot was still the same. Older and showing its age, but still the same. She had spent her whole life here and found a certain romance in the old buildings. The familiarity was comforting, especially after being away at school.

"You remember Mr. Michaels?" Martha asked as they passed the old pharmacy where they had always bought their medicine. There was a hand-painted sign in the window that just said "CLOSED".

"He was always nice to me. Did you know he always slipped me a piece of candy when we went in there?" Evelyn admitted. If she was going to tell secrets she might as well put all her cards on the table.

"I don't doubt it. He gave candy to all the children," she replied, pronouncing it as 'chirren'. "Anyway, he died a couple of months ago and you know who was at the funeral?"

"Aww. That's sad. Most of the town turned out, I'd imagine." Evelyn smiled, remembering the gentile old man with tiny glasses and a ring of white hair around his bald head. His voice was always light and whispery when he called you over to him. He would drop a piece of candy in your hand when your parents weren't looking and give you a clever wink and a smile. As a child she'd thought it fabulously scandalous and always hid to eat her treat so her mom wouldn't find out.

"His boyfriend, or lover, or whatever they call it."

"What? Mr. Michaels was gay?" Evelyn asked, shocked. "He was like a hundred years old."

"Well he wasn't always old, Evie," Martha told her as she steered around a corner. "But it just goes to show you, even in a small town, secrets can hide if people want them too."

Evelyn felt her body tense up defensively. What exactly was her mother saying? That the whole situation with Trae was a secret? Or should be a secret? She certainly hadn't told anyone. Trae probably did some bragging, but that would be deniable enough. Her parents would be the ones left to carry the shame and embarrassment around town if this ever got out. No one knew about the pregnancy even if they believed she'd hooked up with Trae, so there was that. She surely didn't feel the need to spread it around town. Maybe it was her mother's way of assuring her she could still come home in the future without fear of the old biddies pointing and whispering.

Skirting the edge of town to avoid the lunch traffic, the two women rode in silence as they passed a freshly tilled corn field, its fledgling crop standing a foot tall. Lost in thought, Evelyn allowed her eyes to wash over the alternating stripes of green corn stalks and dark earth. It was a disorienting, but not unpleasant, throwback to her childhood. On such a sunny day it had a similar effect to a strobe light that was almost mesmerizing. As the rows began to shorten and taper off, they gave way to a narrow strip of pine trees that ran parallel to the rows, almost dividing the giant field into two halves.

Halfway across the field, near the stand of pines, Evelyn's eyes tried to fix on a shape. Was it a person? Jerking her head around as they sped by, she caught another glimpse of color that her mind matched to the blue jeans and checkered shirt that the girl in the park had worn.

"Stop the car!" She exclaimed, turning in the seat to keep the girl in her sights. The car slowed but didn't stop and the shape disappeared behind the trees. "Stop. Turn around."

"What's the matter with you? I can't just stop. They's a truck behind us."

"Ok, sorry. Just turn around and go back. I thought I saw something in that corn field."

"Probably just a deer, baby. There ain't no place to turn around anyway," Martha told her, irritated as she put a hand to her chest. "Girl, you 'bout gave me a heart attack. Hollering like that."

"Sorry, sorry," Evelyn said, her voice almost frantic. "Up there, there's a road. Turn around, please, Mama."

"Lord-a-mercy, girl." Martha threw her signal on and quickly steered her car off the road, drawing a quick horn blast from the truck behind them as it passed. She backed the car back into the road and headed back the direction they'd just came.

"Up here, just past that line of trees," Evelyn directed. "Slow down a little bit."

"What are you looking for?"

"I saw somebody out there, I think it was the girl from the park," Evelyn explained.

"The homeless girl?" Her mother asked sharply.

"The girl," Evelyn replied as she stared out the driver's side window, struggling to see past her mother. "I know it was her."

"You stop and think it might just be a farmer?" Martha said dismissively.

"No. It wasn't a man, mama. I know it was her. She had on the same clothes as before."

"What does it matter anyway?" Martha's irritation was growing.

"I don't know." Evelyn strained to see as they rolled slowly past the line of trees, but the girl had disappeared.

"I told you it was probably a deer."

"A deer in jeans and a checkered shirt?" Evelyn asked as she fell back into her seat.

"Maybe it was a princess deer, like you, dear," her mother said with a wry smile.

"Maybe so," Evelyn agreed sarcastically, affording herself a final glance over her shoulder towards the rapidly fading tree line. "Have you ever seen her?"

"Who?"

"The girl?" Evelyn asked impatiently. "The girl. That guy at the park said she'd lived here for years and he recognized her. He acted like I should know her if I was from here, but I don't remember ever seeing her. He called her name, Cara, I think."

"Cara?"

"Yeah, that's it. Cara."

"Everybody's seen her, sweetie. She wanders around everywhere. You see her all over town, lurching around, mumbling to herself."

"Has anybody ever tried reaching out to her?" Evelyn asked.

"I know our church helps out people like that with food and medicine and the like. We bring them toiletries and such, but I doubt they use them much."

"Why do you say that?" Evelyn asked, then remembered Cara's dirty face and unwashed hair.

"Some of 'em are crazy, baby. We got a team of men, big men, who take stuff out to some of those people. They say some of 'em just live in squalor. It's sad, but they can't help it because of their minds are gone. Drugs and liquor done ruined them."

"Do you think Cara is crazy? She didn't seem so bad the other day."

72

"I don't know baby. I've seen her talking to herself and swatting at flies or something that ain't there. Stuff like that. A couple of years ago a man claimed she took a plug out of his hand when he was trying to help her. I don't know. You just hear things."

"That seems implausible. If she was unstable enough to bite someone for no reason, they would pick her up and take her for a psych eval. And if she was mentally unstable, they'd have to put her somewhere."

"I don't know about all that, baby. All I know is the men at church told us not to go messing around those folks; that it could be dangerous. I give them a wide berth."

"You know, mama, it's good that y'all do stuff for them, but if they need medical help or psychological help, you're really not solving their problems."

Martha's eyes narrowed. "There's a free clinic downtown. If they need medical help, they can walk in there six days a week. As far as the other, what can we do? Cain't no shrink help 'em if they starve to death or freeze to death."

"That's true but reaching the homeless is more than bringing them food."

"Evie, baby, I know you're all idealistic and full of hope for mankind and all that. I know the folks at school sit up there in their fancy rooms and talk about things like inequality and social injustice, and that's fine. But before you start to lecture me on reaching out to people, because my church only brings folks food and blankets and toothbrushes, you need to realize that in the real world, things aren't as simple as some folks want them to be."

"I'm not lecturing you, mama. I was just saying- "

"I know what you was saying. Our church, and lots of churches 'round here do a lot for people. Ask yourself this, how many banks do what we do? How many of those fancy boutiques you like do as much as we do? When you graduate and get your fancy job, how much time will you spend in the slums?"

"I don't know. I'd like to think I'd help out."

"I'm sure you do sweetie. You're a sweet girl with a big heart and I love that about you. But that's why they call it idea-ology and not I-do-ology."

Evelyn pursed her lips. Her mother's words stung harder than she wanted to admit. The truth was that she hadn't lifted a finger to help another human being since her key club days of high school. She wanted to, but there never seemed to be enough time.

"Look, Evie," Martha reached across the car and rubbed her daughters' leg. "I'm not getting on you. It's just that if all people do is talk about how things should be and never actually work to change things, then things never get better. Faith without works is dead."

"I know," Evelyn sighed. "Maybe that's why I feel like I need to reach out to this girl. Do you know who she is?"

"Not a clue."

"How did I not ever know about her?" Evelyn asked, more to herself than her mother.

"I don't know," Martha answered. "You was in school and running around doing all that stuff girls do in high school. It ain't like folks go looking for her, you know. One minute she's there, one minute she's gone."

Evelyn nodded, agreeing with her mother as her mind began to wander. The girl in the park certainly didn't seen crazy. Dirty? Yes.

Homeless? Maybe, or close to it. Afraid and scared? Definitely. But crazy, no. Riding in silence as her mother drove back to town, Evelyn's mind raced, trying to formulate a plan to reach out to this girl. There had been something about her; something that just seemed to draw her. She didn't know exactly what it was, but there was definitely something there.

Evelyn tossed her shopping bags onto the bed and grabbed her laptop. Opening the computer, she sat down and sat it on her knees, starting it up as her mind raced. Hoping for a clue, her mind went over the facts that she knew, or at least thought she knew. Cara was a longtime resident of Souls Harbor. She probably lived near Truck Smith, or Tuck Smith road. She was about her own age. Female. Caucasian.

Scanning the Souls Harbor home page, she slid the cursor to the "CENSUS" tab and clicked it, hoping to find a list resident names and addresses, but found only demographics and numbers. Undeterred, she clicked on the map icon and bent toward the screen. Expanding the map, she found Tuck Smith road and zoomed in. Again, her search turned up nothing. There were several small, unnamed roads shown that sprang off Tuck Smith, but nothing that looked promising. She knew from experience that there could be hundreds of roads, some passable some not, on any map of any southern town. Some lead to gas wells, some lead to illegal dump sites, some simply lead to nowhere. And off those roads there could be side roads, and mile-long driveways in various stages of overgrowth. There were rarely used camp houses, hunting lodges, and places where people just wanted to be alone, all forged through the thick underbrush and tall pines that threatened to swallow Souls Harbor.

Drumming her nails against the side of the computer, Evelyn racked her brain. Social media of any kind was out of the question. Even if she had her last name, she didn't see this girl as an updating your status type. Frustrated, she sat the laptop on the bed. In the age of technology, it was easy to find someone, anyone, but if they weren't connected it was impossible.

"Nobody's completely disconnected," she told herself, remembering what her mother had said about the men at her church taking food to the homeless. Somebody somewhere knew her. Looking around her room, struggling to find an answer, her eyes fell on her first and second grade yearbooks from Souls Harbor Elementary. They were the only ones that she hadn't checked. Out of desperation she grabbed the first-grade edition and thumbed through it quickly, sparing a glance out the window as thunder sounded in the distance.

Finding her own class, her eyes were drawn to her seven-year-old self. She wore a head full of short braids held up by colorful beads. Smiling, she looked at her own innocent eyes and wide grin. She was a pretty child, with gentle features and light brown skin, and big ole eyes.

A pang of sadness stabbed her heart as she wondered if her baby might have looked like her. It wasn't the first time she'd wondered that, and she knew it wouldn't be the last. Not if it was Trae's baby, she told herself. He wasn't super dark, but he was a lot darker than she was. He was cute, but he did have a touch of ghetto lean to his looks. Now if it had a black and a white parent, probably so. Aaron was a handsome man with a certain ruggedness to his face and she knew their babies would be beyond beautiful. If they ever had any.

The smile left her face suddenly as her eyes wandered over the other pictures on the page and fell on a girl with blond hair wearing a light pink blouse who's smile lit up her face. She noted the girls place on the page and slid her eyes to the list of names on the righthand margin.

Counting down from the top, her eyes stopped at the fourth name on the list, and her heart stopped in her chest.

Caroline Grace LeBeau.

Dumbfounded, her mouth fell open as she stared at the picture. Suddenly her mind began to be flooded with memories of Caroline. They had been best friends. Being one of the few black girls in her class she was a natural target, but Caroline had stuck up for her on the first day of first grade. A white boy, bigger than anyone else in class was teasing her about her braids and calling her names. Unprepared for the cruelty, she started to cry, which encouraging the boy's friends to join in. That was when Caroline appeared from the crowd. She stood between her and the boy with her hands on her hips and gave him what for. The boy tried to act tough, but something about Caroline made him change his mind. He walked away and his friends followed. They sat together at lunch that day, and every day that whole year, as best she remembered.

They became inseparable, playing hopscotch and jumping rope. Evelyn remembered brushing Careline's hair and Caroline trying to brush hers. She wiped a tear from her cheek as a sad smile came to her lips. Evelyn even liked saying her friend's name back then because it sounded French. "This is Caraliiiine Le BO!" she would say every time she introduced her to someone.

"And she's my best friend" Evelyn said aloud, finishing her own childhood introduction as tears rolled down her face. How could she have forgotten her best friend? Her mind groped the recesses of her memory, trying to remember what had happened to them. Why weren't they friends later on? Had she moved? Chewing on her lower lip as her mind worked, Evelyn stared at the picture of the little girl. The woman everyone called "Crazy Cara" had once been her best friend.

"What happened?" She asked the picture, wiping away a tear. The pretty, happy-looking girl with a radiant smile hardly resembled the Caroline she'd seen in the park. That was why she hadn't recognized her. Her transformation was so complete, so severe that she wondered if anything of the little girl in the picture even existed anymore.

Cara sat in the last working rocking chair on the front porch of the shack she called her home as rain poured from the rusty edge of the tin roof above her. Rocking slowly, she began to slip out of a world she'd learned to hate. Her vacant eyes slid down to the blade of the butcher knife gripped tightly in her right hand. While she watched, lightning flashed across the blackened sky, reflecting on the long, sharp blade. She'd been taught many things in her life, most of which she wished she'd never learned, but one good lesson she learned was how to sharpen a knife.

A small voice swam through the murky water of her mind and asked why she had the knife? The truth was that she didn't know. Was it for safety? For protection? But from who? Was it for them? Or was it for her? Did they tell her to get it from the kitchen?

Nodding her head slowly, she returned her attention to the storm. She liked it when it stormed. Then the outside world matched the world she lived in inside her mind; chaotic and frightening. Again, lightning flashed across the sky, illuminating the porch for a few brief seconds. Her blue, unblinking eyes lit up momentarily, then faded back into the darkness.

The charged atmosphere touched an electrical storm in her head, inciting the angry voices hell bent on destruction. But this wasn't her first storm. Sitting, almost catatonic, on the porch she allowed the storm to mesmerize her and ease her into a plane of existence where they couldn't reach her. From high above, she could hear their angry, vile outbursts, but they would soon be impotent and harmless to her. Of course, this would make them even angrier and they would shout louder, and their suggestions would become cruder, and their opinions more disgusting, but they knew they couldn't touch her.

"You got the knife, why don't you use it?" the old woman's voice asked.

"Yeah, stab it in your dirty whore's heart!" the man in her mind urged angrily.

"Do it," coached the little boy's voice. Often, he was as mean and dirty as the old man. There was something about his pre-pubescent voice that chipped away at her. He was just a kid, half her age probably, but he was a bully. "Do it! Stab it in your filthy cunt!"

A chorus of laughter rang through her mind accompanying a clap of thunder so strong she could feel it vibrate the house around her.

Cara continued to rock slowly as the storm outside raged on, bringing flashes of lightning in waves, one after the other. The knife that she'd sharpened on her daddy's old whet stone, gripped tightly in her hand, replayed every flash from the storm. Her eyes stared into the darkness, oblivious to the world around her. She began to sing in a whisper barely audible over the violence of the rain as it hammered the tin roof. With a slow and deliberate tempo, she cast her words into the tempest that surrounded her.

"Miss.... Mary.... Mack.... Mack.... Mack.... all.... dressed.... in... black.... black.... black..."

Lightning erupted in the sky overhead, splitting into three fingers. One of the fingers found something on the ground and struck with a loud report. A deafening clap of thunder followed almost immediately, sending a vibration through the knife as its edge rested against the wood of the armrest.

Cara heard the strike and the thunder, but as she slipped further into her mind it was the muffled snap of a tree branch. The noise didn't startle her, but the vibrations of the knife got her attention. The rocking chair stopped suddenly, and she sat in silence for a moment, her eyes drawn to the knife. There was a slight itch deep in her mind as the hand holding the knife twitched once, then again. The hand went still again, and the itch subsided.

Lifting her eyes back to the raging storm before her Cara began rocking again, continuing her methodical chant. "With…. silver…. buttons…. buttons…. buttons…. all…. down…. her…. back…. back…. back."

Lightning flashed overhead as the electricity streaked angrily across the sky. The world was momentarily as bright as noon on a sunny day, but by the time the thunder rolled across the land it had plunged back into a bitter darkness.

The storm was upon her now, raging with all its fury. Somewhere in the distance, toward town, a tornado siren began to wail but Cara didn't hear it. She was gone.

FIVE

Freddy Jackson sat in the swing on his screened in back porch and waited on his daughter. He'd seen her headlights as she arrived home and heard her go into the house. She'd know he was home and would come looking for him.

After a few minutes she poked her head out the back door. "Oh, there you are."

"You caught me," he said with a smile and took another drink of his beer.

"This thing still hold us?" She asked, joining him on the swing.

"If it'll hold me your skinny butt ain't going to bring it down," he told her as he slid an arm around her shoulders. She leaned into him with a relaxing sigh.

"Where's mom?"

"Bible study," he said flatly and took another sip of beer.

"Guess it is Wednesday. I lost track of the days."

"I thought you was with her," he told her.

"Yeah right," she snorted. "The roof would probably fall in on me. I guess she's down there praying for my mortal soul."

"There's worse things that can happen to a body than have someone pray for them," he told her curtly.

"I know. Sorry. I was just being assy. Actually, I had dinner with Kiera and her parents."

"How are they?" He asked. "Bert's heart doing okay?"

"They're all good. Mr. Walters' doing fine. He had to find another job so money's tight, but Kiera said they're making it okay."

"That's good to hear. I always liked old Bert. He's a good guy. The whole bunch really. Good people." Freddy finished his beer and sat the bottle on the floor beside the swing.

"It was fun hanging out with Kiera, seeing everybody."

"I'm sure it was. Probably did you some good."

"It did. I really enjoyed it." Evelyn turned slightly and looked at her father. After a long day he looked tired. How many hours of pay did he spend on her tuition and books? Even with the partial scholarships she'd earned, the savings account they'd started when she was young, and her working part time, it probably took a big chunk of his take home pay for her education. She was the first person in either of their families to go to college and she was proud of that fact, but it had to be a heavy banner to carry sometimes.

"I don't know if I've properly told you, but thank you, daddy, for all you do for me."

Freddy looked at his daughter, a proud smile sliding across his lips. "Baby, you thank me every time you get up and go to class. Every time you study hard and make a good grade you thank me." He hugged his daughter and kissed her on top of the head. "But you can thank me now by fetching me another beer."

Evelyn hopped up and disappeared into the house, returning with two bottles of beer in one hand and her phone in the other. Giving him one, she sat back down beside him.

"So that's how it is? You just gonna start drinking my beer?" Freddy asked.

"Please, daddy," she begged, giving him her best pouty look. "I'm twenty and I've just finished my third year of college. Surely you can spare one beer for your only child."

"If your mother drives up it better disappear," he warned.

"You're the best," she said, extending the top of the beer to him. "Can you open it?"

Freddy opened both beers and slid his hand back around his daughter as they started to swing again. Watching her take a long drink of the beer, he shook his head. Obviously, it wasn't her first beer.

Propped against her father, Evelyn scrolled through her phone with the thumb of her left hand as she held the beer with the other. She scanned the page quickly and deftly swiped the screen to bring up another.

"I got this theory," he began, "That one of these days, maybe a hundred years from now, that people's hands will be like a mitten. One big ole wide finger to hold the phone and a triple-jointed thumb four inches long to scroll with."

Evelyn nudged him playfully in the ribs with her elbow. "Stop, daddy."

"I just don't see what's so danged fascinating about those things."

"I couldn't live without my phone. Everybody I know is in here. I can call, text, e-mail, surf the web, watch videos, play music. Everything."

"Music?" Freddy asked. "Now that might be nice."

"You want some music?" She made a few swipes on the screen as she took another long drink of beer. "What'cha wanna hear?"

Freddy scratched his chin with his thumb and drank from the bottle as he thought. "Something old and slow; relaxing."

"I need a name, daddy."

"Roberta Flack. Killing me softly," he requested. "That'll do."

Evelyn found the song and hit play. She took another long swallow and settled into her father's side as the soft, soulful music filled the porch.

"That thing sounds pretty good," he admitted.

"I love you, daddy," Evelyn sighed.

"I love you too, baby girl. To the moon and back."

Halfway through her second beer, smuggled past her mother as she dozed in the recliner, Evelyn lowered the music and sat up, looking at her father. There was only so much of the ancient "music" she could take, besides she had something on her mind.

"You know, daddy, I'm really sorry for all that's happened. I guess y'all think I'm not, but I've had months to think about all this and beat myself up about it. The whole reason I even told y'all is to own it."

"I know, baby." He motioned for her to lay her head back down, which she did. "I don't get enough time to sit and hug you anymore."

"I've been through all the social and moral complexities a million times."

"I'm sure you have. It couldn't have been an easy decision for you." Freddy stroked his daughters' shoulder. "To be honest, for your future, it was probably the right decision."

"For school it was. I couldn't finish school and go through a PsyD program with a kid. And then there's Aaron."

"Have you told him?" Freddy asked quietly.

"No. I don't even know if I should, but then I think if he ever found out..." She shrugged, leaving the consequences to her father's imagination.

"Would you rather lose him now or risk it ten years from now?"

"That's the thing. He practically told me not to tell him. I mean, he knows something's been wrong. He told me the other night that he didn't want to know what, and I shouldn't tell him."

"That's easy to say when he don't know what he don't know."

Evelyn sighed, considering her father's words. "Then I think, do I want to tell him because he deserves to know, or do I want to tell him to make myself feel better? Should I compound a foolish act with a selfish one?"

"I can't answer that for you, sweetie. You know that." Freddy squeezed his daughters' shoulder and finished his beer. "A long time ago," he continued, talking in a hushed tone, "I was about your age, maybe a little younger. Anyway, me and some buddies went to the beach. Me and your mama was already engaged. It was about a month before the wedding. We all went down there and partied, acting a fool. I met this girl."

Evelyn sat up, staring at her father in disbelief. He shushed her quietly and gently pushed her head back down to his shoulder.

"So, after the weekend we came home. Me and your mama got married and it's been a good life. Good job, nice house, we had you. Time moved on."

"Did she ever find out?" Evelyn asked in the whisper of a sudden co-conspirator.

"I never told her. She never let on that she knew. There have been moments, like when we watched you walk across the stage at your graduation, when my heart hurts. It hurts when I think what I might have never had. It hurts because I hurt her. It's liked I smudged the 'us' in us, if that makes any sense."

"Believe it or not, I know exactly what you mean. Aaron is a good man, daddy. He's kind and sweet and he loves me."

"He must be a good man if he's caught your heart."

"He is and he didn't deserve for this to happen to him."

"That's probably true, but neither did you." Freddy cleared his throat softly. "I don't believe you ever made the choice to step out on him. You just didn't make the decision not to."

Evelyn nodded, agreeing with her father. He'd preached her whole life about how one bad decision could change your life's path forever. Had she done that? Would her whole life be so different now? With or without Aaron she could still get a BS in psychology and complete the PsyD program at NC. Had it really changed so much?

"You know something, daddy?" she asked.

"What's that?"

"A lot of people think I've got it going on, but most of the time I feel like I'm just holding on for dear life."

Freddy chuckled quietly. "Welcome to adulthood."

"But mostly I'm just scared," she added as a tear rolled down her cheek and soaked into her father's tee shirt.

Freddy squeezed his daughter. "I'm sure you are. You'd be a fool if you weren't. It don't ever stop unless you don't have something or someone that you couldn't bear to be without. I'll tell you, baby, I've done more praying since the day you was born than I ever did in my whole life."

Evelyn rubbed her father's chest and smiled. "Thank you for that too, daddy. They say everything happens for a reason, but I don't know."

"I don't know either. Things happen that try your soul, baby. Terrible things that make you want to quit, but you don't. Years later you look back and say, 'That was getting me ready for this'."

"Maybe so," Evelyn began with a sigh. "But you gotta wonder why I was born to such good parents and some people aren't. Why my daddy isn't an alcoholic and some other baby's is. Why am I here and not somewhere else?"

"I don't know. I'm not what you'd call philosophical, sweetie. I'm not even that smart. That question is way too big for me."

"Stop it, daddy. You're smart."

"If you say so," he said.

"I do say so," she insisted. "I was thinking about this girl I knew in elementary school. How different would our lives be if we switched places at birth."

"No way to know, I suppose."

"Do you remember the LeBeau family?" she asked.

"Sounds failure. Why?"

"I went to school with a girl named Caroline LeBeau. Do you remember?"

Freddy laughed. "Who could forget Caraliiine LeBo? Talk about a blast from the past."

"Apparently, I could because I didn't remember her until I went through some old annuals. We were in class together in first grade and were friends in second grade, then she just dropped off the map. I vaguely remember, or think I do, that she moved away. I don't know."

"Seems like I remember them. Caroline, yes, but not much about the parents."

"Do you know who Caroline grew up to be?" she asked.

"The Governor?" Freddy asked with a laugh.

"No. Cara, here in town!"

"Crazy Cara?" he asked, surprised. "The walking around talking to yourself Cara?"

"Yes. I know it's her. And could you not call her that, please."

"That couldn't be her. Cara is much older than you are."

"No, she's not. She just looks like that because of how she is. She doesn't take care of herself."

"I thought you said they moved."

"That's just it. Maybe they didn't move. Maybe they just took her out of school."

"Why would they do that? Besides, there's laws about that kinda stuff."

"I know, but it is her. She's not in the yearbook after second grade, I've looked. But I know it's her. I saw her up close at the park the other day and I know it's her."

"Okay, it's her. So what?"

"I don't know." Evelyn shrank back into the swing. "I just thought we should do something for her. Shouldn't we?"

"What in the world could we do?" Freddy asked.

"I don't know. When I saw her it just felt like she remembered me."

"Baby," Freddy sighed. "Look, you're a sweet girl with a big heart and that's part of who you are. I know you're in school and all that psychology stuff is interesting to you, but you don't owe this girl nothing just because you was friends in second grade."

"I'm not saying that, daddy. It's just that someone should do something other than laugh at her and call her names."

"Okay, I'll give you that much," Freddy conceded. "But what can we do?"

"I don't know," Evelyn answered weakly, peeling the label from the beer in her hands.

"It ain't your place, Eve. If you really want to help her, call someone that can actually do something for her. Get her into a place that can look after her all day every day." Freddy looked at his daughter and shook his head. "Baby, you ain't no doctor yet. You need to make a few calls and then walk away, get on with your life. Haven't you got enough to worry about without all this?"

"I know," Evelyn sighed, resigning herself to do something. She didn't know what yet, but she had to do something.

Aaron's tee shirt swallowed Evelyn as she pulled it over her head. She got into bed and picked up her phone to text him.

"Hey you."

After a few seconds he replied, "Hey."

"What 'cha doing?"

"Packing," he responded.

"Where U going?"

"Home. I gotta chill with the fam for a few days."

"Beach next week?" she asked.

"IDK yet," he told her.

"Oh, ok." Evelyn looked at her phone suspiciously. Something didn't feel right. "U ok?"

"I'm good, I guess. You?"

Evelyn shook her head. "Not really."

"What's wrong?"

"I'm worried your mad at me," she told him. The minutes while she waited for a response ticked by like hours, allowing her mind to conger up possibilities that she hoped weren't true.

"Why would I be mad?" He finally asked.

"IDK. You seem short with me."

"Told U I was packing."

"I know, but you seem mad." Again, she had to wait for a reply.

"I'm not mad at you, Eve," he answered.

"Want to talk?" she asked.

"Just a bit, still got a lot to do."

Evelyn looked at his reply and shook her head. "Why U being like this?"

"How am I being?" he asked

"IDK. Short."

"I'm just going home. Summer classes start in two weeks."

"Ok. Love U," she told him.

"U 2."

"I don't like us like this." She told him. "I do want to be with you."

"If U hadn't run off, U could be."

Evelyn sighed, frustrated. "I know. Sorry. Really."

She stared at her phone, awaiting a reply, a question on her mind that she was afraid to ask. She finally typed the message and sent it to Aaron. "Are we ok?"

"U tell me, Eve. R we?"

She sat up in the bed and put a hand over her mouth, struggling to maintain her composure. She'd blown their vacation plans and had ran off. Who could blame him for being upset? But she just needed time to think. Was that too much to ask? Why was he acting so put off? Had Kevin told him about Trae? About the baby?

"It it's up to me we are," she finally answered, and then sent "I love you!!"

"I love U 2, Eve."

She stared at the phone, watching for a message that began with "BUT". As each agonizing second ticked by, she began to calm when it didn't come. She rubbed her eyes and gripped the phone again.

"I can come 2 U if you want. Right now."

"I'm only going a few days. M&D want "family time" whatever that is."

"Oh, ok," she replied, dejected. "I understand."

"I don't understand anything anymore."

"??"

"Never mind."

"When U get back, I can join U," she offered. "If U want."

"Kev is moving out."

Evelyn sent a frown emoji. "Why?"

"Flunking out. He's a dumbass."

"Uh, ok." Evelyn's brow furrowed as she studied her phone. "It'll be just us then?" She wanted to steer the conversation to a better place.

"Unless you bring someone else."

"What?!?" she responded. What the hell did that supposed to mean?

"Nothing. Bad joke."

"It was."

"Ok. Sorry. I've gotta go."

"Ok babe. Love U."

"GN Eve."

Evelyn fell back onto the bed, covering her face with her hands and moaned loudly. "Perfect," she said through her hands. "Just freaking perfect."

"Why'd you tell her I was flunking out?" Kevin asked watching Aaron shove his phone in his pocket angrily.

"Because you are." Aaron zipped the duffel bag on his bed and shouldered it.

"I know, but you didn't have to tell her."

"Well, I know how you two like keeping secrets," Aaron replied angrily. "But that's not my game."

"Oh, come off it. Quit being so sanctimonious."

"Shut the hell up, asshole!"

"So that's how it's going to be?" Kevin asked.

"It sure looks like it."

Kevin watched his friend from the doorway as he stomped around the bedroom, gathering things that he'd need on his trip.

"You want to know why I told you now?"

"I really don't care."

"I do, that's why I told you. You and Evie are the couple everyone is jealous of. Y'all are the perfect couple. Honestly, have you guys ever even had a fight?"

Aaron stopped and glared at him but said nothing.

"I told you, partly because I am flunking out and I probably won't ever see you again, but mostly because I wanted to try to talk you out of doing something in the heat of passion and ruining your life."

"Well, ain't you a true friend?" Aaron asked sarcastically.

"I've tried to be. I don't expect you to understand because all you've ever thought of me as is a shallow bastard, and you think you're so smart that I could never offer you advice."

"One of us is flunking out and one isn't. You do the math, buddy," Aaron snapped.

"That's true, I'll give you that. But one of us is about to throw away the chance of a lifetime over one mistake and one of us is trying to prevent it. You do the math on that, buddy."

"How the hell could you hide this from me?" Aaron asked, shaking his head.

"You think it was easy. Evie came to me, she was upset and asked me to keep quiet. What was I going to do, turn her away? Tell her to go to hell? You know, I liked Evie too. She was my friend too."

"Please," Aaron said, "She was a hot piece of tail that you wanted to hit. I know you man, don't forget that."

"If that's what it takes to help you sleep then think it, but it's not true. I care for her too, that's why I helped her. She asked me to, and I did."

"Why are you still talking?" Aaron asked. "Leave me alone!"

"What are you going to do with Evie?" Kevin asked, ignoring his friend.

"Why do you care? You want to make a run at her?"

"Stop it!" Kevin demanded. "You're being an idiot."

"Idiot?" Aaron asked, stomping up to Kevin. "I'm an idiot? That's rich coming from your dumb ass."

"Okay, okay, I'm a dumbass. I'm flunking out of school. Fine! But you're screwing up something special with Evie if you don't even give her a chance."

"A chance at what?" Aaron asked. "A chance to NOT screw around on me. A chance to NOT get pregnant with some other guys' baby. And NOT just dispose of it?"

"Oh, come off it, man! You're gonna climb up on your high horse and look down your nose at HER?"

"What are you talking about? Surely you can't defend what she did."

"So, what? She's just supposed to come to you and say, 'Hey, I screwed up. I got knocked up by this guy back home.' and you'd just be like, 'Okay, I'll raise another man's baby. Another man's BLACK baby?" Kevin shook his head.

Aaron stared at him, shocked into silence. Was that the real issue? Was it just that she cheated or that she cheated with a black man? It couldn't be, she was black. Did it make her seem tainted? Blacker somehow? He'd never been attracted to a black woman before, would it have made a difference if she was darker skinned?

"Screw you," he finally spat angry, but more contemplative now.

"And about the other thing, when did you get so pious?" Kevin asked.

"Pious? What the hell are you talking about?"

"If you're gonna hold her feet to the fire over getting rid of this kid that neither one of y'all probably wanted because of some religious conviction then you'll have to hold them to the fire for letting you bag her for, what, six, seven months? Bet you never minded that."

"You're just being stupid now. Are you trying to get punched in the face? Just shut up."

"Look, just calm down and listen for a minute." Kevin knew he'd given his friend a lot to think about, he just hoped it would keep him busy until he realized that he still loved Evie and she still loved him.

"I've heard enough from you." Aaron pushed past his friend and walked into the living room.

"I don't blame you for being pissed. The whole 'bro before hoes' thing, I get that. But this was different. This is Evie we're talking about, not some bimbo." Kevin followed him into the room.

"What the hell would you know?"

"I know that she loves you. When she came to me, she was scared to death. She kept talking about letting everyone down, how you'd hate her. She said she wouldn't blame you if you did. She was crying and shit. Man, c'mon."

"You really are a dumbass, aren't you?"

"Yes. I think you've made that abundantly clear. Look, you know she's not like that. She made a mistake! Not everybody's as perfect as you."

Aaron shot him and angry look, drawing his breaths in long, angry gasps before he turned headed for the door.

"Stop!" Kevin caught up with him and grabbed his arm, jumping back as Aaron spun with his fist raised. "Just listen for five minutes, for both your sakes."

Aaron shook his head angrily. "What?" he sighed.

"Do you remember when we first met Evie?"

"What does that have to do with anything?"

"Everything. We were at that party. We walked in and there she was. It was like a scene in a movie with light shining down on her and a

96

chorus singing 'aaaaaahhhh'. She was the most beautiful girl I'd ever seen. There was just something about the way she laughed, the way she moved. You were all nervous, so I went up to her. Remember that?"

"Does this story have a point?" Aaron asked flatly.

"Yes, it does. Anyway, I tried my best to hook up with her, but she wasn't having any of my crap. She saw right through me. But then you finally joined us. I saw you guys' faces and I knew you were both hooked. For some reason she went straight to you. I remember y'all sitting at that table in the corner all night, talking and laughing."

Aaron leaned against the wall flicking his keys in his hand impatiently. He did remember that night and a thousand more moments just like that. Those moments when he'd just happened to catch her in the right light, in the right position and she looked almost angelic. He also remembered her body; her smooth caramel skin. He remembered the way her toned muscles rose and fell when she moved, and the way she crinkled her nose when something was gross or smelled bad. He remembered her with a wrap on her hair painting her toenails, her brushing her teeth, the way her eyes shimmered in the sunlight. He remembered everything about her. He remembered that he loved her too, that was why his heart ached so much. Kevin's news felt like a punch in the gut and he still hadn't gotten his wind back.

"I knew she was special, one in a million, and so did you. She still is man. Okay, she screwed up, big time, but that doesn't change who she is. That doesn't change how you two feel about each other."

"Really? I guess I'm just supposed to just shrug it off?"

"No, not at all. Look, I don't know what you're supposed to do. I've never been in this situation. If this was a bimbo, I'd say toss her aside. Plenty of fish in the sea and all. But this isn't a bimbo. It's Evie."

"Right now, I can't see a lot of difference," Aaron spat angrily.

"That's total bullshit, man. Look, she went home at Christmas, had more than a few drinks and was hanging out with some friends. This guy, Mr. Old Boyfriend starts smooth talking and the next thing you know she's made a mistake. I've done the same thing to chicks when I've gone home too. I know, I'm a dog, but it happens. It's not like she just went out and met some random guy. They had history, man. You know how that can be, especially when you go home, and double especially when you've had a few more than you should."

Kevin sighed and looked at his friend. He was hurting, that much was obvious. He held out his hands, palms up, with a questioning shrug.

"Look, just promise me, no, promise yourself, that you'll go home and think about things for a few days. All I know is that Evie is the kind of girl that doesn't come along every day. If you lose her you might spend the rest of your life looking for someone to measure up to her and never find them. As much as this hurts right now, do you want to spend the rest of your life without her? Ask yourself that my friend."

Aaron shook his head. "You really are a dick, aren't you?" He looked at Kevin and sighed. Taking a step toward him he extended a hand and planted it on his chest, shoving him to the ground. "Don't leave a mess."

Kevin sat up on the floor as the door closed. "At least he didn't punch me in the face," he said with a shrug.

SIX

Martha Jackson sat on her living room couch folding laundry. A soap opera played on the television, but she wasn't interested in it. She was watching her daughter. God's grace had taken a single moment in time and produced something a far cry better than the sum of its parts. Her daughter was a bright, beautiful young woman and she was very proud of that. Somehow, she'd gotten very smooth, light skin and a tall, lean body. She normally kept her hair back in a tight ball or a loose ponytail, but today she'd just let it hang freely about her shoulders. It looked better this way, more natural. Evelyn spent a lot of time and money on her hair, both theirs and her own, but she was also rewarded with a long, soft drape that made you just want to touch it, if she let you.

Her daughter had come down late and sat at the kitchen table with her laptop and a cup of coffee. She wasn't very talkative, so she left her alone and let her do her thing, and just watched. The best way to find out what was in a person's head was to watch quietly when they didn't think anyone was doing so. It wasn't spying. It was being an observant mother.

As she watched, Evelyn tucked one long leg beneath her and sipped from her coffee, scrolling through old editions of the Souls Harbor Times. It seemed a tedious and mind-numbing task, but then again folding laundry wasn't exactly the thrill of a lifetime either.

Evelyn stared at the screen of her laptop, but her mind kept going back to her conversation with Aaron. Did he know? Did Kevin tell him? Was that the reason he "moved out"? Had they fought? Surely, he wouldn't betray her trust on something this serious.

She sighed and rubbed her eyes with the thumb and middle finger of her left hand while the nails of her right hand drummed on the table. Surly Aaron would have said something? Ask questions; verify the story? But then again, maybe nothing had happened, and he was just upset with her for not staying and then going to the beach with them. Or he might have had an argument with his family over their "family time" decision. That decision should have gotten her off the hook about not joining them at the beach. She picked up her phone and looked at it. There was no message from Aaron.

Determined to divert her mind from the hundreds of questions, she straightened her computer, sat up straight, and began typing. At least I can find the answers to some questions, she thought as she typed "Le Beau" into the reference index on the site.

The first reference on the list was an obituary dated June 4, 2007 for Lynn LeBeau. Evelyn's eyes swept over the short paragraph.

Lynn LeBeau: June 4, 1982 – June 4, 2007

Lynn LeBeau was killed on a one vehicle crash in rural Hillburn County the early morning hours of June 4, 2007. She leaves behind a husband:

Carey LeBeau, 29, and Caroline LeBeau, 8, both of Hillburn County. Services will be graveside at Meadow View Baptist church on June 6, 2007 at one p.m. In lieu of flowers the family requests help in offsetting the cost of the funeral.

Evelyn furrowed her brow and looked at the obituary again. It was an odd request to see in newsprint. It was, she reminded herself, before the various internet funding sites and if you were broke, that was probably the only way to get the word out. It still sounded tacky and crass though.

The next two references were from the police blotter. On December 24, 2007 Carey LeBeau was arrested on a drunk and disorderly and fighting charge and booked in Hillburn County jail. The second one said that on March 8, 2009 he was arrested for driving under the influence, also booked in Hillburn County jail.

Evelyn shrugged. Bad situation, man loses his wife and turns to the bottle to escape. That was understandable. It must have been rough, she thought as her eyes went to the Hillburn County jail for both bookings. They may have indeed moved out of Souls Harbor, but they hadn't moved far; not even out of the county, apparently.

The next reference was an article about an accident at a concrete plant in June of 2012 that sent Carey LeBeau to the hospital with extensive injuries. The article didn't give any specifics and there were no other articles on the subject.

Evelyn clicked on the last reference tab. Another obituary:

CAREY EARL LEBEAU 1978-2014

Carey Earl LeBeau passed away on August 27, 2014 at his home. According to family, he passed gently in his sleep, having suffered from injuries from an accident years previously. He is proceeded in death by his wife, Lynn LeBeau (2007) and is survived by his daughter, Caroline Grace LeBeau. Services will be provided by Hester funeral home at the graveside, with interment to be at Meadowview Baptist Church at 1:00 Friday, August 29, 2014.

Evelyn counted quickly on her fingers. Caroline would have been 15, 16 at the most, depending on when her birthday was. What would have happened to her? She would have been a minor, someone would have had to be responsible for her, wouldn't they? There must be another relative. An aunt or uncle or someone who took care of her and had a different name or did move her away.

With a sigh Evelyn leaned back in her chair. She'd learned some things, but it led to more questions. She picked up her phone from the table next to her laptop, looked at it, then put it down again. Resting her elbow on the table as her mind began to wander again, she began to flick the nail of her middle finger back and forth with her thumb nail.

"That couldn't be good for them."

"What?" Evelyn asked, turning to look at her mother. "You say something?"

Martha laughed and shook her head. "I said that couldn't be good for your nails to flick them like that."

"Oh. Sorry." Evelyn looked at her hand as if to accuse it of something, then picked her phone up and looked at it briefly before sitting it back down.

"You could text him, you know," her mother told her, folding one of her husbands' shirts.

"What? Who?"

"Honey, you done looked at your phone three times since I been folding this basket of clothes. Unless you expecting the president to ask your advice on something, you're hoping to hear from your man."

"I guess," Evelyn admitted as she turned in the chair and looked at her mother. "He's mad at me I think."

"About what? Y'all have that talk?"

"No." Evelyn rubbed her nose. "I think he's just mad because he wanted me to stay 'till he finished classes then go to the beach with him and his family."

"You gonna meet them before we meet him?" Martha asked, pausing mid-fold, holding a pair of her husband's underpants in her hands.

"I don't know, mama. Nothing was set in stone. But I basically finished classes and took off before he finished his exams. I guess he's got a right to be mad."

"About more than he knows then," Martha said, more to herself than to her daughter.

"Mama, please."

"What?" Martha asked flatly.

"Anyway, he was just short with me last night. I don't know. There's a lot going on I guess."

"And now you sitting here, watching your phone like a hawk, hoping he'll text you?"

"I'm not watching anything. It's just a habit I guess," Evelyn lied.

"Well," Martha began as she stacked the last of the clothes in the basket and stood with it, sliding it to her hip. "You are a daughter, Evie baby, not the Sun. The world don't revolve around you."

Evelyn rolled her eyes but said nothing. It was a phrase she'd heard too many times to count. Her mother believed it was her job to help her daughter "keep it real", whatever the hell that meant. Turning back to the table, she picked her phone up, looked at it, realized what she was doing, and put it down with a "humph". She knew somewhere in the back of the house her mother was smiling because she knew she was right.

103

"Hey there, Mrs. Landry." Evelyn waved to the old black woman sitting on her porch directly across the street from the Jackson family mailbox.

"Hey baby. You mind bringing in my mail for me, hun. Save an old woman a few steps."

"Of course." Evelyn shoved their own mail back into the box and crossed the street. Opening the neighbor's box, she pulled the mail out. It was mostly sale papers and other junk, but there was one letter addressed to Beatrice Landry in the small window.

Evelyn walked up the sidewalk, climbed the three steps, and mounted the porch, all made of concrete and painted dark gray. "Here you go, ma'am."

"Evelyn Jackson!" the woman exclaimed. "I didn't know that was you. Have a sit and stay a while."

"It's me," she said, doing what she was told as she laid the mail on the small wicker table between them.

"You made a doctor yet? Lord, that's all your mama talks about."

"Not yet, Mrs. Landry. I finished my third year. I got one more year then I start on the doctoring stuff," Evelyn answered loudly, simplifying things a bit.

"Mm, Mm, Mm. I don't know how you do it. But you always was a smart one."

"Thank you so much," she said with a smile, exaggerated so the old woman could see. "It's tough sometimes."

"Ain't you a pretty one!" the old woman exclaimed. "Bet the hounds are after you all the time."

"I guess so. But I don't let them catch me." Evelyn and the woman shared a laugh. At eighty-seven, Bernice Landry was Souls Harbor's oldest living African American and the oldest woman.

"But I tell you," Beatrice said, leaning forward, propping her skinny elbows on the arm rests of the rocking chair. "It can be fun to let one of 'em catch you now and again."

Evelyn laughed with the old woman and agreed with her. "So, how you been, Mrs. Landry? Everything going to suit you?"

"Oh, I suppose," she sighed. "Nothing to get riled up about. I woke up this morning, that's something."

"That's everything," Evelyn said, reaching out and rubbing the old woman's wrinkled hand. She had countless pleasant memories of growing up across the street from the old woman sitting beside her.

In her younger days, Bernice Landry had been quite the character. After her husband died only five years after their marriage, she never remarried, and it was rumored that she'd "taken up the company of women". She worked for years at the phone company in town as a switchboard operator until modernization phased the job out. She'd finished out her "working years" as a checkout clerk at the grocery store.

Evelyn was always so amazed to see a woman drink beer, especially the way Beatrice did it-straight from the bottle. She also smoked cigarettes, and she cussed sometimes. To a young Evelyn Jackson she was about the coolest thing she'd ever seen.

"I'll tell you one thing to always remember," she'd told a ten-year-old Evelyn, probably after a few beers. "If a man ever hits you once he'll hit you again, so, if one ever does you stab his ass. Wait 'till that sum bitch goes to sleep and you stab him in the guts. Don't kill him 'cause you'll go to the penitentiary. But stab him in the guts. He will

105

either get the hell out of town or he'll straighten up. Either way he won't hit you no mo."

"You ain't married yet?" Bernice asked, bringing Evelyn back from her memories.

"Not yet. No ma'am," Evelyn answered, still smiling from the memory.

"Any   fellas   looking?"
Evelyn smiled. "I got one on the line, but I'm waiting a couple years."

"Good. You always was a smart girl."

"Mrs. Landry," Evelyn began. "You been here in town a while. Can I ask you something?"

"Why sure, child," she replied, pronouncing sure as "shore".

"Do you remember a family named LeBeau from way back, when I was a kid?"

The old woman rubbed her hands together and sat back against the thread bare pillow in her rocking chair, he lips moving as if she were chewing some unseen food while she thought.

"You know what?" she began. "I think I do." Her eyes narrowed as she talked. "Pretty sure they lived out at the edge of town. Daddy was a drunk, I remember that. I don't reckon I ever seen much of the wife."

"What about the child? Her name was Caroline."

The old woman nodded. "The mom died in a car wreck. They was plenty of talk about that, but nothing ever come of it."

"Talk?"

"You know how folks talk. She had a car wreck on her birthday just at the end of their driveway. Some folks said she did it on purpose. Trying to get away from that mean old man of hers, maybe. Some said he was after her and she just didn't look. Either way the car burned to pieces. Weren't nothing anybody could do back then but wait till the fire department came. They say she burnt up something fierce. Turrible, turrible."

"It is terrible. Guess we could hope the wreck killed her not the fire."

"Don't know either way 'bout that. Folks that come up on it said they heard a girl screaming but couldn't tell if it were the momma or the poor child that followed her daddy out the driveway."

Evelyn sighed sadly. Poor Caroline. Whether or not the wreck killed her mother was probably the least of her worries. Watching her burn up in a fire had to have been traumatic. She was starting to understand why Caroline wasn't your average, run of the mill citizen.

"And the father died at home they said. He'd sustained pretty bad injuries in a work-place accident," Evelyn added.

"Ugh huh. They say a fuel truck exploded. Lord, you could see the smoke all over town. It was all folks talked about that summer."

"The girl would have been fifteen or so when he died. Do you know what happened to her?"

The old woman took in a deep breath and shook her head. "They was some talk about some rich relatives somewhere, but I never saw none of 'em. You'd think if they had rich folks, they wouldn't have to live hand to mouth like they did though."

"They didn't get by so well?" Evelyn asked.

"Honey, you'd not know it now, but back in them days poor black folk and poor white folk was all trash. Around here they was anyway.

So, we tried to help one another, you know. I was working and doing alright myself by then, so I'd get up some stuff and try to help the woman and child out. Never really cared for the man that much. He always looked mad and I kinda got the feeling that if I was ever alone with him, he'd take liberties with me whether I liked it or not."

Evelyn nodded her understanding. If he was that kind of man, would he "take liberties" with his daughter? Probably, she thought. As alien as the thought was to her, it wasn't an uncommon occurrence. In her mind she thanked God again for her father.

Evelyn followed her GPS down the two-lane tar and gravel road, dodging the occasional pothole and unidentifiable roadkill. Left to the mercy of her technology, due to the absence of anything resembling a road sign, she hoped it was right. Swinging into the opposite lane to avoid a series of muddy tracks left by log trucks entering the road, she was glad that traffic was very sparse. There had only been one pick-up truck and an empty log truck to accompany her since she'd left town. She was only six miles from the city limits, but it felt further, more isolated.

Evelyn jumped as the GPS squawked, "In half a mile your destination will be on your left".

"Crap," she said with a nervous chuckle. Hitting the 'mute' button on the tracker she followed the road until the blue arrow made a sudden left turn and stopped. With no other travelers in sight, she rolled to a stop in the road and looked at what might have been a driveway in another life. The police blotter she'd gotten the address from was twelve years old. There was no way to tell if it was even remotely right.

Not wanting to just sit in the road, she nosed her Corolla onto the shoulder, and into the low growth that lined the highway. Expecting to drop off in a hole at any minute she progressed slowly and stopped with a thankful sigh.

"God, I hope I don't get stuck," she whispered, remembering the storm they'd had a few days earlier. She opened her door and cautiously stepped out. There were so many things to be fearful of. Falling down, snakes, ticks, not to mention being a young girl alone on a deserted highway.

"This is how those damned scary movies start," she complained as she pushed through the broom sage and scrub that had grown knee high. Reaching the front of her car, she stopped and looked down at the opening in the trees. It obviously used to be a road, or a reasonable facsimile thereof, but it wasn't now. Along with the scrub and grass, the lane was littered with more than a few young, thin, pine trees, a few almost as tall as she was. Closer to the edge of the lane nearest her, several thistle plants stretched their prickly leaves toward the sun. She had always thought of them as "cow thistle" plants because their vibrant, purplish colored flowers were always visible in cow pastures as they drove past.

"Well," she said as she began making her way through the underbrush, "Here goes nothing."

The driveway was a narrow strip of land between two ten-foot embankments that dropped into a drainage ditch. A rusty culver stuck out both ends, allowing runoff to pass underneath the road. A thick crop of long, dry broom sage grass swayed in the wind above the hard-packed earth and loose gravel that had once been a roadbed.

Just a few steps into the mess, Evelyn also discovered that the gently rustling grass also hid long, sharp briars. Stopping to free herself, she re-evaluated her path, this time finding two faint, parallel tracks that had laid the grass over. Someone had driven over the mess at some point and although most of the vegetation had rebounded, it looked easier that wading blindly through the roadside wilderness.

Proceeding more cautiously, she managed her way through the dense grass and breathed a sigh of relief as she reached the tree line. Here, the grass faded into a thick carpet of pine straw. The passage began to look more like a road, albeit an abandoned one. The two tire tracks continued into the woods and disappeared around a bend up ahead.

The shade of the trees had an instant cooling effect that she welcomed on a day that had turned out warmer than forecasted. Evelyn breathed in the deep earthy smell of the woods, finding it strangely comforting. Although she was anything but a "woodsy" girl now, her family had gone camping regularly when she was younger. This place, with its heavy pine scent and quiet calm reminded her of those innocent days spent alone with her parents, camped alongside the river.

After walking what she thought was a considerable distance, Evelyn looked back to see how far she'd come. Her car sat in the sunshine next to Tuck Smith road probably just a hundred yards away.

"C'mon Evie," she scolded, realizing that she'd been gingerly creeping along. "Get it together." Taking in a deep breath, she forced herself to relax. "What's the worst that could happen?" You could be raped and murdered and chopped into tiny pieces, her mind told her. "Well," she said aloud. "There's that," she added with a nervous laugh.

Continuing at a relaxed pace, Evelyn saw the first hand painted "No trespassing" sign as she rounded a slight bend in the road. It hung on a small pine tree just over head high, slightly askew to the right. The red paint scrawled on the piece of wood was old and faded, but plenty readable. She wondered briefly if the spelling was right, then decided it didn't matter. The meaning was clear.

Pressing on despite the warning, Evelyn continued down the overgrown path. Her eyes scanned the woods on either side of the narrow lane for any movement, her heart pounding in her chest and echoing in her ears, mixing with the sounds of the wildlife. She stopped suddenly as a squirrel bounded out of the woods to her left and scurried across the path, hopping onto a tree on the right. Clinging to the tree, about two feet from the ground, it paused to give her an inquisitive look before hurrying up the tree.

Walking further, Evelyn wove her way carefully through a crop of pine saplings that abruptly appeared in the path. Whoever had driven in here had made it no further than right here, a point brought to her attention by the thorn that snagged her leg and dug into her shin through the leggings she'd worn. Wincing, she freed herself from the thorns and continued, beginning to think the whole journey foolish. What the hell was she even doing here? What would she do if she found Caroline?

Hi, I'm your old friend from second grade, her mind began to mock her. It's been twelve years. Surprise! So, how you been?

Despite all logical thought telling her to turn around, something kept her moving forward. Step by step she worked her way down the lane, picking up several more scratches along the way, but determined to see this through. If she made it to the end of this road, she could return home, satisfied that she'd tried. She could doctor her wounds, fix things with Aaron-if that was even possible- and move on with her life.

Gaining the top of a small rise, on the verge of turning around, Evelyn caught a glimpse of a house. Encouraged, she pressed on, working her way as quickly as possible through the undergrowth, until she finally broke free of the woods and stood in an open meadow. The road continued a short distance, spotted with tall grass that swished across her legs as she passed by, but then simply played out, giving way to a wide swath of bare earth that probably was once a yard.

Evelyn stood in fascination, her attention going back and forth between the clapboard siding house that might have once been yellow and the yard, a veritable minefield of ragged holes that stretched across every square foot of the property with no apparent pattern.

Taking a few tentative steps forward, keep her eyes on the front door of the house just in case, she neared the hole closest to her and peered inside. It was about a foot in diameter and about a foot and a half deep, probably dug with a narrow shovel or a spade. The bottom was partially covered in leaf litter that was still wet from the storm. Swatting a mosquito away from her face, she wished she'd brought some bug spray.

As her eyes swept over the yard, she thought briefly about counting the holes, but quickly gave up. There must be a thousand, she thought, shaking her head. Apparently, someone had been looking for something, but what? Everyone who had grown up in the south had heard stories and jokes about people burying money in Mason jars, but she'd never known of anyone to actually do it.

Stepping with careful deliberation Evelyn placed each foot carefully between the holes, sparing only brief looks around to make sure no one was about. Most of the holes in this area seemed to have suffered the ravages of time, but she saw a few around the edges of the field that might not have been very old. Not that she could exactly tell whether a hole was fresh or not.

It's the strangest situation she'd ever found herself in and her mind raced, trying to find an explanation. Her heart pounded in her chest with a mixture of curiosity and fear, half expecting some old codger to burst through the front door with a double-barreled shotgun and order her off his property, half wanting someone to show up just so she could ask them about all these damned holes.

No one did show up, to brandish a shotgun or otherwise. She was alone with her thoughts and the sounds of nature as she jumped over the last hole and found herself standing next to a porch that sat about waist high. It was severely weather beaten and spotted with various lichen and moss. The last section of handrails along the front had become detached from its post and hung askew, half off the porch. Some of the spindles had fallen to the ground and were busy rotting.

Keeping a careful eye on the windows, most of which were without glass, she skirted the broken railing and rounded the house. Here on the shady side, the siding and overhang were covered solidly with slick, black mildew and the ground was piled deep with the leaf litter cast off by the towering oak tree that dominated this half of the yard.

Evelyn squeamishly made her way through the soft, wet, narrow alley next to the house created by a slight berm and a row of overgrown bushes. She grimaced as each step yielded a squishing, gurgling noise, her foot sinking an inch into the soupy ground. Reaching out to steady herself, she touched the house. The cool, damp of the siding and the slickness of the mildew felt like a fish. She withdrew her hand quickly as a shudder ran through her.

Eager to be out of the mire she hurried her last few steps and emerged into the sunshine again with a sigh of relief. The small back yard, free of holes, felt downright homey compared to where she'd just been. The space was defined by a small shed that was somehow in worse shape than the house and had a dangerous lean to the right. The door was missing, if there ever had been one, revealing an empty pit of dirt dug down about two feet deep. Her grandparents had a similar building that had once been used as a smokehouse.

Next to the shack, in the direction of the lean stood a row of three Rose of Sharon trees, tall and overgrown, but full and lush with fresh new leaves. They will be pretty when they bloom in a few months, she thought, but I won't be here to see them. Turning, she saw the first two signs of life on the whole property, recent life anyway. The stump of an old cedar tree rose out of the middle of the yard, its top worm smooth from use, and a few feet from that the remnants of a campfire.

Looking around again with a growing sense of urgency. Someone had been here, but when? Going to the ashes, she held her hand over the gray embers. Feeling no heat, she poked at them gingerly with her finger. Nothing. It was cold. Sighing with some measure of relief she stood and wiped her hand on her leg, looking around again. There was a small back stoop and a set of steps that looked impassable, but nothing else of interest.

Rounding the back corner of the old house Evelyn was greeted with a panoramic view of the whole property. A sea of holes washed across the land all the way to the tree line. Off to her left she could see the opening in the thick growth where she'd entered this strange scene. She wanted to go back there, make her way back down the lane and get into her car, but she knew that she wouldn't. Instead she stood and stared, her mouth slightly agape, at the multitude of holes. She'd guessed a thousand earlier, but this from this view it was probably twice that. There was something important buried here and someone desperately wanted to find it. She just hoped that they had gotten what they wanted and moved on.

The siding on sunny side of the house had long ago traded the dampness of the mildew for a weathered, gray look. Dry and splintered, it felt like a completely different place. Making her way back towards the front, her eyes scanning the windows, she stepped on the shards of a fallen windowpane. The glass broke beneath her shoe like old bones.

She paused while she considered picking up the glass, then saw several large red wasps staring at her as they stood guard over an empty knot hole in the siding. Moving quickly, but cautiously, she passed them by, thankfully without incident.

Stopping at the third of the four windows on this side of the house, Evelyn stretched to see in, but her eyes barely made it to the dry, splintery sill. One thing became certain: if she wanted to know what was inside this house, she was going to have to go inside. Her mind recoiled from the thought. Here, in the open, she could always break and run if something happened, confident that she could outrun just about anyone who would happen to be in a place like this.

You can't outrun a shotgun blast, her mind told her.

Giving herself a wry smile, she rounded the side of the house and stood at the bottom of the wooden steps leading to the porch. This was her only chance, she knew. There wouldn't be another because, even if she could gather the courage to do so, she wasn't coming back here. She was going to find Aaron and make things right with him no matter what it took. She only had a few days left in town.

Taking in a deep breath, she screwed up her courage and mounted the steps one by one. Once on the porch, she paused for a brief glance at the three rocking chairs, two of which were broken, then went right to the front door. The rusty metal knob was cold in her hand, but it yielded as she turned it, and the door swung open.

Stepping into the shadowy room cautiously, she looked around. Bigger than expected, it was furnished with a short couch that looked like it probably housed a family of rats, two small end tables, one of which still held a small lamp, and a massive stone fireplace. There was a dry musty smell to the place, not completely unlike the smell of an old refrigerator that had been unplugged for a long time. The air was close and warm despite the ventilation through the painless windows. On the floor there were faint impressions in the dust.

Lowering herself into a squat as she looked around the room nervously, she stared at the footprints. They were small, but not the size of a child. A woman, maybe. A size six or seven, she deduced, using her own foot as a guide.

Dusting her hands as she stood, she found another door directly to her right and a kitchen through an open passage across the living room. She headed for the kitchen, if anyone was about, the kitchen would tell her.

The table, large enough to seat eight with its metal legs and an avocado green laminate top, was straight out of the 1970's. On it sat a cardboard box. 'SOULS HARBOR FOOD BANK' had been scrawled on the side in thick red ink.

The knot tightened in her stomach and she spun around quickly, half expecting someone to be there. No one was, but her mind was screaming at her to get out of the house and away from this place. This is no good, she told herself. The box stood as evidence that someone had been here recently; that someone LIVED here!

Her heart thundered in her chest and the first tiny beads of sweat were collecting on her forehead. But what was she more afraid of? That Caroline lived here, or that someone else did?

"No" she told herself aloud, trying to calm down. "Five more minutes."

Moving more quickly now, hoping to search the house and be gone as quickly as possible, she skirted the table and one of the chairs that had been pulled away and now stood in front of the matching stove, she went to the closed door in the corner.

The knob, not as rusty as the one on the front door, but well-worn, turned slowly beneath her trembling hand. The door swung open slowly. A stench crept from the room and washed over her. Grimacing, she

116

turned her head as her hand instinctively went to her nose. The heavy ammonia scent told her that scent was probably urine. Sparing one last look, she saw that the room was completely bare except for an old twin mattress in the far corner and a small chain nailed to the wall a few feet from it. Probably a pet's room, she guessed as she backed away, judging from the filthiness of the mattress.

Moving toward the front of the house, and the front door, she found another bedroom behind the closed door she'd seen earlier. Peeking inside, she saw that it was furnished with what would now be an antique metal bed stead and a dusty, unmade mattress. There was a bedside table and a lamp next to the bed and a small chifforobe in the corner and not much else. It looked like it hadn't been disturbed in years. Closing the door, she turned, her mind made up to leave.

That's when she saw her.

A surprised squeak escaped Evelyn as she turned and found Caroline standing in the open front doorway, her hands hanging limply at her side, her head tilted slightly as she stared back at her.

Shocked into silence, Evelyn stood motionless as her eyes washed over the girl. Dressed in the same oversized jeans as before, she now noticed that they were cinched up tight to her waist. A plain white t-shirt hung untucked from her thin frame, flapping slightly in the breeze. Her hair fell in knotted clumps around her expressionless face.

"Caroline?" Evelyn finally asked sheepishly, careful to not move. She'd been taught that some people with mental illness could misinterpret any movement as a threat and react violently.

The girl stood as motionless as a statue for a moment, then tilted her head in the other direction, keeping her eyes locked on Evelyn's. There was no emotion in her eyes as she looked at her.

"Caroline?" Evelyn asked again. She waited a long time for the girl to answer, then added, "Is that you?"

The girl finally blinked after what felt like an eternity and raised one hand ever so slightly towards Evelyn. Her brow furrowed slightly, and she tilted her head back the other way again. A slight curiosity began to show on her face.

"I'm Evelyn," she told her, this time taking the risk to extend a hand towards her, palm up.

Caroline took a cautious step back but remained in the doorway. Evelyn held up both palms, hoping to show that she wasn't a threat.

Caroline reclaimed the step she'd taken as her eyes locked on Evelyn's.

"Do you remember me?" Evelyn asked. The girl continued to stare blankly at her,

the look of deep thought, or confusion, spreading across her face. How could this be the same little girl she knew from school? None of the vibrance; none of the innocence remained in the girl now before her. The thought that this was a huge mistake slowly began to take root in Evelyn's mind.

Caroline's eyes slowly swept over her and came back to her face as she stared with a cold detachment that send a shudder down Evelyn's spine. Was there even any humanity left in this poor girl, any emotion at all?

"From school," Evelyn continued, feeding the girl clues, looking for some spark of recognition. "We were little together." The girl's face softened slightly, giving Evelyn hope. "Caroline? It's me, Evelyn. Do you remember me?" The girl continued to stare at her without speaking.

Caroline's face eased more, a faint smile pulling at the corners of her mouth. "Evie?"

Her posture relaxed and she closed her eyes.

"Yes," Evelyn answered, on the verge of tears, moved by emotions that she hadn't even known were there.

"Evie", Caroline said again, then collapsed in a heap in the doorway.

"Oh my God!" Evelyn ran to her side and lifted her head into her lap. "Caroline! Are you okay? Caroline!" She looked around at the deserted homestead as panic welled in her chest. "Help me!" She screamed through her tears. "Somebody help us!"

Evelyn's initial panic, which consisted of holding Caroline's head in her lap and saying, "Oh God!" repeatedly, and five minutes of pacing back and forth with her hands clasped behind her head, began to slowly fade, allowing her to regain a measure of composure.

Drawing from the limited training she received as a lifeguard at the city pool her last two summers of high school, she knelt by Caroline's limp body and pressed her fingers alongside her neck. She had a pulse. That was good. But now what? She gently laid a hand on Caroline's chest. Her breathing was shallow, but steady. She was about to stand again, then thought of one more thing to check. Reaching out carefully, she forced one of Caroline's eyes open, then the other. Both pupils seemed normal. Neither were "fixed and dilated". She didn't know what that meant exactly, but she'd seen enough medical shows on television to know it was bad if they were.

Taking out her phone, she dialed 911, but her thumb hovered over the call button. It was the best option, she knew, but it would never work. Her car blocked the only way in, and even if they managed to get by, they could never make it down the long, overgrown lane. And then there was the matter of what she was doing here in the first place? She knew that she should call for help, then if anything happened it would be on them, not her. If she did nothing and Caroline died, then what would she do? Staring at her telephone, she hoped an answer could come to her.

None did.

"Okay, think Evie," she told herself as she stood and began pacing again, this time more slowly and calmer. She probably just fainted, she told herself. Yeah, that's it. She'll wake up any minute now. She paused her pacing and stared at Caroline's limp form.

"You can wake up now," she told her. "Please." Caroline didn't wake up.

Finally, Evelyn's mind settled on a solution. She would have to get Caroline to the road then call 911. They could take care of her and she could go back to her nice, safe life with only a few scratches to tend to.

Kneeling beside Caroline, Evelyn slid her arms beneath her shoulders and knees, intent to lift her. With a grunt, she strained with all her might, but only managed to pull the girl on top of herself as she toppled backwards.

"Dammit!" she cursed as she wriggled out from under Caroline's body. Moving around to the upper body, she slid two hands beneath Caroline's arms, interlacing her fingers across her chest. Taking in a deep breath, she heaved the body up, leaving her legs and thighs to drag on the porch as she shifted their position toward the steps.

"I'm sorry," Evelyn said, grimacing as Caroline's bare heels drug across the rough planks of the porch. Reaching the top of the steps, Evelyn stopped. Realizing the uselessness of her endeavor she leaned against the porch post. Already tiring, she would be lucky if she made it across the yard before she gave out. And there were the damned holes she'd have to navigate through. She'd probably end up breaking a leg or something worse. Then what would she do?

Having little recourse, she half-stepped her way in a semi-circle and drug Caroline back into the house. Laying her down gently, Evelyn shook her burning arms. She was athletic, but even at the gym she'd never tried to move 100+ pounds of dead weight before. Putting her hands on her knees as she struggled to regain her breath in the warm, dusty house, she looked sympathetically at her old friend.

"Guess we're not going anywhere," she told her. Arching her back to stretch it after the exertion, she looked around the old house. Last time she'd come home was Christmas. That didn't turn out well to say the least, and now this. "What the hell am I doing here?" she asked the empty house.

It was raining when Evelyn woke up. She slowly became aware of two things: the first was that the air streaming through the missing panes in the window was cold and damp, accentuating the musty scent of the room. The second was that her whole body ached.

Seated on the floor, across the room from the metal bed where she had managed to wrangle the dead weight of Caroline's limp body, a deep pain had settled into her overworked muscles. Despite the pillow she'd found to sit on, her butt hurt. She stretched and yawned, peering through the darkness. From her vantage point on the floor, she couldn't see Caroline, but she could hear her gentle, even breathing over the soft patter of rain on the roof over their heads.

Feeling around on the floor beside her in the darkness, Evelyn's hand found her phone. She absently swiped the blank screen and it came to life, flooding the room with white light. Squinting, she looked for a message. There was none. She checked the time. It was just past one in the morning.

After getting Caroline settled, she'd used the last bit of her physical and emotional strength to text her parents and tell them she was staying with a friend. As an afterthought, she'd added that it was a girlfriend.

Pushing herself off the floor with a low groan, she rubbed her bare arms and wondered how anyone could survive the winter in this house. It was late spring in Alabama, and the early mornings were still cold.

Switching on her phone's flashlight, she took stock of her surroundings. Caroline was exactly as she'd laid her. Her face was peaceful and calm, lending Evelyn a slight smile. She considered finding a washcloth and cleaning up her face but decided against it for fear of waking her suddenly. "What happened to you?" she asked quietly, shaking her head sadly. Why had the years been so cruel to Caroline and so pleasant to her?

Next to the bed was the table and a lamp. She bent and switched on the lamp. Nothing happened, just as she knew it wouldn't. In a better time, there had been electricity in the house, but not now. The house and its inhabitants had been on a downhill slide for a while.

Sweeping the light around the room, Evelyn followed the beam to the chifforobe. The small latch gave way easily under her fingers and the small door swung open, revealing an empty, dusty hole like a cavity. Cobwebs hung in the light of her phone, collecting the dust she'd kicked up by opening the door. The stack of drawers next to it was likewise peculiarly empty.

Opening another door, barely her own height, she found a few old clothes that had probably belonged to her father and nothing else. Letting the door swing closed, she panned the light further along the wall and found a small, unassuming fireplace. Backed up to the huge one in the adjacent room, it probably allowed heat to pass between the rooms. That is, she thought, IF you had a fire.

Could I build a fire? She wondered, holding the light on the blackened bricks that lined the small fire box. If there was a fireplace, there would probably be firewood. But where? She'd never actually built a fire herself, but she'd watched her father do it a hundred times. How hard could it be?

She headed for the back porch, that was where her grandparents always kept their firewood. Passing through the kitchen, her light fell on the box sitting on the table. Her stomach rumbled noisily, reminding her that she hadn't supper, and lunch had scarcely been much more than coffee.

Shining her light into the box, she rummaged through the canned goods for something she could eat quickly and without much bother. Her hand landed on an apple and she brought it forth victoriously. Yes! Her mind thought as she bit into its red flesh. It wasn't cold, like she liked them, and had turned a bit mealy, but it was sweet and juicy. Her stomach thanked her for each bite she swallowed.

Holding the apple in her mouth and the phone in one other, she opened the back door slowly. The old hinges groaned in the darkness over being disturbed at such an hour but yielded none the less.

Pausing briefly to close the door to the room she'd opened earlier to quieten the stench, she carefully stepped onto the back porch and was greeted by a cool, damp wind. By morning, it would be downright cold, and they would be downright miserable if she couldn't get some heat in the old house.

The beam swept across the narrow porch and fell on a pile of small, dead branches broken into irregular lengths, most small enough to fit into the fireplace. Undoubtedly, Caroline stored them here to keep them out of the rain, and Evelyn was glad she did. She gripped the apple in her teeth again and loaded her arm with the wood. She took it back to the room where Caroline lay and set about finding something to start a fire with.

After a fruitless search of the kitchen cabinets and drawers, Evelyn stood next to the sink and finished her apple, tossing the core out the open doorway. Remembering the fire from the back yard, she knew there was something around to start a fire. She just had to find it. Snapping her fingers as an idea came to her, Evelyn went back out onto the porch and swept the light around again. Sitting on the windowsill above where she'd gotten the wood was a box of matches. She picked it up and shook it. Mostly full. Good. It might take a few.

Back in the bedroom with Caroline, she knelt in front of the fireplace and placed the shredded flaps from the cardboard box in a neat pile then began stacking on the smaller of the twigs. Finally, she struck a match and held it to one of the curled edges of cardboard.

Smiling, she watched the flame slowly grow. "Ha!" She whispered proudly. "First try". When the flame burned out, her smile faded. On her knees and bent forward, she began to feel the pressure on her bladder and quickly realized that she had to pee. Great, just what I needed, she thought. More pressure.

She struck another match and held it to the charred edge she'd lit before, this time allowing the match to burn all the way down, close to her fingers before dropping it. As quickly as she could, she struck another and lit a different piece on fire, then another. Slowly the flame crept up the cardboard and began to lap at the dry branches. Once they began to crackle and pop, she piled on more of the larger ones until she was satisfied that the fire would hold.

Happy with her results, she grabbed her phone and headed for the door. She hadn't seen a bathroom, and even if she had, there was no running water to flush with. Pausing in the doorway, she shone her light into the darkness. Navigating the rickety steps and the muddy yard in the rain suddenly felt very unappealing, but her bladder was beginning to demand release. She looked quickly around the kitchen and found an old pot under the sink. Giving it a quick glance to check for spiders, she sat it on the floor. Pulled down her pants, she squatted over it. Despite the conditions, she was thankful for the relief.

Looking around the shadowy room, Evelyn shook her head, wondering how the hell she'd gone from a nice, warm home to pissing in a boiler in the middle of the kitchen of a shack in the woods. And with a possibly comatose girl she hadn't seen in over ten years to lying in a bed in the next room.

Deciding that she was too tired and sore and cold to worry about that now, she dispatched her urine out the back door, turned the pot upside down on the porch and grabbed the last remaining branches. She went back into the room, stoked the fire and checked on Caroline again.

Neither her condition nor her position in the bed changed at all. Evelyn pulled the dusty blanket up on Caroline's chest and returned to her perch next to the fireplace, thankful for its warmth. Turning off her flashlight, she watched the shadows dance across the room until she faded gently back into sleep.

Evelyn yawned before she opened her eyes. Her body was stiff and achy. Sleeping on the floor, her legs stretched out before her and crossed at the ankles, had taken a toll on her. Wiggling her feet with a low moan, she opened her eyes slowly and lifted her head. She rubbed the pain in her neck and rolled her shoulders to relieve the stiffness.

Blinking away the sleep, she noticed that Caroline sitting on the floor against the wall opposite her. Her knees were pulled to her chest, arms clasped tightly around them. Her chin rested on her knees, and her eyes were fixed on Evelyn in an unnerving stare.

Disguising her alarm, Evelyn smiled. "You're up." Caroline gave no indication that she'd heard. Careful to move slowly, Evelyn pulled her own knees to her and stretched them out again one by one. Readjusting her position on the pillow, she arched her back, stretching the tired muscles. Everything ached and she longed for a long, hot bath.

"You scared the hell out of me, you know," Evelyn said, her mood soured by her sleeping arrangements. Again, Caroline gave no indication that she'd heard her as she stared blankly back.

Evelyn jumped slightly as a piece of wood popped in the fireplace, Caroline never flinched. There were several slightly larger pieces on the fire and more lying on the small hearth in front of it. Caroline had been up for a while.

She slid her hand off her lap and found her phone. A quick swipe of her thumb revealed the time, ten thirty-eight A.M., and a message from her dad that said simply, "Just checking on you." She told him she was okay then slid the phone into her back pocket. Readjusting her position on the pillow, she looked at Caroline, wondering what the hell she was going to do now.

It still wasn't outside the realm of possibility that the girl could attack her, she knew. She also knew that the mentally unstable could sometimes possess strength greater than considered normal for a person of a particular size. In her current state, with her stiff muscles and sitting in a vulnerable position, Caroline could be across the room and on before she had a chance to move. Old friend or not, her position was still precarious to say the least.

Hoping to hide her anxiety, Evelyn let out a long, slow sigh and smiled. "Caroline?" she asked quietly. "I don't know if you remember

126

me, but my name is Evelyn." She thought for a moment than added, "Evie."

Caroline stared at the black woman sitting on the floor of her father's bedroom, her face void of emotion. "I'm not crazy," she finally said, her lips barely moving.

"I know, sweetie," Evelyn answered quietly. There was something almost animalistic about Caroline's stance and the way she looked at her; like a wolf surveying its wounded prey.

Evelyn stared at her, trying to find the innocent, bright eyed seven-year-old she'd known in school. She searched for the girl strong enough to stand up for a black girl in a sea of white faces. She wanted to see a glimmer of that girl, but found only a cold, unceasing, stare and an expressionless face.

The girls sat in silence as Evelyn struggled with what she wanted to say beneath the weight of Caroline's silent stare. She didn't quite know what she expected when she'd set out to find her, but it was more than this. Now, faced with the opportunity, she was at a loss for ideas. The confidence of her classroom was so far away.

The only thing that she knew for sure was that she had to pee again. Glancing out the window above Caroline's head, she saw the rain had stopped. That was good. She wouldn't have to use the pot again.

Finally, out of sheer necessity, Evelyn stirred, this time holding her hands out and showing Caroline her palms. "Look," she began, "I have to go pee. Okay?" Caroline didn't move. "I'm just going to pee."

Evelyn slowly hauled herself up from the floor, her muscles complaining with each movement. She walked backwards toward the door as Caroline's eyes followed her. Pausing in the doorway, Evelyn told her again she was going to pee.

"You don't have to be scared," Caroline told her, only scared came out as "scarred".

"I'm not," Evelyn told her. It was a small lie, but a necessary one. "I'll be back in a minute."

The sunshine instantly began to warm and loosen Evelyn's body as she made her way around the shed in the back yard. Sliding her pants down, she bent astraddle one of the holes and urinated into it, wondering what the hell she should do next. It didn't take a certified psychologist to know Caroline was mentally unwell, but to what extent? She couldn't just leave her to live like this. That would be inhumane.

And what was up with all the damned holes? People who were well didn't dig countless holes in their yard. The odd behavior, the vacant stare, the lowering of verbal acuity, hearing voices, detachment, they were all schizophrenic symptoms. Caroline needed help. Medical and psychological help. That much was clear. How to get her that help wasn't.

Building a plan as she pulled her pants up, Evelyn decided that she had to talk Caroline into seeking help. She had to go to a hospital, that was all there was to it. That was the best thing she could do for her. To just leave her here, knowing what state she was in, was worse than not coming out here at all.

"I'm back," Evelyn said as she slowly approached the bedroom doorway. "Just me." Stepping into the room, she immediately saw that Caroline wasn't where she'd left her. Her heart leapt into her throat as she spun and quickly searched the room behind her, fearful of being flanked. When she didn't find Caroline standing behind her with a hatchet as she half feared, she made her way throughout the house, calling to her.

"Dammit!" Evelyn complained, and stomped the wooden floor with her foot, raising a cloud of dust. There was no chance of finding her in the woods, especially if she didn't want to be found. Angry and disgusted, she walked onto the front porch and surveyed the acreage around the house. It was the kind of dense forest that held secrets well. A person could get lost out here and never be heard from again.

With a desperate sigh, she descended the steps and began picking her way through the minefield of holes, now standing with muddy water. Her foot slipped into one of the holes, sinking into the muddy water. She clambered out, and trudged on, making it to the edge of the woods with no other mishaps.

Caroline watched Evelyn as she walked away from the house. After reaching the tree line, she turned around and looked back, scanning the area. Her eyes swept across where she stood, safely hidden behind the huge oak tree beside the house. Caroline didn't bother to duck behind the tree. Evelyn couldn't see her here in the shadows. This wasn't the first time she'd hidden.

"I only wanted to help you." Evelyn's yell came to her from across the field. "That's all." She waited for a response and when none came, she threw her hands up, turned, and disappeared into the shadows of the tree line as she headed back down the lane toward the highway.

Turning away, Caroline leaned her back against the tree and banged her head against it twice before finally resting it against the rough back. Turning her face toward the sky, she clenched her eyes tightly with an agonizing grimace as tears began to roll down her cheeks. It was the first time she'd cried in a very long time.

SEVEN

Evelyn hit play on her song list and leaned back into the hot bath, sinking into the bubbles. Today felt like a "Bebe Rexha" kind of day. Relaxing in the bath, one hand holding a cold beer over the edge of the tub, she closed her eyes and sighed as "I'm a mess" filled the bathroom.

Agreeing with the song, she wondered how her life had become so disjointed. Six months ago, everything had been fine, perfect almost. She was well onto the path she'd chosen for herself: college, good grades, great guy. She was happy and spoiled and loving life, then it all went to shit.

The feelings that came with not being sure about her future were new and unsettling. Sure, regardless of what happened with Aaron, she could, and probably would, still get her BS in psychology and go into the PsyD program at UNCA. She could take a kick-ass job as a clinical psychologist, but that wasn't what she wanted. She wanted to do all that and marry Aaron and have two or three beautiful babies with him and be the best and sexiest mom at soccer practice. She wanted the dream, all of it.

Her whole life had been geared toward that end. In high school, she worked her butt off and made good grades. She dated, but didn't given herself to all the hungry boys, both black and white, who chased her. Only one had gotten that far. Trae Colvin.

Evelyn pursed her lips as she thought of him. Trae was a handsome, tall black kid from A below average family. He had few plans further in advance than the next weekend, but he was a basketball and baseball standout and a lot of the girls wanted to be with him. There were even a few baseball scouts that dropped by his games to watch. He was charismatic and clever, if a little lazy and self-centered.

Much to the chagrin of her parents, she dated him throughout her junior and senior years of high school, riding the pinnacle of his success until she graduated, and he didn't. Knowing he'd never be true to her while she was away, she broke up with him before she left for college. It turned out to not be as hard as she thought it would be, which she took to mean it wasn't real love, but rather a childish romance.

Not like now, she thought and took a long drink. Things with Aaron were completely different from the start. His maturity showed in the way he treated her, and eventually came to cherish her. He was open with his feelings and shared his dreams with her. He was a man, where Trae had been a boy. Even in their love making, he'd shown her the difference between a man who wanted to keep her and a boy who kept wanting her.

While Bebe charged through the lyrics of her song, "I got you", Evelyn decided once and for all that she was going to come clean to Aaron about everything that had happened. He deserved it. He had always been honest and open with her and treated her with love and respect, something she'd never experienced from any other guy before, with the exception being her father. If they were able to move forward and stay together, great. If not, her conscious would be clear and she would deal with the aftermath as best she could.

"So, what if I'm fucking crazy?" Evelyn sang along with the music. It was the song that introduced her to the beautiful, powerful singer and she'd been hooked since. Although she didn't want to admit it to herself, the lyrics of the chorus funneled her thoughts back to Caroline.

"Girl be out there," Evelyn said, shaking her head. Since meeting Caroline, she was sure that the girl was indeed disturbed, but was she "crazy"? What the hell constituted crazy anyway? A shift from societal norms? Living 'off the grid'? Apathy to fashion? Evelyn shook her head at the thought. "Normal" was a social construct. What was considered perfectly normal in one place might not be so in another.

"Is stomping through the woods, breaking into someone's house and pissing in a spaghetti boiler crazy?" she asked herself. "Is leaving a handsome, wonderful guy, sleeping with a selfish bastard who didn't even get you off, and destroying the evidence crazy? Is talking to yourself crazy?"

Evelyn laughed at herself and shook her head. "This is some mess you got yourself into, girl." She had always been a black or white type person. There were questions and answers. Cause and effect. This new situation unnerved her. The uncertainty of her relationship with Aaron weighed on her. The uncertainty of what to do with Caroline unsettled her. She was a girl interrupted and she didn't like it.

"Are you okay?" Freddy Jackson stood in his daughters' bedroom door eyeing her carefully. Seeing her like this, dressed in a sweatshirt sitting crossed legged on her bed, computer perched on her lap, brought back so many memories. So many times, he'd poked his head into her room and seen her sitting the very same way. The more things change, the more they stay the same, he thought. The only difference now was that she was wearing a UNCA sweatshirt in place of a SHHS one. Whether or not she realized it herself, Freddy knew it was her position for doing some serious studying.

"I'm good," she answered with a smile.

"Mama said she saw some muddy clothes in the laundry room. You get your car stuck or something?"

"No," Evelyn told him. Did nothing ever get past her mother? "It rained yesterday, and I slipped in a mud hole. I wasn't aware that it was a big deal."

Freddy shook his head and smiled. "It's not a big deal. Just wondering. Graceful much?" he asked her, reviving the phrase he'd always used when she had tripped or spilled something growing up.

"I know, right?" she asked with a laugh of her own, her eyes still on the computer screen.

"Okay then. I'll leave you to your work." Freddy Jackson stepped back and drew the door almost closed before pushing it open again. "Love you, baby."

"Love you too, daddy," she answered. Looking up, she flashed him a wide smile before returning to attention to the screen.

Having given up on most of the traditional ways of treating schizophrenia, which she'd diagnosed Caroline with despite not completing a detailed, lengthy mental health exam, she began to investigate a more holistic approach. To her disappointment, although a part of her knew, it was not dissimilar from medical treatment.

Both treatments required the long-term consumption of medicines or supplements as well as long term psychotherapy and regular check-ups. A strict adherence to a regimented plan was a must for both paths and getting Caroline to commit to either seemed unlikely.

Propping her elbow on her knee, her forearm extended up wards, she began to click her nails together as she pondered the legal and ethical complexities of acquiring some Thorazine and slipping it into Caroline's food. Maybe the meds would stabilize her enough to make a rational decision about seeking professional help.

Dismissing the notion because of the sheer logistics of it, Evelyn sighed and looked out the window. "I'm not crazy," Caroline had told her. "You don't have to be scared," but she'd said "scarred".

We're all scarred, she thought, as in having scars. Everyone on the whole damned planet was scarred. It was a part of being alive. Some just had deeper and more obvious scars. Some people's scars still hurt them, some hadn't healed and probably never would. She wondered what scars Caroline carried. Obviously more than she could cope with in a healthy manor.

She remembered Mrs. Landy's recollection of Caroline's mother and how she'd died on her own birthday, and the little girl watching her car burn. Then there was her father, a man that looked like he "might take liberties with me whether I wanted it or not." Would he take liberties with his daughter? Had he? Both her parents had died, scarring enough, but she was apparently left alone at a tender age of 15 to fend for herself in that old house in the woods. Had she reached out for help?

Evelyn thought of the box of food bank groceries on the kitchen table. Someone had, at least, tried to feed her. That was something. Someone must have brought the box to her, knowing that she was destitute.

This piqued Evelyn's interest, giving her an avenue to pursue. Someone somewhere had put her on a list to receive food and someone brought it to her house. That someone might have some answers to the questions that continued to pile up in her mind.

Everyone is scarred, she thought, and the thing that caused most of the scars was that most people were scared. They were scarred because they were scared. It was a poignant thought that resonated in her mind. Everybody was scared of something, whether it had happened in the past or might happen in the future. Everybody was scarred.

The warehouse of the Souls Harbor food bank was a busy place. Evelyn stood in the open doorway of the bay nearest where she had parked and watched as a dozen people scurried back and forth with a sheet of paper in their hand to and from the multitude of shelves that lined half of the warehouse. They would pick something off the shelves and return to the tables in the center and put it into the box. They then repeated the process, going to another place on the shelves and getting another item until the list was exhausted or the box was full.

Many of the team chatted quietly, or remarked something to each other in passing, as they went about their work with bee-like efficiency. Once a box was filled with every item on the list, the list itself would be taped to the top of the box, its flaps folded down in a way that kept them closed, and it was hauled away to a growing stack near the semi that dominated the other half of the warehouse. Another box and another sheet of paper would be grabbed, and the process would begin over again.

"Can I help you?"

Startled, Evelyn and turned to face the woman who now stood at her side. Damn, she thought as she took in the sixty plus year old woman. A pair of half-moon reading glass hung on the end of a hawkish nose. The gold chain connected to them slid around her wrinkled throat and disappeared beneath a mold of gray hair. She wasn't going to be much help.

The woman's hands tucked into the pockets of a pale-yellow cardigan, spread out before her in a slight questioning gesture that was none too friendly as she stared at Evelyn suspiciously.

"Uh. Yeah, I guess," Evelyn stammered, surprised by the woman's standoffish manor. "I was wondering if you could help me out."

"You wanna sign up for food delivery?" the woman asked, her smokers voice dragging over gravel as it left her throat. "Or do you want to sign up to volunteer?"

"Neither, actually," Evelyn replied with a smile. "I was wondering if I could get some information on someone who does receive your generous deliveries though." She hoped her politeness would warm the old woman to her. It didn't.

"We don't give out any information. Confidentiality laws and what not," the old woman barked as she started across the warehouse to what Evelyn assumed were offices.

"Excuse me," she began as she caught up with the woman. She was spryer than she suspected. "But it's an old friend from school and I'd like to help her."

"We accept charitable donations of money and nonperishable food items," the woman informed her, cutting Evelyn off mid-sentence as she continued her march toward her office.

"Ok, but I," Evelyn stopped and watched the old woman walk through the bevvy of activity, the workers avoiding her with a certain skill and precision that reminded her of ants moving around an object that had suddenly fallen into the path of their line.

"Don't mind her."

Evelyn looked around at the young girl that had spoken to her. The girl was thickly built but wore a warm, happy smile on her big brown face. The red bandana she wore over her hair was drenched with sweat.

"Thank you," Evelyn said, extending her hand. The young girl took it graciously and gave her a welcoming shake.

"That's just Miss Maddie. She's been here so long she don't care about nothing but getting the cans out." Evelyn smiled and nodded as the girl laughed at what was apparently an inside joke. "What can I do for you? I'm Katrina by the way."

"Hi, Katrina. I'm Evelyn Jackson and I was just wondering if I could get some information about one of your food recipients."

"I don't mean to be ugly, Miss Jackson, but MS Maddie was right about that, even if she was rude. We're not allowed to give out any information about our clients."

"I understand that," Evelyn began slowly as her mind groped blindly for a legitimate reason for getting the information. While her brain was still conjuring a reason, she heard the words, "I'm from the Department of Human Resources here in town," come out of her mouth. Judging from the girls' reaction, she looked the part convincingly enough. "We're just doing a routine status check on one of your clients and just wanted to make sure the paperwork was still in order." Internally, Evelyn sighed, glad she'd chosen the tan capri pants and white blouse this morning instead of the jeans and tee shirt she'd considered.

"Paperwork," the young girl moaned. "I know the feeling. Paperwork. You gotta do it, but you don't gotta like it." Evelyn laughed and nodded in agreement and followed the girl as she spun on a heel and lead her toward the offices at the end of the building, hoping she wasn't leading her to the old woman's office. She doubted her DHS story would fly with her.

As they neared the office door behind which Miss Maddie had disappeared, Evelyn's apprehension began to mount. She was on the verge of feigning a call or some other excuse to abort the mission when her young guide turned to her right and lead her down a narrow corridor made of boxes stacked head high.

"Mr. Shivers will have the information you need. We are very meticulous with our records around here," Katrina informed her proudly. Pausing at a faded metal door that had probably once been painted safety orange, she looked at Evelyn with a curious gleam in her eyes.

"If you don't mind my asking," she began hesitantly, "But aren't you a little young to be doing casework for DHS?"

Evelyn flashed her a bright smile and slid her hand across her hair, tied back in a low knot. "First of all, thank you," she said nudging Katrina's shoulder playfully. "Actually, I'm an intern. You know how it is, they dump all the grunt work on us."

Katrina gave her a smile that looked forced, telling Evelyn that the girl liked her a little bit less. "Na, I didn't go to college. I'm just a volunteer."

"Well you're doing a great job, Katrina. Thank you so much. Now if you'll excuse me, I really must finish up here and get back. It's like we're pack mules downtown." Evelyn turned from the girl, hoping she didn't pick up on her nervousness, and knocked on the door.

A man's voice yelled for her to come from inside the office and she opened it. "Thank you so much, Katrina. You've been very helpful," she told her and walked through the door, closing it quickly behind her.

"Can I help you, Miss.... Evie?" He used the short e sound.

Evelyn turned and looked at the tall, stocky, black man standing from his desk. Much to her delight, she recognized him from high school. He'd been a year ahead of her and she'd seen him around the school but couldn't remember his name.

"Evie Jackson, how are you?" He asked as he rounded his desk and embraced her, giving her enough time to catch a glimpse of the name plate on his desk.

"Tony Shivers. Wow!" She exclaimed, accepting his motion to sit down. "It's been years. How are you?" She asked, watching him drop back into his chair.

"I'm good. Good," he said, leaning forward on his desk. "You still at North Central?" He asked, using the abbreviated name for the University of North Central Alabama.

"For a while yet, I guess. Go Cougars," she said with a weak fist pump and a laugh. The UNCA Cougars basketball team was a perennial joke in the sports world and everyone knew it.

"I guess you've finished school for the year," he said. "Back home for the whole summer?"

"Na. Just a few weeks. I'm working part time back there. Just visiting the folks," she lied.

"How are they? I don't get to see Freddy that much, but I run into your mama in the grocery store now and again."

"He's the same, I guess. You know, dad. He changes about as quick as an oak tree." She laughed and relaxed into the black faux leather chair.

"So," he said, clamping his hands, palms down onto his desk nervously as he caught himself staring at her. "What can I do for you?"

"Well," she said sheepishly. "I was hoping to get some information on one of your clients." She held up a hand to quieten his objections. There was little doubt that he was going to launch into a spiel about confidentiality and such, just like everyone else had. "I know, I know. But I'm not after anything official. But first let me say how much I admire the work you all are doing here. Every one of you deserve a medal. I've already seen the operation at work AND been told how organized you had this place running. Commendable, to say the least."

Tony smiled. He knew she was feeding him a line of bull, but it wasn't every day that he got bragged on by such a beautiful woman. And, he thought, if it keeps her here long enough for me to make some time with her, all the better.

"I have to say, I do respect the seriousness with which you hold people's confidences, but like I said, I'm not really looking for anything official, mind you."

"Nothing official?" He asked, his eyes darting down to the mounds of her breasts and back to her eyes. "What else is there?" He asked, throwing his hands into the air with a laugh.

"Well, I know this woman who gets food from you guys. I already know she does because I've seen the boxes. Anyway, I was just wondering how she came to be a client. I mean, who referred her to you guys and who delivers the food? She lives quite a bit out."

"Well, you've come to the right place," he boasted as he turned to the computer on his desk. "What's the name?"

"Caroline LeBeau," Evelyn told him. And she's my beeest friend, her younger self added in her head.

Tony typed quickly, hit a few buttons and then leaned toward the screen. "She was referred by Father Thomas Newell, says here."

"Really?" She asked, wondering if Caroline was Catholic. "That sounds a bit odd."

Tony shrugged and returned his attention to Evelyn. "Not really. We get referrals from almost every church in the county. We all do our part to help those poor individuals in need." He gave her a heroic smile and nodded.

"And I'm sure they are appreciative. It's just marvelous what you do here. You must see some awful situations," she told him, reaching out and putting a hand on his wrist.

"I could tell you some things that would make your hair stand up," he said bravely. "They's some really bad stuff goes on right here in our sleepy hometown, Evie. You probably wouldn't believe it."

140

"Yes, I would." She patted his arm then retracted her hand before he could take it in his. "I've kind of taken a personal interest in this one. Caroline LeBeau. Believe it or not we were little together. It's just tragic how she lives now." Evelyn shook her head.

"Well, we're all grown up now," he told her, his voice tinged with a hint of seduction.

"Yes, we are," she said, smiling at him. She cleared her throat and brushed a loose lock of hair out of her face. "Who did you say delivers the packages?" She asked.

Tony went back to the computer. "Looks like Charles does. He lives out that way and usually drops it off on his way home."

"Is there any way I could talk to him?" She asked.

"Na," he said dismissively. "He isn't here today. Besides, he's a little slow if you know what I mean." Tony slid forward in the chair, closing the distance between them as his eyes washed over her hungrily.

Evelyn nodded. "Okay then." Evelyn tried to stand, but Tony had taken her hand. "You know, I always thought you was one of the best-looking girls in school. I get off around five, what say we have a drink or two and catch up on old times?"

"I can't," Evelyn answered, politely, but firmly. "I don't think my husband would like that very much."

"Husband?" Tony asked, surprised. "I hadn't heard. Congratulations." He released her hand reluctantly.

"Thank you, Tony. You've been," she paused as their eyes met. "Helpful."

"Anytime," he said, watching her walk toward the door. "Anytime."

141

Evelyn parked her car on the street in front of St. John the Divine Catholic church and grabbed her phone from the tray in her center console. She'd texted Aaron a simple "I love you, babe" this morning and she hoped the text she'd just gotten was from him. Her heart leapt into her throat when she saw that it was. At least he hadn't ghosted her.

"I love you more than you know, Eve."

She smiled and let out a sigh of relief. Then her phone vibrated in her hand.

"I'm miserable. Wish we could be together."

Her brow furrowed as she stared at her phone, analyzing the text. It was cryptic to say the least.

"When will U be back?" she texted in return.

"Here for a while. May stay a few days longer than I thought."

"Ok." She chewed her lower lip. "Meet me when you get back?"

She sat in her car begging the universe to help her, then realized where she was. She looked out the window at the huge church across the immaculate lawn and held her phone up.

"Can I get a little help here?" She asked. Her phone immediately vibrated in her hand.

"Do you want to?" Aaron asked.

"More than anything in the world," she said aloud as she typed the message, putting the word "anything" in all caps.

Aaron responded with a smiley face emoji and asked if they could talk tomorrow.

"Absolutely," she responded. Aaron's response was another smiley face emoji, this one wearing sunglasses.

Energized by the knowledge that Aaron still loved her, for now, Evelyn got out of her car and started across the wide lawn. Looking skyward, she mouthed a "thank you" just before walking up the steps and into the portico.

Upon entering the vestibule Evelyn was met by a young man dressed in khaki slacks and a while polo style shirt.

"You must be Ms. Jackson", the man said, nodding curtly and extending his hand to her.

"Yes, but please, call me Evelyn." The man's hands were warm and strong as he sandwiched hers between them. "Father Newell?"

"No ma'am," he said with a soft laugh. "But he is expecting you. I'm Roger."

"Roger?" She asked, her face showing her surprise.

"I've not yet taken my vows and dedicated myself to the church," he explained. "If you will follow me, as I've said, Father Newell is expecting you." With that he turned and opened the door she'd just entered through, holding it for her.

Several questions began to formulate in her mind as the man, in his mid-twenties and not bad looking, lead her down the steps, but she decided to keep them to herself. She wasn't here to satisfy her mild curiosity, yet she still found herself wondering if he were a virgin. She knew that Catholic priests took a vow of celibacy, but did that apply to Roger?

The sidewalk swept around the side of the building and sliced through the manicured lawn. Evelyn found herself in awe of the towering stained-glass windows that lined the church as they passed, each one depicting a scene from the life of Christ. They had made it to one with Jesus standing in a boat set upon stormy seas, the others in the boat obviously fraught with despair, when Roger abruptly stopped. Evelyn swerved, but still managed to bump him slightly.

"Sorry," she told him, embarrassed. "I was admiring the architecture."

"It is quite lovely isn't it?" Roger asked, motioning with his hand for her to take an adjacent sidewalk. "This will lead you to the main offices. Father Newell is expecting you."

"Thank you, Roger," she said with a smile. "You've been an excellent guide."

"You're very welcome," he told her. Roger turned and walked away briskly, as if he had better, more pressing matters to attend to.

Evelyn followed the sidewalk to a white painted brick at the edge of the grounds and opened the door. Stepping inside she was greeted by a secretary that politely pointed her down the short hall to Father Newell's office.

"Come in, come in," the priest welcomed as she entered his office. Upon seeing him she now knew why Roger had laughed. Father Newell was old, probably close to eighty. What few hairs he still had on his head were thin and snow white, barely covering his pale gray scalp. Dressed in black pants and a long-sleeved shirt, he looked exactly what she'd thought a Catholic priest would look like, collar and all.

He motioned for her to sit in one of the wingback chairs in front of his desk while he sat in the other. "What can I do you today, young lady?"

"Um," Evelyn began, already nervous, although she didn't know why. "I just wanted to ask a few questions about someone you referred to the local food pantry." Father Newell nodded as he listened to Evelyn talk. "She's an old friend of mine who may need some help, and I'm looking for some information about her."

"I take it you've not been in touch for a while."

"No," she admitted then quickly added, "Father."

The old man chuckled in a warm, pardoning way. "Don't be nervous, Evelyn, did you say it was?"

"Yes, Evelyn."

"I'm a Catholic priest, not a religious fanatic. I know that most people around here are protestant and that doesn't really bother me." He leaned closer and lowered his voice, "I'm even friends with some of them," he said with a laugh. "But don't tell the Pope."

Evelyn couldn't resist laughing and instantly warmed to the man with kind eyes and a soothing voice. "Like I said on the phone, the church referred Caroline LeBeau to the food pantry, and I was just wondering if I could speak with that person."

The priest reached over and pulled a file from his desk and opened it. Reaching for the glasses hanging about his neck, he slid them on his nose and began to read. "Let's see what we can find out here about our friend." His eyes worked methodically down the file line by line, pausing to fold a page up and over the edge, until he had finished.

Dropping his glasses back to his chest, he pursed his lips, shaking his head slightly. He closed the file and slid it gently back onto his neat mahogany desk.

"Firstly, let me say that we referred the food pantry to Ms. LeBeau, not the other way around, and as far as speaking to the person who had referred her, you're looking at him." The priest leaned back in the chair with a quiet sigh.

"Great! That's good. So, you can help me?" Evelyn asked.

"I will help you as much as I can, but first, let me ask you why the sudden interest in Ms. LeBeau?"

Evelyn shrank into the chair. "We used to be friends. It was a long time ago. Second grade."

"Don't sell yourself short, young lady. I was in second grade a long time ago," he said with a smile. "For you, I imagine it feels like yesterday."

"To be honest it feels a little longer than that," she told him with a smile. "Thank you though. But, as I was saying we were friends and then, as best I can remember, she said they were moving, I think. Anyway, we lost touch and, it's sad to admit, I'd forgotten about her." Evelyn began to feel as if she were defending herself until the priest patted his hand in the air before him and nodded.

"You needn't feel bad. You were a child, doing things as children do."

"Anyway," Evelyn continued with a shrug. "I saw her at the park and started snooping around and, to make a long story short, I ended up at her house with her. I'm not a doctor, mind you, but I have just finished my third year of college working toward a psychology degree and it's pretty clear that she needs help. More help than I can give her."

"Ah, psychology," he said with a slight smile, as if remembering something pleasant. "The study of the soul."

"Well, psyche, I guess," she answered with a smile of her own.

"Have you ever read Aristotle's 'De Anima'?" he asked. "On the soul," he added, giving her the English interpretation.

"I have to admit that I haven't, but I've heard that it is part of the post-graduate reading."

"It's a fascinating read. You should really give it a look."

146

"I definitely will," she said.

Father Newell drew in a deep breath and exhaled tiredly. "My apologies, I love the ancient texts. I find them very enlightening. But, back to our friend. Well, you'll get no argument that she needs help, in every facet of her life, poor thing. She's had a very tough go of it to say the least, I suspect mostly at the hands of her father, Carey LeBeau."

Evelyn nodded, but said nothing.

"Her Mother's name was Lynn. I suspect that, being younger than her husband, that she probably didn't have the best of upbringings herself. It was a different time. She was a simple woman, Lynn. Not very educated, unchurched, and pregnant at a young age." He paused as he folded his hands in his lap.

Evelyn shrank under his gaze and the subject of conversation. She could certainly identify with Lynn LeBeau about that.

"Mid-teens, I think, maybe late teens. Probably. The father was a few years older. They lived in a reserve house out at the edge of town."

"A reserve house?" Evelyn asked.

"It's complicated, but more or less the town gave land away back when it was first getting started. In an effort to get people to move here, I suppose. Carey LeBeau's father, or grandfather maybe, homesteaded it so their family can live on it forever, or until the last surviving family dies off.

"So, Carey and Lynn had a baby and I guess all was well for a while then they fell on hard times, as many people sometimes do. Fast forward a while and Lynn, the mother, dies in a car accident on her birthday. People talked but there were no charges filed. That's when I went out and talked to the family. Or better to say talked to the father. I can't remember seeing the girl and there was little in my notes about her. We

147

talked for a while and I helped to set them up with assistance from the county with the power and water and food and such until he got back on his feet again. There was also the problem of the girl not going to school."

He paused to catch his breath and take a sip from the glass of water sitting on his desk. He offered to get her something, but Evelyn refused politely. Watching him drink, she noticed a slight tremor in his right hand.

"So, the truancy officer got involved and it was determined that the poor child was mentally retarded and unfit for education. Can you believe that?" he shook his head.

"Do you think she was? Mentally challenged, I mean?" Evelyn asked as her heart sank.

"I never met her as a child so I can't say either way, but the truancy officer declared her as such, and the school board was satisfied. The case was closed."

"But didn't the father die while she was still a minor?" Evelyn asked.

The priest nodded. "That is correct. And being mentally retarded and a minor, the girl should have been awarded to custody of the state, but she apparently wasn't because she continued to live there alone. People made inquiries and the like, but bureaucracy is the mother of inefficiency, Miss Jackson. It's unfortunate, but people slip through the cracks, I guess. I've made countless trips out there. It's a miserable way to live, but it's her home, apparently. When she became eighteen there wasn't much anyone could do."

"You mentioned that she probably suffered at the hands of her father, can you elaborate any?"

The priest shrugged. "Just the notes of an old man. I jotted down to talk to the girl about abuse if I ever got the chance. I never did. I saw her a few times, always from a distance. There was just a way about her. Something about the way she looked at me. I don't know." He shrugged. "I still pray for that little girl every day."

Sensing the end of the conversation Evelyn stood and thanked the priest, who remained in his chair, begging her forgiveness for not standing.

"Well, Father, she's all grown up now and she needs help. And, forgive me for saying this because you have done so much to help her, but I think she needs more than just prayer."

The old man smiled, unfazed by her comment. "I didn't just pray for the girl to be healed. I prayed that the Lord might send her an angel to protect her." He took her hand in his as he looked up at her, holding it close to her stomach. His blue eyes, still clear and vibrant, stared into hers as a comforting smile tugged at his lips.

"Cura te ipsum, factum fieri infectum non potest." The priest patted her hand and nodded slightly before letting it go. Unsettled, Evelyn, thanked him for his time and quickly made her way out of the office and down the long sidewalk back to her car.

Closing the door behind her, she grabbed her phone. She'd been repeating the phrase to herself, so she didn't forget it, and now typed it into her phone. Something in her told her that he was speaking directly to her, or about her, and not Caroline.

When the translation appeared on the screen of her phone, she stared back at the church, half expecting to see Father Newell staring back at her with a knowing look. Instead she saw a quiet, manicured landscape dappled with sunshine. A mockingbird landed on the lawn, grabbed something hidden in the blades of grass, then flew away.

Shaking her head, she started the car with an unsteady hand. How could he possibly know? She wondered, thinking about the priests' hands next to her belly. There was no way he could. Allowing herself another look at the Latin to English translation, she sighed and drove away with the phrase echoing in her mind.

"Take care of your own self, it is impossible for a deed to be undone."

EIGHT

Despite the argument that her parents put forth when she'd told them about contacting Caroline, Evelyn found herself again on Tuck Smith road. More confident, and with some semblance of a plan, she nosed her car off the road and got out, retrieving a backpack from the back seat. Dressed in jeans, tennis shoes and thicker socks this time, she felt more prepared. Unsure of how things would go, she had also prepared to stay the night.

Stuffing two bottles of soda into the backpack, she hefted it and grabbed the fast food bag from her car and headed toward the wood line. Caroline might not even allow her in, or she might see her coming and hide in the woods, but she was determined to try. Father Newell's words hung in the back of her mind as she pushed through the tall grass and scrub. Gaining the tree line, she stopped suddenly and surveyed the scene before her.

The narrow path that she'd followed before was the ghost of a trail made by the once-monthly food delivery, but now lay before her like a red carpet. The overgrown driveway had been transformed into a wide path that meandered through the overgrown brush and stickers and wove its way through the pine saplings.

Heartened by the obvious sign of welcome, Evelyn hastened her step. The cleared path signaled that Caroline was welcoming her back. It was a good sign. Optimism rose in her chest as she made her way toward the house and she couldn't help smiling.

Evelyn found herself at the edge of the forest sooner than expected. She stopped and looked at the old house, a thin veil of disappointment falling over her face. What did she expect? Caroline standing on the front porch, waving, and yelling for her to come and sit a spell? No, it wasn't going to be that easy.

Picking her way through the pock-marked yard with more ease, Evelyn mounted the steps and stood on the front porch, calling out to Caroline. After a few calls with no answer she slowly opened the door and walked in, announcing herself quietly.

The mattress from the bed had been drug into the living room and now lay along the wall opposite the fireplace, where the couch had once been, the couch was pushed into the corner. One of the kitchen chairs had been slid next to the fireplace, its legs leaving faint trails in the dust. It was something, Evelyn thought. Progress, no matter how small, was still progress.

After searching the house and finding it empty, Evelyn walked out the back door and found Caroline sitting on the cedar stump. Her head was slumped forward, her chin resting against her chest. Her arms sat limply in the lap of her dirty jeans. Evelyn's heart sank at the sight. The sadness and pain emanating from her was almost palpable.

"Caroline," she said softly.

After a moment, she looked up slowly. Staring at Evelyn through a curtain of hair that hung over her face. A tiny smile tugged at the edges of her thin lips, but quickly vanished as her head jerked involuntarily three times. Her lips began to move slightly as if she were speaking to someone in a whisper. She closed her eyes, continued her silent conversation for a few minutes, then stood.

She dragged the dirty hair from her face in a slow, deliberate move and looked up at Evelyn again. "Steps are broke," she warned.

Evelyn nodded, but remained silent. Caroline pointed toward the house, then disappeared around the corner. It took Evelyn a moment to understand what she had meant and by the time she realized, Caroline was standing on the front porch.

"Okay?" She asked, motioning to the mattress, as Evelyn joined her in the front room of the house. Again, Evelyn nodded without speaking as she unslung the backpack and hung it on the back of the chair. Caroline's attempt at redecorating was somewhat baffling, but she wasn't about to criticize the effort.

"Hungry?" She finally asked, holding up the sack of burgers.

Caroline shrugged slightly. She was, but only a little. The truth was that she only ate when her body demanded it, which wasn't very often these days.

"Even if you're not hungry, it's important to eat. Your body needs to be fed." Evelyn took a cheeseburger from the bag and unwrapped the top half of it before offering it to her friend. Caroline reached out cautiously and gripped the burger, leaving the wrapper in Evelyn's hand as she took a step backwards. Unzipping the backpack, Evelyn retrieved the two sodas, offering Caroline one. She shook her head slightly, her eyes glued to Evelyn as she produced her own burger and sat down in the chair.

"I love these things," Evelyn told her around the food in her mouth, hoping that seeing her eat would prompt Caroline to follow suit. The girl was very thin and pale. She knew poor eating habits could be a side effect of mental instability and it was obvious that Caroline ate very little.

Caroline sat on the floor and leaned against the wall near the front door then took a small bite of her burger. Chewing slowly, she watched Evelyn devour her own burger and reach into the bag for another.

"I've got plenty, so if you want more they're here." Evelyn looked around the room. "It's nice," she lied, waving her burger around before her. The room looked and smelled dirty and she was uncomfortable even being in it, much less eating in it.

Caroline took another bite, larger this time, and chewed it quietly. Why was this woman here? she wondered. What did she want? I'll bet she wants me to go to the hospital.

"That's exactly what she wants," the old woman in her mind told her.

"To lock you up and throw away the key," added the old man's voice.

"That's what she wants, or maybe to kill you," the old woman whispered. "She wants to kill you. Kill her first, before she tells everyone about us."

"You should get to her first. Rip her shirt off and let us see those black titties," the old man said with a laugh. "At least let us see them."

After washing down the remnants of her second burger Evelyn wadded the wrapper and dropped it into the bag. "There is more," she told Caroline again. The girl didn't respond or give any indication that she'd even heard her. Sitting in silence as Evelyn watched her, she chewed her burger like a wild animal, suspicious of a trap, but too hungry to care.

Unphased, Evelyn hauled the backpack onto her lap and began rummaging through it. "I've brought some things that I thought you might need or want. Or whatever," she said with a smile. "Flashlight," she switched the light on and moved the beam around the room. "Some miscellaneous toiletries, soap, shampoo and stuff like that, some extra clothes for both of us, a pair of shoes, if you want them."

"I'm not dumb." Caroline sat her burger on the dusty floor beside her and stood, springing to her feet so quickly that it startled Evelyn. "I know who you are." Her head jerked once and her lips whispered for a moment, then she crossed the room.

A chorus of laughter erupted in Caroline's head, mocking her. "I'm not duh-duh- dumb."

"You are dumb, you stupid little snit!" the old woman snapped.

"Good," Evelyn said, her heart racing with fear. Caroline had a distant look in her eyes as she stared, almost unblinking at her. Every motion was slow and deliberate; calculating.

Evelyn remembered going to the zoo as a kid. It had been a glorious day with her parents, until she saw the tigers. One of the tigers paced back and forth on the path he'd worn along the inside of the fence. As he paced, he kept his eyes glued on the crowd, his mouth slightly agape to show everyone his large teeth; to show them just what he was capable of if he happened to escape. It was a look of patient desperation; of a waiting, and wanting, for the right moment to come when he could exact his revenge for being caged. Evelyn felt the big cat was looking directly at her and started to cry. Caroline looked at her with the same desperate, angry look as the tiger and it scared the hell out of her.

"Not gonna hurt you." Caroline stood beside Evelyn, staring down at her for a moment then took the shoes from her hand.

"I know," Evelyn sighed, embarrassed that she'd cringed slightly as Caroline took the shoes. "I'm sorry."

Caroline went back to her seat on the floor and looked at the shoes. Evelyn watched as she slipped the grey and pink pair of running shoes onto her dirty feet and then picked up her burger again and took another bite.

"They'll do," she told Evelyn through a mouth full of food.

Evelyn's stomach rolled over as she watched Caroline eat the burger, and the dirt it had collected from the floor, but she put on a smile. "Good, I really just guessed at the size. I have some clothes too, if you want them."

Caroline looked up from her new shoes and met Evelyn's eyes. "Why?"

"Why?" Asked the little boy's voice. "Have you seen yourself? You look like a crazy person. Wait, that's right. You are a crazy person!" Another chorus of laughter echoed through her head.

"She wants to make you pretty for the good doctors," the old woman whispered. "They want their whores nice and pretty before they soil them."

It was a good question, but one that Evelyn herself didn't have an answer to. Why was she here? Why did she care? Why did she feel compelled to help this woman? She'd obviously survived on her own this long. Was it because she had once been her friend? Because Caroline needed help? That was true, but she knew that was not the answer. Was it some misguided reaction to guilt; some sort of penance for NOT growing up with an abusive father? Was she a curiosity; am embodiment of her studies; a project? Maybe.

Was she trying to make up for what she'd done; to save one life for the one she'd evicted from her womb? Evelyn shook her head and sighed. The real answer was probably somewhere between all of them and none.

"I don't really know," she finally answered. She just wanted to help, but to what end? That too, she didn't know. She had seen a profound sadness and pain in Caroline's eyes that day in the park and she knew, somehow, that she was the only one who could help her; the only one who could alleviate her misery, if only slightly.

Caroline shrugged and finished her burger, leaving Evelyn to her thoughts in an awkward silence as the bright sun shone in through the windows, illuminating the dust moats as they drifted slowly through the light before disappearing back into the shadows. Somewhere in the house a wasp buzzed noisily, bouncing off one of the windowpanes with a repetitive "tick" as it tried to escape from this place. In the overpowering quiet, Evelyn's mind raced, groping for what to do next. Becoming aware that she was in woefully over her head, she began to wish she'd never come.

"You don't talk much," Caroline suddenly told her.

"Actually, I do," Evelyn replied eagerly. "I just didn't want to...." She trailed off

"To spook me. Or scare me?"

"I guess," Evelyn shrugged.

"You're no danger to me," Caroline told her flatly in a voice that sounded like a warning.

"No," Evelyn agreed. "I'm not. I just want to help you."

"How?" Caroline asked, tilting her head to one side.

"That I really don't know. Some food, some clothes maybe. Something. What do you need?"

Caroline frowned and shook her head.

"Look, you cleared the path, didn't you? Obviously, you wanted me to come back by making it easier. There must be something that you need. Or want."

"I did," Caroline admitted then dropped her gaze to the floor between her feet.

"Yeah, the crazy bitch did it. So what?" the old woman asked.

"She lured you in here so we could see what you've been hiding, you stupid black bitch!" the old man added.

"Take your shirt off, you tramp, and show us," the little boy said with a laugh.

Evelyn watched as Caroline shook her head side to side, mumbling quietly to herself for several minutes. Her heart sank, knowing that a few weeks on prescription meds would work wonders for her, if only she could talk her into going to see a doctor.

As the voices quieted, Caroline laid her head against the wall and sighed tiredly. She stretched her legs out on the floor in front of her and closed her eyes.

"Is it bad?" Evelyn asked.

Caroline nodded as a tear rolled down her cheek but said nothing.

"Look," Evelyn began tentatively. "There are medicines that will help you. It will help the voices. That's what it is, isn't it? Voices in your head that tell you to do things." She looked at Caroline, wondering if she'd fallen asleep. "Don't you want them to go away?"

Caroline grimaced as she gave a slight, almost imperceptible, nod.

"What are they telling you to do now?" Evelyn asked.

Caroline shook her head. "No."

"Can you tell me?"

"They say to kill the black whore," Caroline told her in a flat monotone voice, her eyes still closed.

Evelyn recoiled, her heart in her throat, suddenly afraid for her safety. She looked around the room for an escape route, or a weapon.

"No!" Caroline suddenly screamed as she leapt to her feet in a surprising feat of agility. Panicked, Evelyn jumped from her chair, spilling the contents of the backpack sitting on her lap across the floor. Grabbing the chair by the sides of the back rest she raised it into the air. Her chest rose and fell rapidly as she stared at Caroline. She hadn't made a move toward her, but the wild look in her eyes said that she might. She watched as Caroline grabbed two handfuls of her own hair and pulled, her teeth clenched against the pain, tears streaming down her face.

After a few heart-pounding minutes, the anguish left Caroline's face and she sank slowly to the floor, ending up almost exactly where she had been. Her chest rose and fell as she drew in ragged breaths of the musty air. Sweat rose in small pellets on her forehead. One rolled down, navigating its way across her unkept eyebrow and crossed her closed eyelid.

"Caroline?" Evelyn asked, lowering the chair slightly as she took a cautious step towards the pitiful lump of human flesh that had moments ago looked like a raging beast bent on killing her. Her own heart still thundered in her ears as her breath raced in and out of her lungs in frightened gasps. Shit just got real, she thought as she stared at the woman on the floor in front of her. Holy crap.

Caroline moaned weakly and shifted but made no attempt to stand again. Stopping suddenly Evelyn raised the chair again, keeping a watchful eye out for any movement. When none came, she took another cautious step forward. Evelyn lowered the chair, keeping one hand on the metal curve that framed the top of the backrest. As her adrenaline spike slowly began to fade, she'd become aware of the burning pain in her arm muscles. The chair wasn't as heavy as it was awkward to hold aloft.

"I'm so tired," Caroline said groggily. With a heavy hand she reached up and pushed her mop of hair back over her head and looked up at Evelyn with weary eyes.

"I know you are." Deeming the threat gone, Evelyn crossed the room and knelt next to her. The smell of body odor and dirt rose up from Caroline's body, assaulting Evelyn's nose as she bent close to her.

On her knees beside the girl, Evelyn pulled Caroline to her chest and hugged her. "I know you are, sweetie," she told her as she began to rock gently, tears rolling down her own cheeks. In this condition, helpless and pitiful; vulnerable, Evelyn couldn't stop her heart from going out for the poor girl. Like most schizophrenics, Caroline was as much a fragile, harmless child as she was an angry, dangerous monster and that was the mystery of the disease. It was that mystery that had led her into the field of psychology, and it was that fascination, she knew, that would not allow her to desert this poor creature.

Looking at the growing shadows in the room, Evelyn began to feel a sense of urgency. She and Caroline had spoken sporadically all afternoon while she nonchalantly did what she could to make the house more livable, or at least more palatable. The smell of dust and dampness seemed to permeate everything she touched, even to the point that she could smell it on herself. The progress she'd been encouraged by earlier had come to a screeching halt after the episode, leaving their conversation labored and unfruitful.

Under the circumstances, Evelyn wondered if she should stay the night or go home. Her body, aching from sitting in the chair most of the afternoon, voted to go home. Her heart voted to stay. Her mind was on the fence.

Looking at Caroline, squatted on her haunches, elbows propped on her knees, arms extended before her, she wondered if she could ever really make a lasting impression or help in any meaningful way.

Caroline's attention was on the small fire Evelyn had made in the massive fireplace. The weak flames licked through the metal rack that she'd commandeered from the oven to build a makeshift cooking grill. If you had to eat corned beef hash, Evelyn figured, then it might as well be warm.

"I'm going to go pee," Evelyn told her as she stood. Caroline didn't move, but she did nod an acknowledgement. "I'll be right back." Again, Caroline nodded silently.

The air outside the house was cooler and lighter than that inside, especially with the fire, and Evelyn took in a deep breath thankfully. She decided that if she stayed much longer, she'd spend a lot of time on the front porch. Maybe in the one rocking chair that still worked. Rounding the edge of the house, she walked to the back yard. Somehow it had become the designated bathroom area, for her at least. She didn't know where Caroline went.

Skirting the cedar stump in the middle of the yard, Evelyn turned to walk behind the old shed. Out of the corner of her eye she noticed two small mounds of dirt, just beneath the overhanging branches of a large Chinaberry tree, it's leaves gently swaying in the breeze. Telling her bladder to wait, she took a few curious steps toward them. They were both short, less than two feet long, and barely a foot wide. The one on the left was much older and the dirt had settled and faded. A healthy crop of bright green moss had taken hold and was slowly growing its way across it. The mound on the right was much fresher, probably not very old at all.

Bringing her knees together as her bladder began to demand relief, she gave them a curious look as she turned and headed for the shed.

She'd have to ask Caroline about them, assuring herself that they were probably graves of a pet or some other wild animal she'd found.

After relieving herself, Evelyn walked back into the yard, cleaning her hands on one of the wet wipes she'd left behind the shed on a previous trip. Still curious about the two, small mounds, she walked up to them again. Closer now, she could see that each of the mounds had a flat rock, no larger than a book, laid into the ground at the far end. They were definitely graves, but for what? She hadn't noticed any pets the last time she was here, but maybe that did explain the smell in the back room.

"They my babies."

Startled, a quiet yelp escaped Evelyn. Her hand on her chest, she turned to see Caroline standing on the back porch. Her usual, blank expression was gone, replaced by a sad, broken look. After a moment Caroline jumped from the porch and landed expertly on the hard-packed ground.

"They my babies," she said again as she walked past Evelyn and approached the mounds. Unsure of what she meant, Evelyn joined her and stood quietly.

"He took 'em and buried 'em somewhere. Didn't say why nor where. They was borned dead, but he didn't have to do that."

Evelyn slowly reached out and touched Caroline's back. She could feel her cringe beneath her hand, but she didn't move away. "What happened?" She asked quietly.

"They was borned dead, but I loved 'em anyway. They was a boy and a girl, and I loved 'em though they was dead. But he took 'em away from me and buried 'em." Caroline moved to the mounds and kneeled on the ground between the mounds. Tears rolled down her cheek and dripped from her chin, falling onto the fresh earth of the grave.

Evelyn had never seen anyone cry so hard in her life. The alarming volume of the tears broke her heart as she watched, helpless to console Caroline. Her mind searched for understanding as she stood, paralyzed with indecision. It wasn't uncommon for those with mental illness to form unnaturally strong emotional attachment with their pets, but the scene unfolding before her was well beyond that.

"My precious babies," Caroline moaned again as a hand reached out and touched the older of the graves. "I'm so sorry."

Evelyn felt her knees weaken as an understanding struck her with a sudden ferocity that she wasn't prepared for. She reached out to steady herself as she went down, but there was nothing to hold her up. She sank to her knees as tears began to pour from her own eyes.

She ended up with her legs in a tangled heap, unable to control her own weeping as she watched the discharge of raw emotion before her. Caroline sobbed for her own children, her babies, that had been taken from her. Evelyn's heart ached for her, but for the first time she wept violently for her own child that she had so unceremoniously rid herself of. This poor woman, dubbed crazy by the world she lived in, wanted desperately to keep her babies although they were dead, and she, the one called educated hadn't wanted the baby that lived within her own body. Her baby who might have changed the world if it had only gotten the chance. Her beautiful, sweet baby that would have called her mom, that she had silenced, would never utter a word.

A profound sense of loss that she'd never felt swallowed her, pressing down on her like a heavy weight. Evelyn tried to push herself off the ground, but her arms had turned to jelly, and her legs wouldn't respond. The rawness of her emotions overcame her, reducing her to a sobbing heap on the cold, damp ground. Although the heartbreak of watching Caroline had started the flood, Evelyn cried for her baby; for her loss

The grief and pain welled up from a place deep within her that she never knew existed and exploded forth in an uncontrollable wail that rang out through the woods. It was a sound unknown to most people, deep and primal, low and guttural, reserved only for those mothers whose child now lay in the cold earth, gone forever.

The shadows were long, and the sun was slipping down close to the treetops by the time Evelyn hauled her exhausted body up off the ground and clambered up the broken back steps. Part of her wanted to collect Caroline, but she knew she didn't have the strength. Her entire body ached. Her head pounded worse than any hangover in history as she struggled on unsteady legs toward the porch. Grabbing the rickety handrail, she bent and heaved, but produced nothing. She cleared her throat and spat as a vile tasting liquid burned her throat and mouth.

The emotions that she'd denied and suppressed for so long had forced themselves out of her body with such force and suddenness that she couldn't begin to control them. She'd wept for herself, for Aaron, her parents, her plans, and once on a particularly rough night, Trae. She'd wept for everyone and everything except for the baby itself; the unrealized life that would never be.

Summoning all the strength and determination that she could scrounge from her spent body, she managed, somehow, to propel herself into the house. She staggered through the kitchen, her mind reeling as if she'd been drugged, and into the living room. Looking at the dirty mattress, her tired body almost talked her into laying down, but some small flicker of her old self won out and she dropped close to the fireplace. Folding her arms across the seat of the chair, she laid her heavy head down and fell asleep almost immediately.

"September twenty-seventh." Evelyn spoke solemnly into the darkness. She was astraddle the chair now, her arms folded across the back, propping up her chin. She knew that Caroline was in the room because she'd heard her come in some time after she had, plodding loudly over to the mattress and dropping on it heavily. She knew that Caroline was awake because she'd also had a bad dream, mumbling aloud about an hour ago and woken her. Since then the girl had rebuilt the fire to stave off the chill that had settled on them in the night. Evelyn heard her moving about restlessly on the old mattress and sensed her pass in the darkness more than once. She was awake, and probably like her, alone with her thoughts.

"That's when my baby would have been born." Evelyn spoke quietly, woefully. "For the rest of my life I will wonder what it might look like; wonder if it was a boy of girl."

"What happened?" The horse voice crept across the room, almost a whisper.

"I have a boyfriend in another town," she began, almost mechanically. "I came home for Christmas and slept with my old boyfriend. I got pregnant."

"Oh."

Evelyn was thankful for the mercy of not having to explain further. "I thought it would be best, you know. I thought it would ruin everything. My parents had a plan for me. I had a plan for me. Every fucking body had a plan."

"There is no plan," the voice answered with an edge of bitterness.

"I think I'm beginning to understand that now," Evelyn agreed. She still felt very tired but wasn't sleepy. She felt like crying but was cried out. She wanted to scream and fight and curse, but she didn't have the energy.

165

"Are you hungry?" She finally asked. There was a long pause before Caroline answered.

"A little." It was a sheepish, almost child-like voice answering in the dark.

The two women sat in front of the fireplace, legs crossed, facing each other and ate a peanut butter sandwich on stale white bread that the people of Souls Harbor had donated to the food pantry. The two women, emotionally drained, stared alternately at the floor, then the flames of the fire. Talk was scarce, but there was a mutual appreciation of each for the other's presence. Bonded in pain, they shared a common thread. Knowing, first-hand, that someone else was also suffering, made each of their own suffering somehow bearable. Like soldiers in the hellish confines of a heated battle, both thankful not to be there alone.

"Do you hate me?" Evelyn asked quietly.

"Why?"

"For what I did to my baby?"

Caroline looked at Evelyn and then stared into the flames for a while. "I don't really understand, not all of it, but I don't hate you."

"Sometimes I hate myself."

"Don't. It's not good." Caroline picked up a twig from the hearth and absently tossed it into the fire. "I hate myself all the time."

"You shouldn't." Evelyn told her. "You didn't do anything wrong."

"I'm weak." Caroline stared at the floor, her hair covering her dirty face. "I wish mama had killed me before she left."

"Don't say that, sweetie." Evelyn wanted to comfort her but couldn't find the energy.

The two women sat before the fire for a long time in silence before Caroline looked up.

"You're very pretty."

Evelyn looked up at Caroline with a hollow laugh. "I seriously doubt that, right now." She tried to smooth her hair, now barely contained in the tie behind her head.

"You are," Caroline insisted with a slight smile.

"You are beautiful," Evelyn told her.

Caroline shook her head. "I know I'm ugly."

Evelyn didn't think it possible, but the words hurt her heart even more. "You are not ugly," she insisted, wondering how many times in her life Caroline had been told that she was ugly.

"That's why people treat me like they do, because I'm ugly."

"Caroline," Evelyn reached out and put a hand on her knee. "You are beautiful. You have to believe that. You are beautiful and strong. You're the strongest person I've ever met. Don't let anyone ever make you feel like you're not."

Caroline pushed herself back, out of reach of Evelyn's hand. She began to pick fiercely at her thumb nail. "My pa said only thing that'd help my face was the back of a shovel. So, I asked why he kept coming to my room at night sometimes then. He got mad and beat me with his belt, then he hurt me and hurt me and hurt me."

Evelyn closed her eyes and sighed; her suspicions confirmed. She leaned forward and took Caroline's hands in hers to stop the savage assault on her thumb nail. Moving closer, she gently placed the tips of her fingers under her chin and lifted the girls' face to hers.

"Caroline," she began, "There are bad people in this world, and they hurt other people. I don't know why, but it happens. Maybe because they're miserable and want to make other people miserable. Or they're just cruel or hate themselves. I don't know why people do what they do. But that doesn't make YOU bad. It doesn't make YOU ugly. It makes them ugly."

"Why?" Caroline asked, closing her eyes tightly, pushing out a single tear.

Evelyn wiped it away with her thumb. "I don't know, sweetie. I wish I could tell you why, but I don't know." The two women embraced tightly in front of the fire, each sharing in the others pain.

This was also one of her reasons for her going into the field of psychology. The hope of reaching the unreachable was the impetus of all her hard work and dedication; to calm the savagery brought on by the mind. The one thing she hadn't counted on was the reciprocity she'd found. In the moment, Evelyn wondered who was helping whom. Sitting in the flickering light of a dying fire, Caroline gently weeping in her arms, the words of a song fluttered into her mind.

'So, what if I'm fucking crazy?'

NINE

Evelyn woke with an unsettling nervousness that she couldn't explain and an incessant desire to be somewhere, anywhere, other than in the old house. The ugly walls of the room felt closer, making it hard to breathe. Trying to diminish the urge to run, she told herself that it was just a need for a hot shower and toothbrush, but she knew it was a lie. There was an oppressiveness to the old house, as if all the bad memories were trapped in the dry dust that settled on everything.

"I have to go," Caroline eventually said flatly, a similar nervousness seemed to have settled over her as well.

"Okay," Evelyn said thankfully. "Me too. But I'll come back if you want."

Caroline said, "Okay," as she turned and walked through the front door.

"Wait!" Evelyn ran to the open doorway. "If I was able to get my hands on some medicine that would help you, with the voices I mean, would you take them?"

"They're mean and I hate them," Caroline told her over her shoulder.

"So, yes?"

"Okay." Caroline turned and walked off the porch without looking back. Her even, monotoned voice and her black, expressionless stare was back. Evelyn watched her round the edge of the house and disappear. Hurrying back inside, she emptied the backpack, slung one strap over her shoulder and exited the house in a rush, glad to be rid of the weight of its presence.

The air outside was cool and refreshing, lightly scented by the pines. Taking a few deep breaths as she wove her way across the yard, the weight of the house slowly diminished. Dirty and tired, she just wanted to be home.

The old house disappeared slowly through the pines as Evelyn made her way down the path. She took a deep breath and released the pain of the previous day through a slow exhale. Her mind quickly shifting gears, Evelyn decided to check on Aaron.

"Hey you," she texted.

"Hey yourself," he replied, almost immediately.

"How are U?"

"Ok. Drank 2 much last nite."

"Hangover?" She asked, adding a googly eye emoji and smiled. Aaron rarely ever got "drunk" because he couldn't stand the hangovers. He was a real baby when he didn't feel good.

"Big time." Aaron added the vomiting emoji for emphasis.

Evelyn scrunched her nose at the thought of the vomit. "What U doin?"

"Bed. U?"

"BION, strolling thru woods," she told him, abbreviating Believe It or Not.

"Really?"

"Yes."

"Why? You get lost? Lol."

"Looooong story. U wouldn't believe it if I told U."

"Sounds fun."

"Kinda nice. Quiet. Peaceful."

"I'm sure." Aaron answered. He'd spent a lot of time in the woods growing up, deer hunting, before college. "Big fight with M&D. They are ASSY."

"Sorry. Can I help?"

"Doubtful."

"Wish I was there."

"Not here." Popped onto her screen. "Be back in a few days," followed by "at NC."

"Join U?" She asked, chewing on her lower lip. Looking around, she watched a blue jay light on a low hanging limb at the edge of the roadway. It looked at her for a moment, its head tilted to one side in a way that reminded her of Caroline.

"You want to?"

"I do," Evelyn answered. She smiled then added, "LOTS."

"Leaving here by Thurs."

"Thought you were staying longer??" She replied.

"Was, but I've come to a decision."

Evelyn stopped and looked at her phone inquisitively. "What decision?"

"That my life without you is miserable."

Smiling, she replied, "You didn't already know that? LOL," as she started moving again.

"I guess I did. Just reaffirming it I guess."

"Good to know because I love you more than a rabbit loves carrots. Lol."

"Wow, hillbilly much?"

Evelyn laughed. "When in Rome."

"Well, I'm getting out of Rome soon. I'm leaving Thursday."

"Be there Thurs night." The planned reunion elevated her spirits. "Rest up."

"You better. Lol." he responded.

"Get some sleep. Sorry U don't feel good."

"Better now. Some."

"Love U, babe."

"Miss U."

Evelyn's heart soared. "Know you're tired. Sleep."

"I am. Watch for bears."

Evelyn stopped suddenly, looking around at the woods that surrounded her. "Bears?" she asked him. "Really?"

"Lol. Just kidding. No bears."

"Butt," she typed and added an emoji with its tongue sticking out.

"TTUL?", Aaron replied, asking if they could talk later.

"You better. Now rest."

She finished her walk to the car feeling much better than when she'd started it. Nearing the road, she watched as a log truck rattled past, empty. Following it, an old light blue pick-up truck slowed, allowing the passenger to get a good look at her.

172

Hoping it wouldn't stop, she stared back as the gray-haired black man older than her daddy leered back at her. She shook her head angrily and breathed a sigh of relief when the brake lights finally went out and the truck sped off, its occupants undoubtfully discussing what sexual exploits they'd like to have with her.

"Jerks," she said, shaking her head. Getting into her car she kept an eye on the truck. Something about it gave her the creeps.

"That smells good," Evelyn said as she approached her father, standing in front of his grill waving smoke from his face.

"Hey baby doll!" He stepped out of the smoke and gave her a one-armed hug, kissing her lightly on the cheek that she presented to him. "Smoking a butt for supper tonight."

"I can tell," she said, watching him close the lid and wipe his hands on that he'd just pulled from his pocket.

"I missed you last night," he told her, flipping the rag onto his shoulder.

"I told y'all where I'd be, daddy."

"I know. I still missed you," he told her. "Come and sit. Let's talk."

Evelyn watched him sit at one of the patio chairs and drink from the can of Coke on the table in front of him. Reluctantly joining him, she braced for a lecture.

"I just worry. We both do," he began. "How safe is this whole thing with this girl, Eve?"

"It's fine, dad," she insisted. "I'm not going to a crack house or a-" she paused as she struggled for the right words, waving her hand in a circle before her face, "or a place where gangs hang out."

Her father looked at her with an incredulous laugh. "First of all, you in college and that the best you can come up with? And secondly, I don't see how nothing good can come of this. That girl ain't right. She might snap and slit your throat in the night or something. You don't know."

Evelyn shook her head. "Well, I'm tired, catch me after a nap, Mister Wordsmith. And secondly, I love you dad, and I appreciate your concern, I really do. BUT you don't know what you're talking about. That poor woman hasn't hurt anyone, ever. If anything, it's the other way around." She didn't feel the need to tell him about the episode Caroline had had, or what the voices were telling her to do. If she did, he would probably do something rash, like call the cops.

"That may be so," Freddy conceded with a sigh. "But I just don't like it. I worry about you."

She reached out and put a hand on his arm. "Daddy, I'd be in more danger at a frat party than I am with Caroline. Now, I'm gonna go talk to mom. She inside?"

"Wait," Freddy called, watching his daughter climb the steps to the back deck. "Frat party? We do need to talk!" Evelyn waved to him over her shoulder and laughed. "We gone talk about this. I know where you live!" he called as she opened the door and went into the house.

"And so, I pretty much got up and came home," Evelyn said as her thumb wiped condensation from the glass of sweet tea cradled in her hands. She looked across the table at her mother. Martha Jackson stared back at her daughter, tears welled in the corners of her eyes for a moment then got up, came to her, and enveloped her in a tight embrace.

She had watched her daughter struggle to come to grips with the affair she'd committed, heard her talk about her fear of disappointing her parents, watched her worry about the effects it would have on her relationship with that white guy, Aaron, but she hadn't seen her pour her heart out about the pain of loss for her unborn child. Whether by her own doing or not, she had lost a child; lost the potential of what that child might have been. It had been that acknowledgement; that pain, that she herself had been waiting on from her daughter.

Evelyn's depiction of her day and night with Caroline broke her heart, for both women. As a woman herself, she knew the pain that could be wrought upon them. She had experienced it herself, albeit not anywhere close to the extent that Caroline had.

A sense of shame also settled into her heart. She'd seen that poor girl countless times on the street and had never stopped to extend a hand to her. She'd spent countless hours in church, listening to and reading God's word and had passed by "one of the least of these" on the street without so much as a second thought. She had been the Pharisee who had passed on the other side of the road so as to not see that helpless victim, but her daughter had been the good Samaritan who had stopped to help. Convicted by her own hypocrisy, she said a silent prayer for forgiveness.

Caressing her daughters' back as she held her, pride began to outpace her guilt. Her daughter had put a face to the name. Her daughter had reached out, against her own objections, and took a hand of a wretch and lifted her up. It was a beautiful thing to know about your child.

"You okay, baby?" Martha asked as she released her daughter from the tight embrace and took a seat next to her.

"I don't know, mama. What's okay?"

"I don't know either. I guess it's what you make it."

"Well, I've got a few days to figure it out. Aaron will be back at school Thursday and I've GOT to be there."

"Why?" Martha asked her.

"He's taking a Criminology class this summer, so his load won't be so heavy in the fall. He went home for a while, but he's going back up Thursday to get ready for classes next Monday."

"And you have to be there?"

"No, but I want to be there, mama."

Martha pursed her lips and looked at her daughter with a sigh, resigning herself to the fact that she'd have to stop referring to Aaron as "the white guy".

"You really love him, don't you?"

"I do, mama. And he's crazy about me. If y'all ever met him I'm sure you'd love him too."

"Maybe so," Martha answered doubtfully. Black or white, she doubted any man would ever be good enough for her only child. "Does he know?"

"No, but I'm going to tell him. I don't know how he'll react, but he deserves to know. I don't want our life built on a lie. He deserves to know the truth."

Martha closed her eyes, remembering a biblical quote attributed to Pontius Pilot. It was her time to ask a philosophical question. "What is truth?" she asked.

Evelyn looked at her mother, unsure what to say as her mind jumped to the secret that her father had told her. Did she know? Had she always known? She thought about it a moment and decided that she did, although she'd never brought it up. Maybe leaving her husband to carry the weight of his secret had kept him from making the same mistake again. Maybe she had allowed the weight of his own shame to be his punishment all these years.

"I love you so much, mama," Evelyn finally told her, throwing her arms around her mother's neck.

"I love you too, baby," Martha told her, patting her on the back gently. "More than anything else in the whole world." She knew that she was helpless to do anything to aid her daughter with her white boyfriend; with Aaron, but she would move the world to help her daughter any other way that she could.

"Now you go and get out of those clothes and take a shower. You smell like an old house and you dirty."

"You'll get no argument from me there," Evelyn said as she stood.

"And wash your head. Mama will fix your hair when you get out."

Evelyn stopped and turned back to her mother with a smile. It had been years since her mother had done her hair. "I think I'd like that."

Martha Jackson watched her daughter disappear down the hall and sighed heavily. Pushing herself up from the table, she grabbed another can of soda from the fridge and headed out the back door to talk to her husband.

Caroline stood in the front room of the house she'd grown up in and looked around. It hadn't seemed possible, but it felt even lonelier than before; more lonesome. She avoided coming inside unless the weather was bad, but she was drawn in by the supplies that Evelyn had left. Not that she needed them. She wanted to be near them because they brought her nearer to Evelyn's presence. It was the first time in a long time that a kind heart had graced this hellish place.

Kneeling next to the hearth, the fire long burned out, she looked at the neat pile of things that Evie had been left for her. She lifted the flashlight and shoved it, handle first, into her back pocket. There was a half dozen cigarette lighters, two more packs of the wet wipes, another pair of jeans and a clean tee shirt, two large bottles of water, band-aids, antibiotic gel, a small bag of toiletries, and a mirror not much bigger than her hand.

Gently pushing the other things out of the way, Caroline picked up the mirror hesitantly. She never worried about how she looked. It never mattered. People didn't like her because she was ugly and there was nothing she could do about it. It had always been that way and always would be.

Lifting the mirror before her, Caroline stared blankly at her reflection. Evelyn's words echoed in her mind. "You're beautiful". Caroline shook her head. She wasn't beautiful. Evelyn was, but not her. In the mirror a hand slowly came to her cheek, her fingers lightly touching the smudge of dirt that marred it just below her eye. Tilting the mirror to follow its progress, she watched her fingers brush over the tangled mop of hair that framed her face. How long had it been since she'd washed it? Or brushed it?

"Oh, it's looking at itself," mocked the little boy's voice. "Ugly old Cara found a mirror."

"Good thing no one else can see her," the old man laughed.

"She wants to look pretty so the boys will come and dilly with her more," the old man laughed. "She likes it when they dilly with her."

178

"She wants to be pretty like the black whore so they can whore it up together," she old woman growled.

"Or be pretty so the darkie will dilly with her." A chorus of laughter erupted in Caroline's head.

With a sudden jerk, her hand threw the mirror across the room. It struck the wall and ricocheted halfway back across the room before falling to the floor, face up. As soon as she'd done it, Caroline regretted it. It was a gift from Evelyn. How could she break it? She'd be mad now! She might not ever come back!

"You crazy bitch!" screamed the voice in her head. "You crazy, ugly bitch!"

"Now you can't get pretty for your woman whore."

"No!" Caroline cried to the empty room as she went to the mirror. She fell to her knees and bent low as she began to pick up the broken shards hurriedly, uncaring that a few of them had cut into her fingertips. She had already gathered several of the broken shards when she caught a glimpse of herself in the pieces of mirror still holding in the pink, plastic frame. She looked at her face, fragmented, broken, pieces missing, and unconsciously tightened her hand around the broken ribbons of glass.

Was that really her? Could it be the Caroline that her memory clung to? The little girl in a light blue sun dress with white daisies on the shoulder straps. Was this the blonde hair that her mother washed and brushed every night? Was this the face that her mother kissed and sang to? How could that little girl with hope and promise turn into the monster that stared at her from the mirror?

"You get to choose, Cara," Lynn LeBeau told her daughter. "No matter what happens in your life, no matter where you go, and I hope it's a hell of

*a long way from this miserable place, you get to choose who you are."
Her fingers danced gently around the red welt beneath her left eye
which had*

*already begun to swell, a remnant of the beating she'd taken from her
husband.*

*"You get to choose who you are, in here." She pointed to her chest
just above a small rip in her blouse, another remnant of the fight. "You
remember*

*that, and that Mama will always love you. Not only for the rest of my
life, but for the rest of yours too. Mama loves her precious, beautiful
girl. You   remember that."*

"I'll remember, Mama. I promise."

*"I hope you do, baby. I hope you do." She stood and walked to the
door hoping to hide her tears.*

*"Mama," Caroline called, stopping her mother in the doorway.
"I'm so sorry that daddy ruined your birthday cake. I wish you would
of had a happy birthday."*

*"It's okay baby. Any day I get to be with you is like a happy birthday
to Mama. You get some rest now. You got school in the mornin'."*

She didn't make it to school that Monday morning or any that whole
week. She'd been too busy preparing for her mother's funeral. She woke
up crying and went to bed crying. The doctor wanted to give her some
medicine to make her stop crying, but her Daddy told him to leave her
be. He was content to let her cry while he sat on the porch and drank his
whiskey.

"No!" Caroline stood suddenly and threw the bloody shards of glass
at the mattress in the corner. She spun on a heel and ran from the house,

leaping over the back steps and continuing past the old shed until she reached the woods.

Reaching beside her Evelyn picked up her phone as it vibrated on the bed next to her. Sitting in her usual position she swiped the screen absently and put it to her ear, her eyes glued to the computer screen in front of her.

"Hello."

"Hey sweets!"

Jolted from her studies by Aaron's voice in her ear. "Hey sweetie," she answered, a smile breaking out over her face as she moved the laptop to the bed and leaned back against the pillows, careful not to mess her hair.

"What 'cha doing?"

"Not much. Just doling some reading," she told him.

"Sounds boring," he said with a laugh. "But you like it, though."

"I do," she admitted. "It's a fascinating read by a phycologist who talks about not using antipsychotics to treat patients with mental illnesses."

"Wow, you really get into that stuff, don't you?" he asked her.

"I have to admit that I do. I'm a nerd."

"A beautiful nerd," he told her.

"You're too sweet. My mother did my hair today, it feels awesome!"

"My mother called me a heathen today," Aaron laughed. "Trade moms."

"No way, but I'd bet she'd do your hair if you asked," Evelyn teased.

"Sounds like you had a better day than me." He sighed heavily into the phone. "I don't even know why I came home. I can't wait to leave."

"Me either. I miss you."

"I've come to realize that being away from you really sucks."

"You just now realizing that?" she joked.

"Na," he answered, "I've known it, just lately accepted the truth."

"Well, I'm glad you finally came around," she laughed.

"I am too," Aaron cleared his throat. "So, what have you been up to besides strolling through the woods and getting your hair fixed?"

"You wouldn't believe me. It's such a long story."

"I've got all night. Lord knows I'm not going back downstairs 'till my folks' party is over."

"I'm sorry you're not having a good time, babe."

"I am too, but it makes me look forward to seeing you even more."

"Baby, I love you."

"I love you too," he told her. "Now let's hear that story."

Over the next hour Evelyn filled him in on the story of Caroline LeBeau. She told him all her suspicions and what she'd come to find out from Caroline. She cried some, when she told him about Caroline's babies, carefully dancing around the subject of child loss. They laughed together when she told him about Roger, the not-yet-vowed priest. She purposefully left out what Father Newell had told her just before she left. Through all of it Aaron listened patiently, interjecting his opinion at times, and let her finish her tale.

"Wow," he finally said. "All I've done is argue with my parents and drink too much," he told her when she'd finally finished. He loved the excitement in her voice when she became passionate about something; how she talked a little faster and tended to ramble sometimes. He wished he was lying in bed beside her as they'd done so many times.

"What are you all arguing about?" She asked, wanting to give him a chance to vent.

"I don't know," he sighed. "Just stupid crap. It's not important."

"You sure. I can listen as well as I can talk you know."

"I know, sweets, but I don't wanna talk about them."

"Okay. Well, what you think?"

"About the girl? That's wild. I can't believe it. You're more badass than I thought you were."

Evelyn laughed. "It's nuts though. I still remember her standing up to a bully for me in second grade, and to meet like that after all these years. It's just nuts. It's like we started at one place, our lives went in totally opposite directions, then we met back up."

"Wild stuff. So, is she going to see a doctor or what?"

"I don't know. There's so much to consider, so many environmental factors to look at before you could even begin to pick the right meds. Or go without meds, who knows. To be honest, I just barely even know what the hell I'm doing. It's like the blind leading the blind here."

"Well, if she's hearing voices, she probably needs meds."

"I know, but there's voices and there's voices. I mean, I hear my mom's voice in my head all the time."

"Wieeeerdooo," Aaron joked with a laugh.

"Yeah?" Evelyn retaliated playfully, "She's saying don't be taking yo panties off for that white boy no more."

"Okay, okay. Everybody just calm down. Do not! I repeat, DO NOT listen to the voices in your head. They are baaaaad voices."

Evelyn laughed loudly, covering her mouth with her hand. "I don't know, they can be pretty convincing."

"Well, I'll just have to be more convincinger than they are."

"There's that North Central education. Your parents must be so proud."

"I think my education is the least of their worries right now," Aaron told her, the playfulness gone from his voice.

"I'm sorry. What are they mad about?"

"Just stupid crap," he told her after a hesitation. "They're stupid."

"You don't want to talk about it?"

"Not really. I mean," he paused again. "It's really nothing. They're not happy with my educational choices and my major."

"Why? That's a great field."

"Parents," he sighed. "Who knows what the hell they're thinking?"

Evelyn agreed, but she felt like there was something he wasn't telling her; something he didn't want to tell her. Her mind wandered to the race issue. It had never specifically come up between them. They'd never discussed it. He knew he was white and that she was black, and so did she, so the need never arose.

"Is it because I'm black?" she asked quietly, sitting up in the bed.

184

"Oh no," he assured her. "I haven't told them that. I thought I'd wait 'till Thanksgiving and do a whole 'Look who's Coming to Dinner' thing."

Evelyn shook her head as his laughter filled her ears. "You're impossible. But seriously, they do know right?"

"Of course," he told her, still laughing. "I showed them your picture months ago."

"And?"

"And they asked if you were black? I pretended that I hadn't noticed and flipped out."

"Stop," she said, laughing with him. "Seriously."

"Okay, okay. Yes, they know. I did show them a picture. The one with you in the park, by the fountain."

"Good, I looked good in that one."

"Mom was surprised, I guess. Dad said you were hot after mom left the room."

"Well, now we know where you get your impeccable taste from."

"I guess so because you are hot."

"And you are wildly gorgeous, for a white boy."

"I guess that'll have to do." There was a brief silence on the phone then he said, "Eve, I love you."

"I love you too. God, I wish I was with you now."

"Well in a few days all your dreams will come true."

"A few days?" She asked.

"When I go back to NC? You are still coming up, aren't you?"

"Yes, yes. I guess I just spaced a second. I'll be there. I wouldn't miss it for the world."

"Good. What are you going to do with your patient then?"

Suddenly struck by the finiteness of her time left in town, Evelyn wondered the same thing.

"To be honest, I don't know."

"Well, you got a matter of days to figure it out and get that girl into a hospital or something."

"I know," Evelyn said, suddenly torn. "But I will be at NC Thursday night."

"Just how crazy is she anyway? I mean there's 'crazy', then there's 'Craaaazy'. Maybe you could bring her along," Aaron suggested playfully.

"Yuck! First of all, you're sick. You are a sick individual. And second of all, she probably hates men and would probably gut you like a fish, so there's that."

"I'm just kidding," he said, laughing again. "Unless…"

"Stop it you perv," she laughed.

"Okay. You know you're all I need," he told her.

"I'm all you can handle," she told him.

"I'd really like to handle you right now."

"Hmm," she began, seductively, as she settled back into the bed. "Please, tell me more."

TEN

Evelyn pulled her car off the road and stopped. Getting out, she hefted the backpack onto her shoulders and followed the thin footpath through the tall grass and into the woods. Completing the path quickly, she found herself in front of the old house once again. She needed to broach the subject of medicine and possibly a doctor visit today. The timeline had been condensed and she didn't have the luxury of waiting. After today she had only four days before she left, with Thursday being a spa day so that she looked nice when she saw Aaron. The clock was ticking.

She traversed the yard without a misstep, leaping and jumping the holes expertly until she finished at the base of the front steps, which she bounded up quickly. "Lucy, I'm home," she called out as she walked into the living room of the old house. "Good morning."

Her eyes swept the room, finding it empty. Moving through the house she checked every room, except what she'd come to think of as the "stinky room" and found herself on the back porch. Caroline was nowhere to be seen.

"Well," she told the empty house as she turned, "Might as well get started." She shrugged the backpack and took out some cleaning supplies, tackling the daunting task before her determined to make a difference.

By the time Caroline appeared in the front doorway Evelyn had found an old straw broom, swept the living room and kitchen, used a hand pump to inflate the two single air mattresses she bought and made them up with sheets and a blanket, and was in the process of dusting. She stopped, her hand in an old sock drenched in lemon-scented polish and stared.

She stared at Caroline with a mixture of surprise and joy. Caroline had bathed, somewhere, and washed her hair. She stood now, dressed in the jeans and pale green t-shirt Evelyn had left for her. Her hair was brushed back and tied up in a neat, clean ponytail. A few shorter, blonde locks fell across her cheek in a casual, playful way.

"Oh my God!" Evelyn exclaimed, going to her. "You look amazing!" Noticing the rag tied haphazardly around her left hand, Evelyn lifted it in hers. "What happened?"

"I cut it," Caroline informed her blankly, pulling her hand away.

"Okay," Evelyn said suspiciously, deciding to not press the issue right now. "Anyway, you look great!"

"Thank you," Caroline said sheepishly as she and Evelyn exchanged a brief, slightly awkward embrace. "I used the stuff you left for me."

"Great. You do look amazing. Here, let me see you, girl." Evelyn made slight adjustments, tugging at the hem of the shirt before examining the jeans. They were an old pair she'd outgrown, but they fit Caroline well. "The pants a little loose in the back," she told her. "My butt's a little bigger than yours though," she laughed. "But that's not a bad thing."

Finishing her tour around Caroline she smiled and nodded her head. "You look amazing!"

"Thanks." Caroline tucked the stray locks of hair behind her ear and allowed a slight smile to escape. "It's been a while. I was nervous."

"Don't be. Really, you look great."

"You're always so pretty and I…" she trailed off as she surveyed the room.

"You were beautiful before and are more so now. So, whaddaya think?" she asked, following Caroline's gaze around the room.

"Cleaner. Smells better," Caroline told her.

"What do you say?" Evelyn went to the old mattress and gave it a kick. "Wanna get rid of this thing?"

"I'd like that," Caroline said, a pall washing over her face as she joined Evelyn.

"Good, because the couch is next," Evelyn told her.

Not wanting to guess what secrets and bad memories the dirty old mattress held, Evelyn helped her tilt the mattress up onto its side and they slid it out the front door. The bright sun outside fell on the old thing for the first time if forever and lit the plethora of stains for the world to see. Exposed in the light of day the stains, most of which looked like faded blood, stood as a testament to the pain Caroline had endured silently for so many years.

Evelyn intentionally showed no indication that she'd seen them. Caroline was in a good mood. There was no reason to dredge up old injuries right now. The two women wrangled the old mattress to the far end of the porch toward the shady north side of the porch and pushed it up and over the rail.

"Well," Evelyn panted. "Out of sight, out of mind." Dusting her clothes, she looked at Caroline. She looked genuinely happy to be rid of the mattress; of the constant reminder of what her father had done to her. It had stood as a testament to his power over her, of his strength and her weakness.

189

"Thank you," Caroline told her, dropping her gaze to the floor, embarrassed.

Taking the girl by the shoulders, Evelyn investigated her face and shook her head. "You don't have anything to be ashamed of. Nothing that happened to you is your fault, Caroline. Accepting that is the first thing you must do. Don't let anybody, or anything that happened to you define who you are now."

A slight smile came to Caroline's thin, pink lips. "Thanks. My mama told me something like that once."

"Your mama must have been a smart woman," Evelyn said, ushering Caroline back inside the house.

"Not really," Evelyn said, checking out the closest of the air mattress with the edge of her foot. "Not smart like you."

"Book smart is one thing. Street smart is another. You don't have to go to college to be wise, Caroline."

"I guess." She sat down on the kitchen chair next to the one Evelyn had brought into the room from the kitchen.

"I know," Evelyn assured her as she approached the girl from behind. "You know, my parents never went to college. I'm the first person in my whole family to, but my mama knows a whole lot more important stuff than I do." She absently began to gently pull Caroline's hair through her fingers. It was long and shiny after being washed, more golden than she'd thought.

"My mama used to do my hair all the time. In the summer we'd sit on the porch for hours while she worked her magic. I used to love it. It takes a long time to do a black girls head and when I was little, I used to fall asleep while she was doing it. I'd sometimes wake up while she was carrying me to bed and ask if my hair was pretty. 'It was pretty to start with, child. It's just fixed now' she'd say."

Evelyn smiled at the memory. "She hadn't done it in a long time. I go to the salon now," she said with a shrug. "But she did for me yesterday." Evelyn's hand went to her hair, patting the wrap gently. "And I remembered how nice it was."

"Mama used to brush my hair. She kept hers short, but always wanted mine to be long. She brushed it out every night and every morning."

"Isn't it wonderful when they do that?"

"It was," Caroline said with a bittersweet smile.

"Want me to do you?" Evelyn asked. "I brought a brush."

"It's okay," Caroline told her. "You don't have to."

"I want to," Evelyn said, putting a hand on her shoulder to stop her getting up. "I'm not as good as my mama, but then again she never done white girl hair either."

Caroline shrugged. "If you want."

"Have you ever thought of leaving here?" Evelyn asked as she pulled the brush through Caroline's hair.

"Don't have nowhere to go," Caroline answered, her voice low and calm.

Evelyn drew in a deep breath as she continued to brush her hair. "I'm sure there is some place."

"Like a hospital?" Caroline asked suspiciously.

"No, not necessarily."

"My mama left here in a pine box that daddy couldn't pay for. I don't even know where she's buried. My daddy died in that very room right there," she pointed to the room with the metal bed frame. "My babies never left here. Why would I leave?"

"I don't know," Evelyn began tentatively. "It seems like there's a lot of bad memories here for you."

"I suppose," Caroline said with a shrug. "Some good ones too."

Evelyn wanted to change the subject and not press the issue, but she needed to move forward somewhere. She finally breached the subject from a different angle as she swept a swatch of hair into her hand and began brushing it gently.

"Caroline, how are the voices?"

"Still there."

"They still tell you to kill me?"

"Not today," Caroline answered flatly.

Evelyn cleared her throat nervously. "Okay. You know that's not good. The voices I mean."

"I've always known that. Everybody thinks I'm crazy, don't they?"

"It doesn't matter what they think. Do you think you're crazy?"

Caroline thought for a while. "Sometimes," she finally answered.

"Did they make you do that?" Evelyn asked, referring to the bandage on Caroline's hand.

"Not really. The mirror fell and broke."

"It's okay. It was cheap anyway."

"Are you mad?"

"Not even a little bit," Evelyn assured her. "You want a ponytail, a knot, a bun, braids?"

"I don't know what those are. You pick."

Evelyn looked at the waterfall of hair before her. "Let's do a braid. It'll be easier to manage."

Caroline shrugged, remaining quiet as she picked nervously at the edges of the bandages.

"Mostly they scare me and are mean. I hate them," she finally said almost in a whisper.

"Are there many?"

"Three mean ones and a nice one, but they don't hardly ever let her talk. She's scared of them too."

"Who are the mean ones?" Evelyn asked as she separated Caroline's hair into three sections. "Do they have names."

"No. They're just there. Even when they're not talking, I can feel them."

"I'm so sorry. Caroline, there are places that can help. Medicines you can take to make them go away."

"No. I can't go."

"Why not?" Evelyn asked softly.

Caroline sat still and quiet for a long time while Evelyn braided her hair, keeping it tight to her scalp as it progressed over the crown of her head and began its way down the back. Evelyn worked slowly and methodically with firm, but gentle hands taking care to stroke Caroline's mane lovingly.

Her mind strayed to a study she'd read about kids in a war-ravaged Kosovo orphanage. The kids, mostly starved of human contact by the cold but efficient nuns who fed and housed them, had developed several personality traits, not the least of which was a Dissociative Identity Disorder, involving a distorted view of reality and the feelings that multiple people lived inside their heads. The amazing part of the study was that most of them, particularly the younger ones who had spent longer periods at the orphanage, had developed a stern father figure personality, and a mother personality who was kind and gentle. These identities hadn't been rooted in real parents, because most have never met their parents or were too young to remember them. The personalities were created entirely in the child's mind from some innate social construct, and each set of "parents" were different from those imagined by other children across a wide spectrum ranging from strict and overbearing to warm and loving.

"My mama died on her birthday," Caroline finally said. "And I guess my babies did to, kinda."

"I'm so sorry," was all Evelyn could manage without bursting into tears.

"I found two of 'em. One is still out there. I've been lookin all over."

"Were they...?" Evelyn asked, not wanting to vocalize the rest of the question, asking if they were her fathers' children.

"Most likely."

Evelyn wiped a tear from her cheek as she struggled to finish the braid. "You poor child."

"The last one tore me up bad. There was lots of blood after it come out. It wouldn't quit. My daddy took me to a clinic and made me tell them I was with a boy and got pregnant because I was a whore. The doctor said I couldn't ever have no more babies. "

"Didn't he do anything? The doctor?"

Caroline shook her head. "He didn't care. We didn't have no money, so he fixed on me some and sent us home. Didn't even ask where the baby was."

Evelyn drew in a deep breath to compose herself. There was little wonder that Caroline didn't trust men, not to mention doctors. How could a person be so failed by society? Were things so bad as to allow the systematic and life-long failure of another human being to go unnoticed?

"Is that what the holes are?" Evelyn asked. "Looking for them?"

Caroline nodded quietly. "Want me to show you?"

"If you want to," Evelyn answered, unsure what to expect.

Caroline stopped just short of the tree line just past the rectangular, settled patch of earth that Evelyn had assumed was a garden. Large grasses had reclaimed the soft, sandy plot in big patches, giving it an almost desert-like feel. At her feet sat a small rock about the size of two of her fists. On its surface there was a worn slash as if someone had struck it with a metal object very hard some time ago.

"What is it?" Evelyn asked.

"I don't know. Maybe something. Maybe nothing."

"Looks like it could have been marked. Do you think....?" Evelyn trailed off, not wanting to say it.

"Could have been struck by a plow and throwed outta the garden."

"And it could not be."

Caroline stood and stared down at the rock. "Found it yesterday. I was scared to dig it up. Don't know why."

Who wouldn't be? Evelyn thought. If it wasn't what she hoped for, it would be yet another disappointment. If it was, then her work was done. All three babies would have been found. To someone with mental deficiencies, and even some without, the routine of a certain labor could be comforting, even if it was a fruitless one. It was a reason to get out of bed in the morning; a motivation. Caroline was probably afraid of what would happen if that motivation was taken away, her only goal in life finally realized.

"When my daddy was sick, before he died, he couldn't get out of bed. I had to give him his medicine and wipe his ass. He was still mean to me, so I made him tell me what he did with my babies. He refused to, so I threw his pills out the window. He hollered all night and cried. He cried and begged like a baby."

Evelyn moved closer and slid an arm around Caroline's waist. She gently lowered the girl's head to her shoulder as they stood in silence and stared at the rock. It was strange that such an innocuous-looking stone might prove so significant in someone's life. Small and roundish, half buried in the ground, it had sat in its cradle for years, undisturbed, and possibly marked the resting place of a human being. Today, right now, it was the most important rock in the world.

"I watched him suffer, you know. I listened to him beg, and I did nothing. He even promised to show me, but I waited. I wanted him to suffer. Does that make me a bad person?"

"No, sweetie," Evelyn told her, fighting back tears. "Not even a little bit."

"I gave him his medicine the next day and I put him on the bedspread and drug him around the yard. I made him watch as I dug. When I found the first one, I took him back in and put him in the bed. I didn't want him to see me cry ever again."

"He got a little better, enough to sit up anyway. I asked him to tell me where the other two were, but he was a bastard and wouldn't tell me, so I threw all his pills out the window and locked him in his room. I heard him moving around some. Screaming and crying. He started to beg and swore he didn't remember.

"He did say that one was under a rock with a mark on it. I never knew if he was telling the truth or not. He was so bad to me, Evie. As bad as the devil could be."

Evelyn hugged her as she began to cry. "If you ask me, he got about half of what he deserved."

"He screamed for two days and begged me to kill him. I went in once and he'd fallen on the floor and had shitted his pants. Something in me thought it was funny and I laughed at him. He laid there on the floor in his own shit and piss and died without a soul in the world caring. That's how he died. Alone."

"Good!" Evelyn exclaimed through her tears. "Fucking good! He deserved every bit of it. I hope he suffered all the way to hell."

"He did," Caroline assured her through her own tears.

"Good!" Evelyn was surprised at the severity of her anger and the strength of her pain. They were at the level reserved only for those who hurt the ones you loved.

The two women embraced, both carrying the burden of the same great pain, at the edge of a ruined garden and cried together.

Evelyn knelt beside Caroline, watching as she began to dig slowly, moving her hands carefully in the dark soil. She'd not allowed her to

197

dig and, assuming it was something she had to do herself, Evelyn remained silent. Caroline's hands dug and clawed at the earth, removing it by the handfuls until she'd reached the depth of two feet.

Finally, she stopped digging and sat back against her heels revealing a small bundle of a dark cloth at the bottom of the hole. The bundle was smaller than she expected, leaving Evelyn to assume it was a preemie birth, or a result of very poor nutrition. There was no smell of decay, as she'd expected, only that of freshly churned earth.

"Are you okay?" she asked softly, knowing Caroline wasn't.

Caroline didn't answer but sat with her dirty hands clasped in her lap, staring down at the baby in the hole while tears began to roll down her cheeks.

With gentle hands Caroline got beneath the soil-incrusted shroud and lifted it and its contents out of the ground carefully. Shifting her position, she sat back on her butt, crossing her legs, and cradled the bundle of cloth to her chest.

Evelyn slid in behind Caroline and hugged her, laying a tender hand on the bundle. She didn't cry, but her heart broke for her friend. Looking at the bundle, a certain solace settled over her. The baby was finally with its mother; the mother with her child. It was the close of a horribly painful chapter in Caroline's life and she prayed its end would allow for a new one to begin. One that would lead to a certain healing that her friend so greatly deserved.

"We have to rebury her," Caroline said, standing abruptly. "We don't have much time."

"Um, okay," Evelyn said, hurrying after Caroline, who was already plodding across the garden.

"What can I do?" she asked.

Caroline shook her head as she hopped and jumped her way across the wide yard, avoiding the holes she'd created in search of the prize she now clutched to her chest.

"Look. I can use a shovel," Evelyn said, struggling to keep up. "I'll dig while you sit and hold- "her voice hung in her throat, not knowing what to call it. A baby? A body? She settled on "the baby."

"Thank you."

Evelyn stabbed the spade into the ground alongside the other two graves with a grunt. The ground here was compacted and interlaced with roots. The emotional toll alone was enough to make it a difficult task but creating a hole in the ground to serve as an eternal resting place for another human being was back breaking work for a girl with little experience with a shovel.

She tried to fit the small casket, made of layered cardboard, into the ground several times only to find she'd grossly over-estimated the depth and width of the hole she was digging. Lugging the box out, she dug more and tried again. Again, it didn't fit so she hauled it out and dug more in what was beginning to feel like an endless cycle of failure.

Finally, her arms and back aching, the small casket struck the bottom of the hole with a dull thud. Sticking the spade into the pile of fresh dirt, she motioned to Caroline and stumbled over to the cedar stump. She sat down with a heavy sigh, checking her hands for blisters.

Caroline rose slowly, crying softly as she walked to the grave. She slid to her knees, kissed the bundle of dirty cloth, and lowered it into the casket. Closing it with a thick cardboard lid. She stood and sighed, her eyes locked on the piece of cardboard that would keep the dirt away from her baby's remains. The letters OOD BANK stared back at her from the box that had once brought her groceries.

"Should we say something?" Evelyn asked, her breathing returning to normal.

Caroline nodded. "Now I walk through the valley of the shadow of death, I will fear no evil. The Lord is my Shepard, He will guide me." Caroline fell silent for a moment, wiping tears from her cheeks "That's all I remember."

Rubbing Caroline's back softly, Evelyn stood beside her friend. "I remember it," she said. "May I?"

Caroline nodded silently, her eyes on the tiny makeshift casket.

"The Lord is my Shepard; I shall not want. He maketh me to lie down in green pastures: he leadeth me beside still waters. He restoreth my soul; he leadeth me in the paths of righteousness for his name's sake. Yea, though I walk through the valley of the shadow of death, I will fear no evil, for thou art with me; thy rod and thy staff they comfort me. Thou preparest a table before me in the presence of my enemies. Thou anointest my head with oil; my cup runneth over. Surely goodness and mercy will follow me all the days of my life. and I will dwell in the house of the Lord forever."

When she finished reciting the psalm, Evelyn closed her eyes and said, "Amen."

ELEVEN

Evelyn woke slowly. She'd slept well, considering she'd spent the night on a twin sized air mattress. She wanted to roll over and go back to sleep, but the soft light filtering through the open windows told her that morning had arrived. Caroline was already up and about. There was still a nervousness about sleeping so soundly while the girl crept around the house, although she hated to admit it. It couldn't be helped though, she'd been exhausted last night, both emotionally and physically and apparently Caroline slept very little.

She knew in her heart that Caroline would never hurt her herself, but her mind knew that she wasn't always in charge of the things she did. How horrible must it be, she thought, to be controlled by something within your own mind? How long had she suffered like this?

Sitting up with a yawn, Evelyn wished for a steaming hot cup of coffee to help stave off the damp chill that had settled over them in the night. She rubbed her arms and dug in the backpack for the sweatshirt she packed for just such an occasion. Sufficiently dressed, she pushed herself up from the mattress and went to the front door. Opening it, she found Caroline.

Stepping onto the porch, her bare feet protested the cool dampness of the porch's floorboards. A low fog hung over the area, shrouding everything in an opaque veil so that the surrounding trees were relegated to vague, dark shapes in the white mist. In the quiet, she could hear a chorus of water droplets falling to the ground as the moisture settled on everything around them. The ground looked as if a light rain shower had passed through in the night. She hadn't heard a thing.

Yawning again, she stretched as she thought about the camping trips her father had taken them on when she was younger. The mornings on the lake were just like this, cool and foggy, and quiet. For a moment, the old place didn't feel as repulsive as before. In the still quietness, it had an almost peaceful feel.

Lost in her thoughts, Evelyn's mind slipped to an article she'd read entitled, "Brain Fog". The author noted how the human mind, in an effort to survive in a difficult world, always masked the pain we felt over time. It was why mothers could remember that childbirth hurt but couldn't remember the exact pain in a physiological mind trick to encourage multiple births by the same woman. It was a survival tactic that allowed human beings to suffer unspeakable trials and continue to function, at least on an elementary level. It was the author's position that psychoses occurred when the brain's mechanisms were thwarted by chemical imbalance or the sheer size of the trauma punched through the brain fog and overcame the coping mechanisms of the brain, enabling one to remember the actual pain in full detail.

"I like this time of day."

Evelyn looked around and found Caroline in the rocking chair. Her knees were pulled up to her chest, wrapped in the blanket Evelyn had brought for her bed.

"It's nice," Evelyn agreed sleepily. "If I had some coffee, it'd be perfect." Looking at her friend, she thought that the latter of the options in the article applied to Caroline. The sheer amount of trauma and the thoroughness of her abuse, both mental and physical, had broken through her brain fog and surfaced in an ugly, dangerous psychosis.

"Sorry," Caroline told her with a shrug.

"Don't sweat it. No biggie," Evelyn told her as she leaned against the door frame, scratching beneath her breasts absently as another yawn escaped her.

"Are you going back home?"

"Not right away. I really don't have any plans. Do you want me to?"

Caroline shook her head. "No."

"Well then, I guess I'm staying a while. You hungry?"

"I could eat."

"Let's see what we have?" Evelyn said as she started back into the house. She stopped and turned back to Caroline. "Would you be opposed to going into town for breakfast?"

"Oh, no," Caroline replied instantly, fear rising in her eyes as she sank further into the blanket.

"It's okay." Evelyn went to Caroline's side. "We will be in the car. It will be safe, I promise."

"Evie, I don't wanna."

"Do you trust me?"

"I suppose," Caroline answered, almost a whimper.

"Either you do, or you don't. I trust you," Evelyn said, being intentionally firm.

"It's just that…" Caroline trailed off as she turned away and to the edge of the porch. "I just don't want people to treat me so bad. Not today."

"I promise you, Caroline, nobody is going to notice you. People in cars don't pay attention to other people in cars."

Caroline's sigh told Evelyn she was making headway. "Look," she told her, "I promise that if anyone says anything, I will turn the car around and head right back here and won't bother you about it anymore."

"Ok, if you promise," Caroline agreed, still unsure.

"I do. Yay! Coffee!" Evelyn exclaimed, clapping. "I'll get dressed."

Caroline reached out and took Evelyn's hand as they rounded the bend in her driveway, bringing the highway into view. Allowing herself to be led like a child, she walked tentatively toward Evelyn's car. Beside but slightly behind Evelyn, she took in a deep breath and exhaled slowly.

"I don't understand. You've been in town a million times. Why are you so nervous?"

"I don't know. It feels different now."

"How so?" Evelyn asked.

"I don't know. It's just different."

"Oh," Evelyn said, nodding. "It's because I'm black isn't it?"

Caroline looked at her, confused.

Evelyn burst out laughing. "I'm just kidding."

Caroline continued to stare, still confused.

"Really? No? See, it's funny because you're, well you, and I said it was because I'm black."

Caroline shrugged, still confused.

"Never mind. Let's just go."

Evelyn felt Caroline's grip on her hand tighten as they drew closer to the road.

"It's going to be okay. I promise."

Caroline forced a smile, but said nothing, her eyes locked on the road in front of them.

Evelyn held Caroline's hand tightly as they emerged from the woods and walked to her car. Once inside, Caroline seemed to calm some. She sat in silence, staring out the window as Evelyn backed onto the road and steered her car toward town.

Evelyn said a prayer in her mind for an uneventful trip. This would be Caroline's first big step toward rejoining the world. If it went wrong, there was virtually no chance of getting her somewhere safe before she left to meet Aaron.

As Evelyn rolled her car toward the drive thru window, she patted Caroline on the leg. "So far so good," she told her. "See. People just going about their lives."

Caroline answered with a quick nod, clasping her hands in her lap. "My heart races."

"That's not always a bad thing."

"Well, I'll be. Evie Jackson," came the voice from inside the open window as a young man with greasy blonde hair leaned toward her holding her sack of food.

"Charles," Evelyn said, putting on a smile. "How are you?"

"I'm good," answered, lowering his head to look at Caroline. "Who's your friend?"

"Caroline," Evelyn told him with a nervous smile.

"Hi, Caroline," he said.

She nodded nervously and managed a quick wave of her hand before turning away and looking out the window.

"Ok, here you go, ladies." He handed Evelyn two large coffees and a medium soda. "Y'all gonna be hanging out anywhere later?" he asked.

Bending down, he looked at Caroline. "Evie can be a nerd sometimes, so you might have to drag her out. We could get a drink and meet better."

Surprised, Evelyn looked at Charles, then at Caroline. She was staring back at her with a look of bewilderment painted on her face. "We're not in town long, sorry."

"So, you two go to school together or what?" Charles asked, directed more to Caroline that Evelyn.

Evelyn was about to answer when the car behind them issued a polite beep of the horn. "Sorry, Charlie, gotta run," Evelyn told him, using the phrase that everyone in school had worn out on him. She pulled away from the window quickly.

"I guess you know him?" Caroline asked.

"We were in high school together. He was one of those 'gamer' kids. Always playing video games and stuff. He's kinda cheesy, but harmless," Evelyn informed her. "But he sure had his eye on you."

"No, he didn't. If he did, he probably recognized me," Caroline told her, wringing her hands nervously.

"Okay," Evelyn began, sensing her anxiety. "It's over. Let's just breathe and calm down. Nothing to worry about here."

"When people look at me, I don't like it. My skin feels like its crawling or something. It's like they can see things on me that I can't see."

"It's okay now, sweetie," Evelyn said, putting a hand on her shoulder.

"It's like they can see into my head and they know what happened and they blame me."

"That's not it at all, he probably just thought you were pretty."

"Please stop. A damned boy humping all over me is the last thing I want."

"I know. I'm sorry. I didn't mean anything like that." Evelyn handed Caroline the bag. "I was just saying he thought you were pretty, which you are." She tried to stroke her hair, but Caroline shrank away from her touch.

"Caroline, do you want to know what I see when I look at you?"

"Not really."

"I see a beautiful young woman who has been dealt a shitty hand in life. I see a woman who has endured unspeakable horror and neglect and is now afraid. Afraid to love because everyone you've loved has hurt you. I see an amazing human being who has survived all that and is still beautiful inside and out, who just needs someone to actually care."

"Inside or outside, I'm just," she paused while she stared out the window. "I'm just." She didn't finish her sentence but shook her head as she looked out the window.

"Okay, let's just not talk about that anymore if it bothers you. Let's eat."

Caroline frowned as she took one of the bacon biscuits out of the bag and unwrapped it. She didn't want boys to think she was pretty. She didn't want them to even notice her. It was no good. When men noticed her, it only ended one of two ways: they either were mean to her or they hurt her.

"Something wrong with the food?" Evelyn asked, sipping her coffee.

"No," Caroline answered around a mouthful of food. "It's that I don't want boys to look at me that way."

"I understand." Evelyn took another sip of coffee and let out a slight moan of pleasure. "I do, really. I just wanted you to realize that you are pretty. I could say it all day, but I guess validation from someone else, even if it was Charlie Hubble, just reinforced what I was telling you."

Caroline shrugged as she continued to devour the biscuit. "I guess."

"Okay, well that's done with. We've got food, I've got my coffee, now what? You want to go back?"

"I don't know," Caroline said, sipping her soda enthusiastically. "It's been a long time since I rode in a car. Can we do that?"

"Oh, sister, you are looking at the road trip queen," she said with a playful laugh. She rolled all the windows down in the car as she sped under a yellow traffic light with a triumphant "Woohoo!" Wind filled the car, ripping at their hair and lifted a napkin into the air between them. "Okay," she continued with a laugh as she rolled the windows back up again. "I was going for the effect, but it's still a little bit chilly for that."

Caroline looked at her from across the car with a thin smile. There was no denying she loved her new old friend, even if she did act a little strange sometimes.

It was late afternoon, with Evelyn's gas mostly depleted, before they decided to return. Evelyn was getting tired of driving and Caroline was beginning to fidget in her seat. Evelyn steered her car back onto Tuck Smith road with a sense of accomplishment. She and Caroline spent most of the day away from the house and nothing happened. Caroline seemed to have had a great day, laughing loudly several times. They'd eaten fast food for breakfast and lunch and the extra calories seemed to perk her up. She looked lighter; less strained and it wasn't just the new clothes and clean hair. She genuinely looked happy, and that made Evelyn happy. It was a huge step in the right direction.

"How was your daddy to you growing up? Did he ever, you know?" Caroline asked, watching the scenery pass by outside the car window.

"Lord no! No. Nothing even remotely like that. If anything, he was the opposite. He's a wonderful man, and to be honest, I feel lucky to have had him as my dad."

"You are lucky then," Caroline said. "How was your mom?"

"She's a great mom. Strict when I needed it, loving when I needed it too. Really, I had an ideal childhood. We all love each other very much."
"Sounds great."

"It is. I'm lucky is all. Nothing I did to get them."

"Lucky draw I guess," Caroline said with a sigh.

"But lots of people overcome traumatic childhoods, Caroline. There's therapy and medicines and support groups. Lots of stuff for people like…" Evelyn stopped herself from saying, "people like you", and instead said, "People who have gone through a crappy childhood."

"For crazy people?" Caroline asked.

"They do, but you're not crazy, Caroline. Look, I can't even pretend to scratch the surface of knowing what you've gone through, but here you are. You survived. You outlasted that bastard. You watched him die. The only way he can hurt you is in here," Evelyn tapped the side of her head. "And only if you let him. You're stronger than he ever was."

"Stop!" Caroline exclaimed suddenly as the car topped the last hill before her driveway.

"What? I was just…"

"Stop!" she demanded again. This time Evelyn followed her gaze to the old pale blue pickup truck backed into the place where she'd been parking her car.

She slowed the car, her eyes franticly scanning the roadside, hoping it wasn't the same truck she'd seen earlier. There was no sign of anyone. So much for hoping it was just someone picking up aluminum cans alongside the road.

"What the hell?" she asked as she drew closer. The dents and scratches along the sides of the truck bed told her that praying for it to be someone different was useless. It was the same truck, and the same two who had slowed to stare at her that day.

A shiver went up her spine as she remembered the lascivious grin on the man's face. Slowing more as she approached, she edged the passenger side tires off the blacktop and onto the shoulder before coming to a bumpy stop far enough away from the truck to afford them an escape. Staring at the empty truck, a sickening feeling tied her stomach in a knot. She'd led them straight to Caroline's door. Before she'd started parking there, it would have been near impossible to recognize the old driveway. And even if you did, it looked abandoned. There would have never been a reason to give it a second thought. But they'd seen her and her parking spot and now they had a reason to be curious and her gut told her it wasn't a good.

"What do we do?" Caroline asked, close to panic.

"Okay, let's just calm down," Evelyn said, speaking to herself as much as Caroline. "We don't know what they want."

"Who is it?" Caroline asked, pleadingly.

"I don't know, but I saw them pass by the other day. They were staring. I didn't think much about it then."

"Oh my God! That's why they're here. They came to get us!"

"Nobody's getting us as long as I got something to say about it. Look at me!" She grabbed Caroline's arm. "Look at me! We can handle this."

"We gotta hide. Get outta here. Run hide!"

"No!" Evelyn snapped. "They will not scare us away. Today you learn to fight back."

"No, no. Please," she begged. "I can't. I can't do it!"

"Yes, you can."

"No, I can't. I'm not you! Don't you understand that? I'm not you!" Caroline reached for the door handle, but it was locked. "Let me out. I gotta hide!" She began slapping her palm against the window rapidly, her eyes full of tears.

"Okay, okay. We'll go." Evelyn finally said. There was no other choice. Caroline was on the verge of a full-fledged meltdown. She released the brake and floored the accelerator. Gravel flew into the grass as the car leaped forward, gained purchase on the pavement and sped away.

"We're good now," Evelyn said as they put distance between themselves and the truck. "We're okay now. Try to calm down." She spared a glance at Caroline and found her rocking gently in the passenger seat, sobbing.

"Oh, sweetie, I'm so sorry," she said. "This is my fault. I'm so sorry." Shaking her head as she sped toward town, Evelyn felt her anger begin to boil in her chest. Dammit! She cursed in her mind. Those assholes had undone all the progress shed made today. Caroline was thrown into a tailspin just by their presence and she knew it was going to be a long night.

"No!" she said and suddenly slowed, drawing a long, angry horn blast from the car behind them as they swerved into the other lane and passed her.

"What are you doing?" Caroline asked, fear dripping from her voice.

"I'll tell you what I'm doing," Evelyn nosed the car off the road. After checking for traffic, she turned the car around on the highway. "We're going back and standing our ground."

"No, no. We can't. Please," she begged.

"Caroline, when we were kids you stood up to a playground full of kids for a skinny little girl named Evelyn. Well, that little girl has grown up and it's time to return the favor. That courage is in you, still. I know it is."

"No. I just want to hide. Leave me alone." She pulled frantically at the door handle.

Her eyes set in a defiant stare, her jaw clenched angrily, she pressed the accelerator and sped back toward Caroline's house. The anger swelling in her chest was for herself as well as Caroline. Those men had no reason to be there but to terrorize what they probably thought would be two helpless women. They were bullies who probably did crap like this to people like Caroline their whole miserable life.

"If you don't stand up to these guys, they will come back and keep coming back. People like that are animals, Caroline."

Caroline didn't hear. In her mind, the voices were roaring again. One hand was pulling on the door handle while the other slapped the window with an open palm in a desperate attempt to escape.

"You stay here," Evelyn said as she screeched to a halt, half on, half off the road. She grabbed Caroline by the shoulders and shook her to stop her struggling. Caroline immediately went docile and covered her face with her hands to shield herself from the blow she assumed would come next.

"Look at me!" Evelyn pulled Caroline's hands away from her face and held them firmly. "You are safe. No one is going to ever hurt you again."

Caroline stared at her with distant, vacant eyes, mumbling incoherently.

"I promise you, Caroline. It's over. That time is over."

Putting on her emergency flashers, Evelyn spared another glance at Caroline then got out of the car. Going to the trunk she retrieved the softball bat she'd used in high school and slammed the lid angrily.

Stomping up to the truck she raised it and smashed out the passenger side window. It felt good to strike back. Glancing back at her own car, she hoped Caroline was watching. She needed to see this. She needed to know that it was okay to fight back.

Walking to the front of the truck, she smashed everything glass, and gave the grill a few swings for good measure. Continuing her round, she broke the driver's side window and the back glass out of the truck before finally lowering the bat with a satisfied smile. It was a strong message, but she wanted them to know that she meant business.

Opening the driver's side door, she was greeted with a sickening combination of years of body odor, stale beer, and cigarette ashes. She grimaced, her stomach turning over. The inside of the truck was filthy; covered in old beer cans, food wrappers, and cigarette butts. It wreaked of sickness and filth.

Undaunted by the putrid odor, she leaned inside with the bat and smashed the instrument panel and everything in the dash that she could destroy with the short, compact swings that the close quarters afforded her. After doing enough damage, she exited the truck. Sucking in deep breaths of air, she realized that she'd been holding her breath.

Looking at her handywork, she nodded in approval, a smile sliding across her lips. She had one more message to send. Climbing onto the hood of the truck she looked back at Caroline as she took a tube of lipstick out of her pocket. Kneeling before the only unbroken glass she'd left on the truck, she rolled out the red lipstick and scrawled a message for the men before hoping down and picked up her bat.

From the safe confines of Evelyn's car, Caroline had regained enough of her composure to stare at her friend in disbelief. The sight of her friend standing on the hood of the truck was the must triumphant thing she'd ever seen.

"Are we leaving now?" she asked when Evelyn slid into the car, a nervous smile pulling at the corners of her thin lips.

"NOW, we can go," Evelyn told her with a laugh as she pulled onto the road. Driving past the battered truck, her smile widened as she looked at the "DON'T EVER COME BACK ASSHOLE!!!" scrawled across the filthy windshield in her "get his attention" red lipstick.

"Today, class, we learned what happens when you mess with a black woman who plays softball," she laughed. Beside her in the car as she sped down the old two-lane road, Caroline smiled. It wasn't a huge, happy grin, but a sly little smile that told Evelyn she was glad she'd done what she did.

Evelyn's thumb pressed the button to send the text, "I think they got the message," to Aaron and looked at her friend, asleep in the passenger seat. After filling up, she had driven a hundred miles north on the interstate before Caroline had calmed down enough to talk, and another hundred miles back south before they could laugh about the situation.

Eventually, she'd grown too tired to drive and pulled into a rest area for a bathroom break and to get some rest herself.

Caroline told her she thought she'd gone crazy, and Evelyn guessed she had, if only temporarily. She couldn't decide if she wanted revenge for women everywhere who suffered at the hands of men like the one who had leered hungrily at her or if it was more personal; if she wanted to prove to Caroline that a woman could fight back. It was probably both but might have also simply been revenge on the dirty look the man had given her, reducing her to a piece of meat he wanted to have sex with.

She'd absorbed "looks" like that from people her whole life. Hungry, lustful looks from men of all ages, both black and white, and even a few women; their eyes groping at her body. She'd gotten "looks" from men and women, both black and white, that said she was "out of her place" or "bougie" or "uppity" or a "sellout" all her life. She was a woman. A woman who had never flaunted her beauty, her intelligence, her strength, or her blackness before anyone, yet those are the things everyone seemed to take issue with. She just wanted to be Evelyn Jackson, but the world always wanted to add a tag to her; a description.

"If they didn't, then they're crazy."

Evelyn smiled at Aaron's response. They'd been texting while Caroline slept for a while, as she brought him up to speed on their day. It was an eventful one, to say the least, and she was tired.

"What now, slugger?" Aaron asked.

"IDK. She probably won't go anywhere else but home."

"Do U think it's safe?" he asked.

"IDK, but it's the closest."

"I'm worried, Eve. Should I come?"

Evelyn smiled. "I don't think so. Caroline vs men and all."

"Yeah, but still?"

"I will be ok."

There was a long delay. "Please don't let yourself get hurt."

"Promise." Evelyn smiled. Aaron's concern was comforting.

"Eve. Please be careful."

"I will." Evelyn sighed as she looked around the rest area, dreading either of the two prospects that lay before her. They could either sleep here or they could return to Caroline's house. Neither sounded very conducive to getting much sleep.

She laid her head back against the seat and closed her eyes. Her body made the decision for her as it immediately began pulling her towards sleep. She felt her phone vibrate as Aaron asked if she was falling asleep but was too far gone to answer. By the time it vibrated again, the text "Guesso. GN Eve," appeared. She'd fallen into an exhausted sleep.

Evelyn looked in the mirror and crinkled her nose at her reflection as she untied the braids from the back of her head. After smoothing each one between her palms as best she could, she retied the ends together behind her head and smoothed the top to flatten some of the frizz.

A toilet flushed behind her and Caroline walked out. Evelyn watched her reflection as she moved to the bathroom door and stood, waiting. She washed her hands and pulled several paper towels from the dispenser on the wall.

"You okay?" she asked Caroline as she dried her hands.

Caroline nodded, but said nothing, watching as Evelyn opened the door with the paper towels, blocked it with her foot, and tossed the towels in the trash.

"You ready?" Evelyn asked. Caroline walked out the door without saying a word.

Outside, in the fresh air of late spring, they walked down the long sidewalk of the rest area towards Evelyn's car, where they had spent the night.

"You gotta talk to me, Caroline."

"I'm confused."

"About what?"

Caroline shrugged. "I don't know. Just confused is all."

"That's not much help."

"Sorry," Caroline replied quietly, her eyes cast downward.

"Don't be sorry." Evelyn stopped and reached out for Caroline's arm. "You don't have anything to be sorry for." Caroline turned and started walking again without saying a word.

Catching up Evelyn looked at her friend and sighed. "I'm the one who should be sorry. I pushed too hard. I, I don't know."

"You don't be sorry."

"Fine then, nobody be sorry." Evelyn wasn't in the best of moods after an uncomfortable night sleep. The two women walked the rest of the way to the car in silence.

"So, tell me," Evelyn began again as she got into her car, strapping on her seat belt. "What is bothering you?"

"Really?" Caroline asked with a smirk. "Everything is bothering me. I'm crazy, you remember?"

"Stop it. You're not crazy. Sure, there are some things we could work on, but you are not crazy. If anything, you're sick."

"And sick people go to the hospital, right?"

"Look, I don't know. To be honest, I don't know what the hell I've been doing all this time. I'm just flying by the seat of my pants, hoping I don't screw something up so bad it can't be fixed."

Caroline looked at her friend and surrendered a slight smile. "I'm glad you did or are. Whatever, you know what I mean."

"I do," Evelyn said with a smile of her own. "I'm just worried about you. I don't want to leave you unless I know you'll be okay."

"Leave?"

Evelyn closed her eyes, angry at herself for bringing it up this way, especially so soon after the incident yesterday. "You know that I will have to go back to school? Right?"

Caroline's eyes fell to her hands as she started picking at the hem of her tee shirt nervously. "I guess I knew. I figured; I mean."

"But not today," Evelyn said, patting her leg.

"Okay," Caroline responded, picking lint off the front of her shirt.

"Let's get some coffee, some breakfast, and go see what those assholes did to your place."

"Okay," Caroline responded, still picking at her shirt.

"About what I expected," Evelyn said, trying her best to sound nonchalant, as she and Caroline stood just inside the open doorway and surveyed the damage. The beds had been tossed about and their clothes lay strewn across the room. Judging from the open cabinet doors, the men had searched the house looking for something of value. "After they didn't find us," her mind told her.

"Just a little clean up." Evelyn walked into the room, picking up the dirty clothes she'd left folded on the now overturned chair by the hearth. Up righting the kitchen chair, she piled her jeans, shirt, and socks in the seat, instantly noticing that her panties were missing. A sickening shutter ran through to her as she thought about the men touching her under pants. "No biggie," she added, hoping to reassure herself as much as Caroline.

She swept the room with her eyes and quickly found the white cotton panties tossed into the corner. Going to them she touched them cautiously with her foot. Bile rose in her throat as she felt the stiffness of the cotton. It didn't take a genius to know what someone had used them for. Putting the back of her hand to her mouth she turned away and coughed, gagging the remnants of her coffee back down into her stomach.

Picking up the broom, she swept the panties out of the room, through the kitchen and into the "stinky room". She slammed the door quickly, and turning, forced a smile for Caroline's sake. "Guys like that are animals. Sick bastards. They're not all like that."

Caroline raised an eyebrow slightly as she stared at Evelyn disbelievingly, but said nothing. Instead, she quietly began to gather the clothes she'd worn yesterday and pile them with Evelyn's, once again picking up the damage wrought on her life by yet another mean, spiteful man.

Her heart churning with a mixture of anger and frustration as well as sadness and pity, Evelyn closed her eyes and said a prayer for them both. One step forward, two steps back, she thought. Every time. Every damned time.

Determined in the face of yet another setback, Evelyn righted her own air mattress, thankful that it hadn't been punctured, and grabbed up the sheets to dress it. Her hand landed on the wet fabric and recoiled instantly. Waving her hand before her nose, the unmistakable smell of urine struck her nose as she evicted the sheets from her hand.

"They pissed on the bed?" she growled, standing. "They had to piss on the fucking bed. Really? Jacking off in my fucking panties wasn't enough? They had to piss on my bed too?"

Caroline watched as Evelyn kicked and stomped the bed covers and the mattress, venting her anger at the men onto them. She watched for the whole tirade, unflinching as Evelyn raged against the injustice, until she'd finally released enough anger to calm to a mild anger. The mattress now punctured and deflated lay in a heap against the wall and the bed covers were dirty and marked with the footprint of her shoes. Her eyes followed Evelyn as she stomped out the front door.

Caroline went about picking up the living room, gathering the clothes and putting things in place. She was scared. The men who'd done this weren't strangers to her. They'd often come through the woods behind her house and looked for her. Most times she was able to elude them. Sometimes not. They sat around their shack and cooked up something in a strange contraption then smoked it until they simply fell out. If they'd been smoking, they were weak and clumsy, easy to get away from. If they hadn't been, they were mean and angry. It didn't look like they'd been smoking today.

Finally, after giving Evie time to cool down, Caroline walked to the open door and leaned against the jamb. Evelyn was sitting in the chair, rocking back and forth quickly in short, angry movements.

"Never seen nobody rock mad before," she finally said.

"What?" Evelyn stopped rocking and looked at her, then looked down at herself. Realizing that was exactly what she'd been doing, she shook her head. "Well, I'm mad as hell and this is a rocking chair," she added, a smile coming to her lips. "It was bound to happen."

"You was about to take off across the yard, I think," Caroline told her with a laugh.

Laughing herself, Evelyn realized how comically she must have looked. She shook her head and let out a frustrated sigh. Becoming part of Caroline's world was harder than she thought it would be. It was just so foreign to her, so surreal.

In her "normal" life it was inconceivable that someone would do this to her. People like these men kept their distance. She was beyond their reach for the most part, but Caroline wasn't. Never in her life had she felt such degradation. What audacity they showed, using her panties for a happy ending. HER panties.

Approaching Evelyn, Caroline stood in front of her and pulled her close, pressing Evelyn's face to her chest. "It's okay," she said. "You're not crazy, you just have issues." Laughing loudly together, the two women held their embrace for a long time.

Evelyn appreciated the hug. She'd just gotten a taste of treatment that Caroline would probably consider insignificant and it troubled her deeply. How could anyone withstand the abuse and neglect for so many years? There was no doubt that Caroline was much stronger than her.

"What the hell is wrong with people?" Evelyn asked.

Caroline stroked Evelyn's hair, "I wish I knew."

TWELVE

Evelyn swam slowly toward consciousness as a smooth hand gently caressed her face. She smiled and let out a soft moan, nuzzling the hand against her face, partially dreaming, partially hoping it was Aaron and the last week had been a dream. Suddenly her peaceful sleep was interrupted by a firm, but gently slap.

"Wake up, sleepy head." Martha Jackson looked down at her daughter and shook her head.

Evelyn opened her eyes and, blinking away sleep, saw her mother's smiling face hovering inches from hers. "Really?" she asked, pulling back.

"You ain't got time to sleep all day. Get up."

"What's the matter with you?" Evelyn asked, trying to roll over on her parents' couch. She'd left Caroline shortly after lunch, which consisted a power bar and bottle of water on the front porch of the old house and had been making call after call since. She called every halfway house, group home, and facility that appeared in the electronic phone book in her phone within a fifty-mile radius. Finding a place for an undiagnosed, unmedicated woman suffering from schizophrenic conditions, who survived sexual abuse, who also has a severe distrust of men, and who happens to be destitute was proving harder than she thought. Every one of the places had disqualifying conditions: male staff, they required strict medical adherence, they only took insured patients, or they just flat out said "No".

"What's the deal with your friend?" Martha asked.

"I don't know. We've made progress, we've had setbacks, and we've made progress again. I've introduced her to fast food and sodas."

"Well, a fine doctor you'd make. I don't think I ever heard of the burger and fries treatment," Martha told her as she disappeared into the kitchen. After a moment, she reappeared with a glass of tea. She sat by Evelyn and took a long sip. "Getting hotter outside. In a month, it'll be murder."

"Mama, I don't know what to do. Here it is Monday afternoon, and I'm no closer to securing a place for Caroline than I was last week."
"Well, sitting here and fretting ain't gonna get nothing done. Have you talked to anybody?"

"I have," Evelyn held up her phone. "I called everywhere. Talked to everybody. They're either not right for her or she'd never go in the first place. A couple places just flat out said no. That's what I was doing. I guess I dozed off."

Martha smiled and laid her hand against her daughter's cheek again. "Baby, I been seeing you go through hell since you got here. First all that with Trae then the baby, and that would have been enough to wear anybody down. Then you went and got yourself all mixed up with this girl and her problems. It's no small wonder you're so tired. You gotta give yourself a break."

"My problems are nothing compared to hers, Mama. I told you. I just thought I could help her, but to be honest, I don't know if I've helped her or made it worse." Evelyn rubbed her temples to sooth the headache forming between them. She couldn't deny the mental and physical fatigue was wearing on her. She felt like she was fighting battles on every front of her life: dealing with the whole issue of her affair and the baby, flip-flopping on whether she should tell Aaron or not, telling her parents, then there was Caroline and the plethora of problems she brought with her. What she wanted to do was get into her car and drive away from all of it; to go to Aaron and pretend none of this ever

224

happened. She wanted to make love to him and lay beside him and forget about everything but being together.

Martha sighed and looked at her only child. "I just hate to see you all tore up. You gotta promise me to come back when all this is over and we can have a good visit, like we used to."

"I promise, Mama." Evelyn leaned against her mother and relaxed into her embrace.

"It's little wonder you tired. Sleeping in that old house, basically living like an animal. Its plum crazy."

"Mama," Evelyn pleaded.

"I was just saying. We worry about you. Your poor father hasn't slept a good night since you been home. We just want to know you're safe and happy, like you used to be."

"I know, mama. I'm sorry. I know this whole trip has been one big problem after another for y'all."

"Oh, honey, you're our daughter. You been worrying the hell out of us since the day you were born. That's what kids do to they folks, even if they're great kids like you."

"Thanks, I guess," Evelyn said with a short laugh.

"Anyhow, maybe I did something to help you out, maybe I didn't."

Evelyn sat up suddenly. Her first thought that her mother had called the hospital, or the police, or both on Caroline and had her committed for a psych eval. "What'd you do?"

"Ease yourself, child. Me and your daddy talked about something."

"Mama, it's nice, but there's no way Caroline would live here."

"What? Hell naw! You must be the crazy one if you think we gone move a stranger up in here, especially not one that'd be apt to freak out in the middle of the night." She shook her head, cutting her eyes to her daughter in disbelief. "She'd be all creeping around the house in the dark like a thief in the night."

"Good grief, mama. She' not Charles Manson."

"But she's got problems that'd keep us up at night. I tell you that."

"Okay, mama, what then?" She had thought about the prospect of moving Caroline into her old room but was holding it as a last resort. Now, given her mother's reaction, even that was out of the question. One more card off the table.

"There's this place. It's about fifty miles from here. In the middle of nowhere. These folks got a hundred acres of land and they got this place built right in the middle of nowhere. It's a place for women to go and "heal", is what the little pamphlet said."

"I've called everybody in the book, mama."

"They ain't in the book, smarty pants. People only know about them by reference I suppose. They said we could come and look at the place if we wanted."

"What? Really? What kind of place is it? Is it a secure facility? A psychiatric hospital?"

Martha stood, wincing at the pain in her knees. "I don't know, baby. Get yourself ready. We got time to go look at it. I figured you'd know what questions to ask better than me."

Evelyn smiled as she sprung from the couch. This place was her last chance. If she couldn't get Caroline into this place she'd be left with a very difficult decision, and in her heart, she already knew the answer.

"Your destination is on the right," chimed Evelyn's GPS. Following the directions, she turned off the road and stopped at a large metal gate. The forty-minute drive had been a pleasant one. With mother and daughter's spirits soaring, they'd talked the whole way and had covered every topic from "old timey" soul food to dating a white man, a topic Martha found more than a little uncomfortable. It was like the old days, when she had driven her mother to the UNCA campus for their first visit. Optimism was high, despite the cauldron of unknowns simmering in their stomachs.

"It's looks ominous," Evelyn said, leaning against the steering wheel and looking up at the sign above the large, ornate grate. "One Safe Place Women's Retreat," she said, reading the sign. "Sounds kinda odd to call a place a retreat that's locked behind such a big ole' gate."

"You think rich folks don't have a gate in front of their neighborhoods. They seem pretty happy. It's probably just to keep out the riff raff, like us," Martha replied with a curt laugh.

"Touché. But now what do we do?" Evelyn asked.

"I don't know. I didn't know they'd be a gate."

"I didn't know they'd be a gate," Evelyn repeated, playfully mocking her mother.

Ignoring her daughter, Martha pointed to a small sign affixed to one of the brick columns that bordered and supported the gate. "Says to push the button. Go push it."

"You go push it. It's on your side. I gotta drive through when it opens."

"Go push the damned button. My knees hurt."

"Fine," Evelyn relented, getting out of the car. "Your knees always hurting when you don't wanna do something," she mumbled as she rounded the hood of the car.

Rolling down the passenger side window, Martha stuck her head out. "What was that? I didn't hear you."

"I said I forgot about your knees, mama," Evelyn lied and pushed the button as instructed by the handmade sign, written in blue ink and covered with wide strips of tape to protect it from the elements.

"Can I help you?" squawked the box.

"Uh, yes. We called earlier. Martha and Evelyn Jackson."

"Okay. Yes. Just pull through the gate when it opens and park in the area to your left. Someone will be with you shortly."

"They're coming," she told her mother as she dropped back into her seat. "I hope they're not hippies."

"What does it matter to you? It's your friend that's gotta live here. Gotta be better than where she is now. If she likes it, I say good."

"I know. I was just thinking out loud."

It only took a few minutes for the golf cart to arrive. It paused temporarily for the driver to press a code into a keypad atop a short pole inside the gate, then proceeded to the small, unpaved parking lot and waited.

By the time the gate opened, and Evelyn pulled into a spot next to the cart, the two women riding in it had gotten out and awaited them near the back of her car. The driver, a short, stocky brunette wearing a pair of khaki shorts and a pastel blue tee shirt emblazoned with the words, "YOU'RE SAFE NOW" across her ample bosom was smiling happily. The other woman, a tall, very thin blonde with collar-length hair and dressed just like the driver wore a more cautious look.

"Hi there," they both greeted the women as they got out of the car. "Nice to meet you. I'm Joan. This is Brandy. So glad to meet you two lovely ladies."

Martha introduced them both and everyone exchanged pleasantries. "I guess you two didn't drive all the way out here just to meet us, so let us show you both the place." The Blonde's voice was pleasant, yet measured, as if she'd done this spiel many times before. "We will be touring the grounds in the trusty old golf cart," she added, motioning for them to take a seat. "We call her Bertha."

"And away we go," Evelyn said and followed Martha into the back seat.

Allowing Brandy, the blonde, to drive Joan turned in her seat as they backed out of the lot. "I think you'll find our place here to be just perfect for your friend."

"I hope so. She's had a pretty tough go of it lately," Evelyn thought for a second and added, "Her whole life really."

"Poor thing," Joan said, shaking her head. "You'll find that all the women here have had traumatic lives. We are well prepared for even the worst cases."

"Well, you'll get a great girl who's had a pretty bad time."

"We have an onsite licensed medical doctor, but we rarely have to dispense any conventional medicines here. We prefer a more holistic approach. Quite a few of the ladies do take a low dose anxiety medicine for a while when they first get here, though. Most find it beneficial while they acclimate. We do what's best for the individual and let them be the guide to their own wellness."

"What kind of cases do you currently have here?" Evelyn asked, skeptical.

"We don't have 'cases' or 'patients' here, Miss," Brandy interjected. "We have people here who are suffering, and we do whatever it takes to help them feel better."

Rebuffed, Evelyn leaned back in her seat, sparing a glance at her mother. Martha put a hand on her daughters' leg and gave her a few quick pats. It was her "Shut up and listen" pat that she used in church when Evelyn was a fidgety youngster. As she'd expected, her daughter's protective side was doubtful, but she needed to like this place. It might be Caroline's last chance.

Evelyn settled into her seat, resigned to doing just that. She watched the scenery pass as they rode down the long, winding, tree-lined path toward what she hoped would soon become Caroline's new home.

Despite her initial hesitation, Evelyn tried to tour the place with an open mind. The grounds and the facility in general were impressive, nothing like the gray Orwellian prison she'd imagined. On paper, it looked perfect. But they didn't live on paper. She knew it would be hard to get Caroline to leave the only home she'd ever known, albeit one with a lot of bad memories. She knew from experience that old habits were hard to kick.

"As women," Joan said, holding onto the rail as they rounded another corner, "Our roles change many times in our lives. From daughter, to girlfriend, to wife, to mother, and grandmother and so on. We believe it's in these changes and the expectations that come with them that women sometimes lose themselves. Those fundamental shifts in our identities leave tiny cracks through which some of us can slip. This place was built for those women who slip through the cracks."

Evelyn nodded in agreement. Caroline surely fit that bill. What was it that Father Newell had said? Bureaucracy was the mother of inefficiency. "How long to women generally stay here?" she asked.

Joan shrugged. "It depends on what she needs. Some stay a few months, some a few years, and some just live here. It becomes a safe place for them, and they don't want to leave."

"Thus, the name of the place, huh?" Evelyn asked.

Brandy spared her a quick look. "The world can suck sometimes. A lot of times, really. No matter who you are or what you do, everyone needs a place to feel safe; a place to heal. We all need a place to recharge. When a woman can't find a place like that out there, we provide one for them here."

"We prefer to think of this place as a safe port in the storm of life. Sort of a harbor for the poor souls who have lost their way."

Evelyn looked at her mother, an eyebrow cocked quizzically.

"Is something wrong?" Joan asked, noticing the looks on the women's faces.

"Oh no," Martha told her. "It's just that we're from a little town called Souls Harbor."

"Isn't that interesting?" Joan said with a wide smile. "It's perfect."

"So?" Evelyn asked, sitting on the front steps of Caroline's house, flashlight held aloft as her friend perused the booklet that she'd brought back with her. "What do you think?"

"I don't know," Caroline told her nervously.

"It's a nice place," Evelyn began to gently nudge her in the direction of choice. "You'd have a cabin with two other women who've had similar experiences as you."

"What does this mean?" Caroline asked, pointing to a word on the pamphlet.

"Self- sufficient? That basically you all take care of yourselves as much as possible. Gardening and working together on repairs. But also, you'd be on your own as much as you wanted. There's no set schedule or anything like a hospital."

"What about this?" Caroline pointed to another word.

"Convalesce?" Evelyn asked, leaning closer. "It means to heal. To get better."

"That sounds nice." Caroline smiled as she stared out into the darkness.

"It's your choice, sweetie." Evelyn lowered the light to the steps and wrapped an arm around Caroline's shoulders. "But it's got a lot more comforts that this old place."

"I know. It's just that..." She trailed off with a sigh as a tear rolled down her cheek.

"Oh sweetie, I know it's hard for you." Evelyn hugged her tightly. Leaving her parents' house and going off to college was the hardest thing she'd ever done. She now realized her parents' house had been her "safe place". She could feel it when she walked in the door. It had always been the place she'd come for safety and security, for love and compassion. Home was what it was, whether you lived in a mansion or a shack.

"Ultimately it's your decision. It's your life, Caroline, and you have to take charge of it."

"I don't know what to do," she admitted. "I never even considered leaving, but I don't know why."

"It's okay to be scared, Caroline. It's normal. It's a scary thing to move away from the only thing you've ever known. Sometimes though, you don't realize how bad things are because that's the way they've always been. But sweetie, this place is bad for you. I can feel the badness that lives here, and I know you can too, probably a thousand times more than me."

"I remember once, when we were in school, after I first met you, one of my daddy's friends came over and told him about me being friends with a black girl, only he used some other words. Mama was gone somewhere. It was on a Saturday morning and this guy comes over and tells daddy standing right over there." She motioned into the darkness with her hand. "So, daddy calls me outside and asks me about it. Told me not to lie. I told him it was true. He made me pull my dress off right there in the broad day light, in front of this guy. As I was standing there naked, I saw them look at each other. It was a look I'd never seen before. I can't really explain it, but it looked mean and twisted. Daddy grabbed me by the hair of the head and beat me with his belt. He didn't beat me hard, but hard enough, and I remember looking at the man. I don't even know who it was, but he had this grin on his face. It was like he was enjoying the whole thing; like he liked seeing me like that, naked and ashamed and getting beat.

I remember looking at the man. His lips were dry and cracked and he hadn't shaved his whickers off. While I was looking at him, he kinda licked his lips and we was smiling. The front of his pants was sticking out. I remember thinking how weird that was. I didn't know why, but now I do.

"After a while my daddy let me go and told me to get cleaned up and get dressed. When Mama came home, I told her about it. Her and daddy had a big fight. Daddy hit her some that night, but I heard them in the bed later. It sounded like he was hurting her somehow. I wanted to run in and save her. I wanted to DO something, but I didn't. I was afraid of my daddy, I think after that night, she was too." She sighed and spat into the darkness. "I think that was the first day of my life I was scared, I mean really scared, and I guess I've been scared ever since."

"My God, baby. Bless your heart." Evelyn hugged Caroline as she sat, staring into the darkness. "I'm so sorry."

"That's what's out there, Evie. Bad people. Mean people. People that want to feed off my shame; off my body; off my soul. They's been so many people feedin' off me that they ain't much left."

Evelyn swallowed hard. "There's enough of you to love," she said, stroking her hair. "There are also people out there who will love you, who will help you. The right people can help you get back some of what's been taken away from you."

Caroline shook her head. "Maybe for a little while, I guess."

Evelyn recoiled slightly, the guilt she felt in the pit of her stomach bubbling up. She was as guilty as anyone else of leaving Caroline, maybe more so because she had gained her trust; she had broken through the walls that she had built, and Evelyn knew she'd leave too.

"Don't be mad," Caroline continued as she put a hand on Evelyn's thigh. "I don't blame you. Everybody leaves. My own Mama left. That's what she was doin' on her birthday when she died. She was leaving us; leaving me. She knew how mean daddy was, but she left, and she didn't take me. She hauled ass up that driveway without even turning the car lights on. Guess she didn't want daddy to know. I was standing right there by that porch rail watching her tear outta here. They said she pulled right out in front of another car without her lights on and the car couldn't stop. She died right there on the highway."

234

Evelyn wiped away her own tears and put a hand on top of Caroline's. Not knowing what to say, she sat quietly and thought about the priest's account of that night; about the fire and the screaming. Sighing heavily, she gripped Caroline's hand.

"I always thought my mama was beautiful, but she left me with a mean man who didn't mind his friend seeing me get belt whipped naked. She left me with a man who did stuff in bed to her that hurt her. She knew that and she still left me with him." Caroline sighed and blinked away her tears. "She loved me, I know she did, but she left me anyway."

"I'm so sorry you had to go through that, Caroline. My heart just aches for you. I wish I could take it all away, I really do, but I can't." Evelyn raised Caroline's hand to her lips and kissed the back of it, holding it to her cheek. "I wish I could make it better somehow."

Pulling her hand free, Caroline leaned forward, propping her elbows on her knees and held her head between her hands. She shook her head slightly as she stared down at her feet.

"My daddy made me cook and clean. He made me take Mama's place in the kitchen and in his bed, I guess. He beat me and he fucked me, but he never left me."

"Oh baby, you can't make excuses for that man," Evelyn snapped.

"Excuses? No." Caroline told her. "It's just what happened. Sometimes he bought me pretty dresses, and every now and then, he'd take me out to a fancy restaurant. We even saw a movie once in a theatre for my birthday."

"Caroline, stop it. You were a child. You can't blame yourself."

"I was maybe ten or eleven, we sat in the back, way over to the edge. He put his hand up my skirt and fiddled with me, but I didn't care. I let

235

him do it while I ate popcorn and watched a cartoon movie about toys that are alive. I like the cowboy. He was funny."

Evelyn sprang up and looked at Caroline. "You stop it!" she snapped angrily. "You were a kid! Ten freaking years old and he was abusing you. You didn't have to fight him for it to be wrong! He was a sick, perverted son of a bitch! Don't you understand that. It wasn't your fault! You were just a kid."

Caroline shrugged. "I guess so."

"There is no guessing to it. He raped you, he beat you. He was a freaking monster and I can't even begin to imagine what that does to a kid's head, but you can't think any of it was okay, or that any of it was your fault. That's just... "Evelyn caught herself before she said "crazy".

"Crazy?" Caroline asked, finishing her sentence for her. "I'm crazy, don't you remember?"

"You're not crazy." Evelyn sat back down with a sigh.

"I'm just sick?" Caroline asked. "I have 'issues'?"

"I don't know." Evelyn threw her hands into the air and let them fall to her lap as she sat back down beside Caroline. "I don't know anything anymore. I'm tired, I'm frustrated, I'm hungry. I need a bath. I'm worried about you. I'm afraid for you." She shook her head and rubbed her eyes with her fists like a child. "I care about you, Caroline. I want to help you. I want you to be safe, and better, and happy."

Caroline got up and knelt in front of Evelyn, taking her face in her hands. "You make me happy. Why don't we just stay here? I could make you happy. I know I could." She bent forward and kissed Evelyn on the lips tenderly.

Paralyzed by shock for a moment, Evelyn felt Caroline's lips press softly against hers as her hand slid around the back of her neck, beneath her hair in a gentle grasp.

"No. No!" she exclaimed, scurrying backwards on the porch. "What the hell?" she finished as her back struck the wall of the house.

"Isn't that what you wanted?" Caroline asked.

In the low light cast by the flashlight laying on the porch, Evelyn could see a glossy, crazed look in Caroline's eyes, and it scared the hell out of her. Her lips were stretched into a strange, maniacal smile as she slowly mounted the steps.

"No, that's not what I wanted!" Evelyn exclaimed. "Not at all!"

"Oh, come now, Evie," Caroline said as she mounted another step. "You know you did. Everybody wants to fuck me. That's what I do, you know. My daddy did, his buddy did, a few guys in town did, those two guys in the truck did." She grabbed her crotch angrily. "It's this stinking cunt that causes all the problems. All they want to do it fiddle with it. That's what you want too, ain't it?"

"Caroline, stop it!" Evelyn demanded as she struggled to her feet. "Stop it right now!"

"It's okay, baby. Don't be scared." Caroline stepped onto the porch. "I'll treat you very good. I'll make sure you're happy here. You can do anything you like to me. What do you want to do to me?"

Evelyn held out a hand to stop her as Caroline drew closer. "Stop it!"

Caroline's smile broadened as she took Evelyn's hand and pressed it to her breast. "Is that what you want, daddy? Do you like touching me?"

"Caroline!" Evelyn screamed, feeling her friend's breast pressed harder against her hand.

"I'll let you fiddle with me if you let me fiddle with you," Caroline's free hand reached down, moving towards Evelyn's crotch. "You'll like it. "

Caroline stopped as Evelyn's free hand landed hard on the side of her face, snapping her head to the side. She took a step back, reeling, but Evelyn slapped her again before she could react.

"Stop it!" she screamed through her tears.

Caroline shook her head as if to clear it. The smile was gone from her face, replaced with the vacant, distant expression Evelyn had seen before during her psychotic episodes. Her eyes, glossy and empty, stared at Evelyn from a thousand miles away.

Caroline sank to her knees, her eyes still locked on Evelyn's. "I'm sorry, Mama. Daddy just liked me better."

Evelyn edged along the wall, keeping her eye on Caroline and a safe distance between them. Her mind still reeling, trying to make sense of what just happened, she worked her way around her friend and bent for the flashlight. Shining it on her, she saw that Caroline hadn't moved. She was down on her knees, eyes staring out the end of the porch into the dark night.

Backing her way down the steps unsteadily, Evelyn kept the light trained on Caroline. Reaching the ground, she paused for a moment and watched her friend. There was no movement at all from Caroline except for the shallow rise and fall of her breathing and an occasional twitch of her head.

Sparing a cautious look at the ground behind her with the light to look for the holes, Evelyn backed away from the steps. It was a slow and agonizing process she repeated many times as she worked her way through the yard. Every time she shined the light back of the porch, Caroline was still kneeling just as she had been.

Finally, after what felt like an eternity, Evelyn's light showed that she'd cleared the edge of the mine field of potential broken knees. She stood in the darkness and shined the light back at the house. Near the end of its reach, it cast only a faint light on the porch, but it was enough to see that Caroline was gone.

The drew in a sharp, frightened breath, sweeping the light back and forth across the yard quickly. Her heart pounded in her chest as she looked for Caroline, but she was nowhere to be found. She turned and ran into the darkness.

Evelyn paced the length of her bedroom, her hands clasped behind her head. During a restless night she'd read countless articles about sexual psychosis and its prevalence among women having suffered sexual abuse as a child. The articles all sounded so cut and dry; so clinical, so matter of fact. Caroline had suffered a psychotic break. That much was clear. It was probably brought on by the pressure she felt to move to the retreat and the fact that Evelyn was leaving. That was why she'd tried to talk her into staying with her at the house, it would solve both problems that had been thrust upon her.

Caroline's own self-view as a sexual object, to be used however one saw fit, was the catalyst for her behavior. She would be willing to give herself to anyone who could solve her problems. In her own mind, Caroline thought the only thing of value she had to offer was herself, so she'd offered it. That, too, was part of the psychosis. Although Caroline didn't have any control over her actions and probably wouldn't remember them, Evelyn couldn't get the feeling of being kissed out of her mind. The smile on Caroline's face, distant and alien, haunted her. Her friend was sick and needed help now more than ever.

She knew all these things, but it didn't alleviate the fear still residing within her chest. She had been afraid, very afraid, for her own safety.

The person behind the empty eyes she'd looked into wasn't Caroline at all, but some manifestation of the pain and evil poured out on her whole life. That person was desperate. That person could have hurt her.

She closed her eyes and sighed, remembering the strength in Caroline's hand as it wrapped around the back of her neck. Caroline could have just as easily grabbed her by the throat and choked her to death.

"Think," Evelyn told herself as she sat on the bed and began to rub her temples. She couldn't turn to her parents for help. If she told them they would probably call the police and have Caroline committed for a psyche eval, but that would only further her idea that everyone eventually abandoned her.

Caroline would surely not go willingly and that would result in a forced committal and she'd either hurt herself or someone else. She closed her eyes tightly and shook her head as the image of Caroline, confined to a bed by hard restraints, screamed and cursed her name.

It was up to her and she didn't have a clue about to what to do. Should she just stay away and let her be? Caroline made it this far on her own. Should she call the woman's retreat to see if they could help? That was a possibility, but did they ever make "house calls"? Could she risk another visit alone? Should she? What would she do if she found her still lost to a psychotic break? What would she say if she wasn't? Her heart broke for her old friend; for her babies, but what could she do? She hadn't hurt her. The people who bore all the responsibility were already dead. There was no one left to punish for what had happened to Caroline.

Except Caroline herself.

"AHHH!" she growled and flopped down on her bed. "What the hell am I going to do?" she asked the ceiling. "I can't deal with this shit," she said and grabbed her phone. Scrolling through her contacts list, she looked for someone to talk to but couldn't find anyone that she actually *wanted* to talk to. With a heavy sigh, she dropped it to the bed and stared at the ceiling again.

Feeling restless, Evelyn pushed herself off the bed and walked into the living room. She flipped on the television with no intention of watching it and dropped onto the couch. With her dad at work and her mother out, the house was quiet and still and took only a few minutes to drive Evelyn off the couch.

"What am I going to do?" she asked herself. Pacing again, she looked for something to do, something that would occupy her while she thought. She walked the length of the hall and back, then headed for the door. There was nothing outside for her to do, but at least it would be a change of scenery.

She walked out the door and was halfway down the sidewalk when she saw the piece of paper tucked beneath her windshield wiper.

"Not now, Trae," she complained, assuming he'd left her a note. She eyed it contemptuously as she rounded the hood of the car and snatched it from beneath the wiper blade. Looking around, she saw no one about.

Opening it at the fold, she immediately saw that it wasn't from Trae, but part of her wished it was. That would have been easier to deal with. It was written in a ragged, childish scrawl that said, "I'm so sorrie. I'm better now. Pleese come see me again. Are you still my friend? I'm sorrie." It was signed "Cara".

Evelyn fell against the car and rubbed her eyes with her free hand as she stared at the note. How could she deny such a cry for help? She knew she couldn't, yet she hesitated. There was a part of her that dreaded going to the old house with its dusty, smelly interior and its sad, run down porch. The whole ordeal had already taken an emotional toll on her she hadn't even fully explored yet. There was just so much pain in that house that it permeated the walls and seeped into everything and everyone that walked in it. It was a bad place where bad things happened, and she wished she never had to see it again.

But that was where Caroline, not Cara, was. She could feel the desperation. The pain in the note was almost physical. The fact that Caroline had signed the note with the name her father called her spoke volumes. She was scared, and hurting, and alone.

Caroline was the only other person in the whole town other than her parents that knew she'd gotten pregnant and had terminated the pregnancy. She ruined a three-hundred-dollar softball bat on an old truck for Caroline and drove hours on the interstate for her. She'd slept on the floor, slept in her car, and not slept at all for her. She'd dug a grave for one of her babies, for God's sake! How could she forsake her now, when she needed her most?

Finally, ending the pretense that she wasn't going to go, she dug her key out of her back pocket and got into the car. "Lord," she prayed as she started the car. "Please, please, please help us both."

When her phone began to ring as she backed out of the driveway, Evelyn looked skyward questioningly. Was this an answered prayer? The caller ID on her phone told her it was Sandra Bailey, her psychology professor. Maybe it was after all.

"Hello, Professor."

"Hello, Miss Jackson. How are you today?" The woman's voice was authoritative and calming.

"Good, good. Thanks for calling me back. I really hate to bother you, ma'am." Evelyn said.

"It's not a problem. Your message said you wanted to discuss something?"

"Yes, ma'am. Uh, I guess I'll just jump right in." As Evelyn drove slowly down the tree-lined streets of the neighborhood she'd grown up in, in the back of her mind she wondered how many secrets the nicely painted front doors hid.

"There's this girl, young woman. Actually, she's my age. Anyway, there is a history of severe childhood trauma, sexual, physical, and emotional abuse. Also, there is a presentation of hearing three distinct voices."

"That sounds troubling," she professor said. "A friend of yours?"

"Of sorts. Well, yes. She is a friend," Evelyn admitted, both to herself and the professor. "She also presents with apparent self-harm, as well as severe social withdrawal centered around an unnatural mistrust of men."

"Well, given childhood sexual abuse, that wouldn't be unusual. How is she doing with her meds? Any adverse reactions?"

"Well, that's the thing. She isn't on any meds."

"That's odd. What facility is she in?"

"She's not in one, ma'am. That's the problem."

"Well, she needs to be. You're a third year, right?"

"Yes ma'am. I know she needs help, but she is adamantly opposed to any hospital. She has an attachment to the house where she grew up."

"Look, Evelyn, you know very well that she needs medical attention. The self-harm alone could get her in a thirty-six-hour suicide watch admit whether she liked it or not."

"I know. I've been talking to her about going to the hospital, but I think an involuntary committal will do more harm than good, long term."

"Miss Jackson, I'm sure you mean well, but judging from the limited knowledge I have of this girl, she needs to be in a secure facility with a trained medical staff."

"I couldn't agree more, but as much of her psychosis is caused by her history of abuse, being left alone at an early age has also played its part. She stays by herself and has for years, since she was fifteen. She's barely literate and wants to stay isolated."

There was a sigh at the other end of the line as Evelyn rolled to a stop at a traffic light. "Look, Miss Jackson, I cannot give a diagnosis over the phone with second-hand testimony, but it sounds to me that this girl has a serious mental illness. Whether it's from childhood trauma or severe social withdrawal doesn't matter. Self-harm is very serious. Surely you know the suicide rate among people in his country with mental illness. It's practically an epidemic."

"I know." Now it was Evelyn's turn to sigh. "It's just that she's so scared of the doctors and she trusts me. I can't just turn her in. I just don't know what to do."

"I don't know what to tell you. You know the first step is to get her looked at by a trained professional. Even then, it's a crap shoot sometimes until you find the right combinations of meds and therapy. There are lifestyle enrichment paths, education, social rehabilitation. Hell, they can teach her to read. All of these are esteem boosters that she needs. It's a long and arduous road, but it all begins with a professional interview. You know that."

"I know, ma'am. I just thought there might be something I could do while I keep trying to convince her to seek medical help."

There was a pause. "Are you in a position to see this person regularly?"

"Yes, almost every day." For now, her mind added.

"All I can suggest is to keep talking to her about getting help from a professional and proceed with extreme caution. Miss Jackson, we've talked a lot this semester and I know you're a smart girl. You're a very promising student."

"Thank you, ma'am. I've had a bit of a personal issue the last half of this semester."

"I've noticed. But like I was saying, you're a smart girl. You know just enough to be dangerous. I've seen students get pulled into situations like this before. You just want to help, or someone needs free advice, whatever the situation. But I can tell you that it always blows up in their faces, every single time. Miss Jackson, talk your friend into getting help. Professional help. I've seen seasoned doctors struggle with difficult patients. In my honest opinion, you don't have a snowball's chance in hell of helping this girl as things are now."

Evelyn grimaced at the reproach. "That's what I've been trying to do. It isn't easy. I don't want to betray her trust though."

"Do you want to cut her down from a tree?"

"No." Evelyn steered around a corner and headed toward Tuck Smith road. "Is there anything I can do? Anything I can say to nudge her along?"

"Now, you'd know that better than me, seeing that you know her."

"Well, I'm doing my best to help her. I just wish I could do more. Every time I make progress with her, something happens, and it all goes away."

"Thus, the need for a facility where her surroundings can be controlled."

"I just wish there was something I could do to help her."

"There is, Miss Jackson. I don't mean to be blunt, but you can stop playing doctor and be her friend. A friend would make sure she gets the help that she needs. The professional help that she needs."

"That's what I'm trying to do," she said, smarting from the directness of her professor's comment.

"Miss Jackson, I know you want to help this girl. That is a good sign that you've chosen the right career path, but situations like this are simply out of your reach. Nothing against you. I don't know anyone who could help her without her being admitted to a facility. The simple truth is that from the sound of things, your friend is unstable and potentially dangerous, to herself and to others. You have a duty to inform the proper authorities about her. Whether she hurts herself, someone else, or even you; you don't want that on your hands. Now do you?"

"You're right. I just hope I can get her to go voluntarily."

"You know, Evelyn, that I'm not a religious person, per se, but if she doesn't want to seek medical help then I'd suggest you start praying for her and proceed with extreme caution."

THIRTEEN

Evelyn stopped in her tracks, her face frozen in horror, as she passed the tree line and caught sight her friend. Walking toward her with her arms extended like a child running to their parent, Caroline looked like she'd been to hell and back.

Caroline's hair was out of the French braid she'd wove into it and hung in a dirty, tangled mop. The tee shirt was covered in dirty blotches and a large rip ran a few inches down from the neckline as if she'd tried to tear it off. What was left of the collar was stained with dark blood. The right knee of her jeans was torn, revealing a fresh scab of dried blood and her hands were as filthy as if she'd been digging in the ground all night. But it was her face, dirty and tear-streaked beneath a series of long, deep scratches, that truly broke Evelyn's heart.

The wounds on her face were obviously self-inflicted in a fit of self-loathing, undoubtedly brought on by her departure last night. As she'd done with everyone else who had hurt her, Caroline had punished herself for driving her away. Guilt swamped her as she looked at the ferocity with which she'd attacked herself. There was an almost animalistic savagery to the scratches, leaving Evelyn to wonder how it was possible to hurt one's own self so badly.

The scratches began on her forehead and ran down across her eyebrows, over her eyes, and ended on her cheeks, leaving four dark, bloody gouges on each side of her face that matched perfectly with jagged fingernails on each of Caroline hands. They were going to need some immediate attention to stave off infection, if that was even possible. Hopefully the first aid kit she'd brought on one of her previous trips was still intact and could be found.

"Oh, Baby," Evelyn said as she went to Caroline and embraced her, both women beginning to cry.

"I'm so sorry. I'm sorry," Caroline sobbed. "Please forgive me."

"There's nothing to forgive, sweetie," Evelyn said, wiping away her own tears. "You couldn't help it."

"I'm sorry, please say you forgive me," Caroline cried, sobbing violently against Evelyn's shoulder.

"I forgive you. I forgive you," Evelyn assured her. "I'm sorry too. I'm sorry for leaving like that. I was just scared, and I panicked. I'm sorry."

"It's my fault, like always. I'm so sorry."

"None of this was your fault," Evelyn told her. Wrapping her arms around Caroline, holding her tightly, she let her cry. It was all she could do. "None of it was your fault."

Standing in the open field, surrounded by the holes Caroline had dug in search of her dead babies, while the girl sobbed against her chest like a child, Evelyn looked up at the blue sky overhead and made her decision. There was no way she could leave this girl until she was safe. Her own life's trajectory might change because of it, but she'd survive. If she left, Caroline probably wouldn't.

After a long while, as Caroline's sobs began to subside, Evelyn gently pushed her back, holding her by the shoulders. "Let me look at you," she said.

"Please, don't," Caroline said, shielding her face from view with her hands.

"You're gonna need some cleaning up and some ointment put on those. The quicker we get them taken care of, the less chance they will scar. Now let me see." She gently pulled Caroline's hands from her face. Trying not to wince, she examined the deep, ragged scratches. Her friend looked like she'd been attacked by a wind animal and in a way she had. Sadly, it had been herself.

"How bad is it? I've been too afraid to look."

"It's not good," Evelyn told her. "But they'll heal okay."

"I don't know what happened. All day they were talking to me, whispering at me. Nipping at my heels. I could feel them crawling around inside my head, like rats. Usually they just scream at me to do stuff, or say dirty stuff, but it was different this time."

"It's okay now," Evelyn told her, knowing that she was mostly to blame for the break this time. She pushed too hard. She insisted on going back and making a statement with the guys in the truck. Her anger and pride had put those scratches on Caroline's face as sure as if she'd physically attacked her herself. She wanted to contain everything within her predetermined window of availability then run back to school feeling like she'd accomplished something.

Caroline turned as Evelyn tried to console her, not wanting to be consoled. Not yet. "I was there on the porch, but not really. I couldn't do anything to stop what was happening. The old man in my head was in charge. I remember now who he is. It's the old man from the yard, the one who watched my daddy beat me. The one who enjoyed seeing me naked and hurt. My daddy's friend. I don't know his name, but it was him."

She wrapped her arms around herself, squeezing tightly. "He was saying stuff and the others were going along with it. He wanted me to do stuff to you. He wanted me to hurt you while he watched. He called you names. Dirty names. Bad names. They wanted me to hurt you, but I fought them. I fought as hard as I ever fought because I didn't want to hurt you. I think that's what stopped them hurting you. I've never really fought back before. When they attack like that I usually run and hide. They were so loud, screaming like wild animals. They never been so loud."

Caroline paused to gingerly wipe a tear from her torn face. "I have this place that I can go. They can't get to me, but it's like a cage. I go and sometimes I can't get out for a while. Sometimes days, I think. Really there's no way to tell how long. But I couldn't go there because I knew they'd hurt you and do the things he wanted to do to you. I knew somehow you had to go away before I got too weak to stop them, so I kissed you. I knew it wouldn't hurt you, but that it might make you run away. The old man liked that. How they hooped and hollered. But when I let you go, they turned on me and..." she paused, collecting her thoughts, "and they attacked me. By then I was too weak to run away, so they set in on me. But the whole time I was just glad you got away. That's what helped me."

Evelyn approached Caroline from behind, embracing her around the waist. "I'm so sorry, sweetie," she told her, laying her head on the back of Caroline's shoulder. "It must have been horrible. I can't even imagine." She was grateful. If not for Caroline's strength and concern for her, it might be her face that was gashed and torn. It might have been her body beaten and abused. Things might have been done to her that she dared not even imagine. Instead of spending a restless night in her comfortable bed, she might have spent the night going through mortal hell, like Caroline had.

Placing her hands atop Evelyn's, Caroline asked, "Can you stay?"

"I can stay," Evelyn told her.

"I'll go to that place if you want me to."

"It's not that I want you to. It's just that there are people there, twenty-four hours a day, seven days a week. People who can help you more than I can. Other people who have been through what you have that can help lead you to where you want to be. I just want you to be safe, Caroline. You're not safe here."

"I know," Caroline agreed, casting a wary eye toward the house. "Last night proved it. I almost hurt the only person who cared about me that didn't have to."

Evelyn gave her a tight hug. "But you didn't." She didn't want to know how close she'd come.

Caroline smiled as the wind lifted the stray hair from her face. She was proud of herself for the first time in as long as she could remember. Maybe her whole life.

"What say we get you cleaned up?" Evelyn asked, her eyes turned to the western sky and the beginning of storm clouds on the horizon. "Besides, looks like it's gonna be a rainy night."

Evelyn pushed a second pot of rainwater onto the grill in the fireplace, brought the first off with the cleanest rag she could find, and sat down in front of Caroline by the fire. Crossing her legs, she brought the small camping lantern between them. She looked at Caroline's face, and pursed her lips, trying to keep her emotions from showing on her face. The scratched looked horrible and she couldn't imagine the prospect of having such wounds, especially on her face.

"This might hurt a little bit," she warned her as she dipped the rag into the warm water and began dabbing the wounds on Caroline's face. "Tell me if I'm being too rough. I haven't had much experience at this."

"It's fine," Caroline told her flatly. She'd begun to not think of herself as ugly. Not pretty like Evie, but not ugly. Now this. They did this to her on purpose to make her look ugly again. They were afraid of losing her.

Washing out the bloody rag, Evelyn looked at Caroline. "Penny for your thoughts?"

Caroline shrugged as Evelyn began gingerly wiping the dried blood from her face again. "That's about all they're worth."

Evelyn continued her work, folding the rag as it became soiled. "They're your fears, you know,"

"What is?" Caroline asked, watching her friend wash the rag out in the pot.

"The voices. Well, not necessarily your fears, but things that you're scared of."

"Is that what they taught you in school?"

"Not in so many words, but yes, pretty much. You've been through a lot, a whole lot, it's not unusual that you have these manifestations in your mind to represent the things that have hurt you. It's a mixture of unfounded guilt, and anger at yourself for being powerless, and a reliving of the sexual abuse. To be honest, there's no way anyone could go through so much and not have some issues."

"So, I would be crazy if I wasn't crazy?" Caroline asked as a slight smile tugged at the corners of her mouth. "Is that what you're saying?"

"I guess so." Evelyn shrugged. Surveying the wounds on the left side of Caroline's face, glad that they weren't as bad as they had originally looked. They were still bad, and a few places might scar permanently, but minus the dried blood and dirt, they looked much better. She applied a thin layer of antibiotic salve to the wounds and started on the other side of her face.

"Do you want to talk about what happened?" she asked quietly.

"Not really, but I guess you can tell it was bad."

"I know it was, sweetie." Evelyn drew in a deep breath and exhaled slowly, struggling to maintain her composure. This woman, this "crazy" woman had sacrificed herself in order to save her. That was love. Pure, genuine love, and thinking about it almost moved her to tears.

The women sat in silence as Evelyn cleaned and doctored the right side of Caroline face and did the same for the scratches running across each collar bone that framed the tear in the collar of her shirt. There wasn't much she could for the abrasions and the multitude of bruises except give her the two pack of ibuprofen from the first aid kit.

"You would make a good doctor," Caroline told her.

Evelyn laughed. "If I were a doctor I wouldn't be cleaning and medicating these scratches. I'd say, 'Clean these up and put this medicine on it', then I'd leave, and a nurse would be doing this."

"Well, you would have made a good nurse then."

"I actually thought about being a nurse," Evelyn told her as she washed the rag out in the blood tinged water and wrung it out.

"Why didn't you?" Caroline asked as Evelyn got up and tossed the water out the front door.

"I don't know. They also have to do a lot of stuff I don't have the stomach for. I don't really do the whole poop and pee thing, if you know what I mean. Don't get me wrong, I'm glad someone else is willing to do it. It's just not my cup of tea."

Caroline shrugged. She tugged at the legs of the running shorts Evelyn had slept in the last night she stayed here. They were obviously shorter than what she was used to, but they and the t-shirt were far cleaner than the mud-caked and bloody clothes she'd had on.

Cringing slightly as a clap of thunder exploded overhead, she cast her eyes to the window. "I love storms," she said flatly.

"Really?" Evelyn asked, returning to the fireplace with a fresh pot of rainwater. She slid it onto the fire, pulled the other off then raised the lantern to the mantle to better light the whole room. "You ready?" she asked.

Caroline spun around, lent back on her elbows, and bent her head back over the empty pot between Evelyn's knees.

"Tell me if it's too hot, now." Evelyn slowly dipped the water out of the pot and poured it over Caroline's hair, collecting it in the empty one below. "Too hot?"

"It's good," Caroline told her, her eyes closed.

"Anyway, I never liked storms when I was a kid. I remember running into my parents' bedroom and climbing up between them on stormy nights. It was the most secure place I've ever known. It was the safest I ever felt."

"I'll bet," Caroline said flatly. "I feel safer when you're here."

"I don't know why. I'm a fraidy cat."

"I don't know. You seem pretty brave to me." Caroline closed her eyes and allowed her hair to be washed. "You ever ask your parents if they was afraid of storms? They might have been as scared as you."

Evelyn laughed. "I've never thought about that. Guess I just assumed they weren't because they didn't act scared." She used the last of the travel sized shampoo on Caroline's hair and began to work it into a lather.

"That feels good," Caroline admitted.

"Girl, I love getting my hair done. I'll be about ready to fall asleep I'm so relaxed."

After a long pause, Caroline looked up at Evelyn for a moment then reclosed her eyes. "I kinda lied to you earlier."

"About what?" Evelyn asked.

"About the kissing thing."

Evelyn's hands stopped, covered in lather. "And?"

"I kissed you because I love you." Caroline sighed. "Not like that. Not dirty. It was just seeing you so concerned and worried about me. Nobody's ever worried about me. You are the only friend I've ever had, and I love you. I was just overcome. I'm not used to being around people, not close anyway, and I really didn't know what to do."

Evelyn went back to washing Caroline's hair, assuming the role of hairdresser and listening.

"I used to imagine you. After I stopped going to school, I mean. I wondered what you might be doing. What you might look like. I always dreamed you as a beautiful lady in a fancy dress that drug behind you when you walked. I sometimes watch people's television through the windows. I couldn't hear nothing, but I remember this one movie. There was a beautiful woman coming down a big, fancy set of steps. She seemed to float down them, so easy and smooth like. She had this dress that spread out across the whole stairs and just rippled as she come down them. That's how I always pictured you'd be now."

"You mean like this?" Evelyn asked with a laugh, holding up her hands covered in shampoo lather.

255

"You know what I mean," Caroline said with a laugh. "I guess I always wanted you to be my sister, if I had one."

"I always wished I had a sister," Evelyn agreed. "I pretended my dolls were my sisters. Of course, I was the oldest, so I was in charge."

"That's hard to believe," Caroline joked with a laugh.

"Here's a free tip- don't piss off the woman doing your hair," Evelyn said with a grin then began rinsing Caroline's hair.

"What I meant to say was that I didn't kiss you just to run you off. Part of me wanted to kiss you to show you how much I loved you."

"Like a sister, right?"

"Yes, like a sister." Caroline thought for a minute. "I see girls kissing girls before, but it wasn't like that. Or maybe it was. I don't know a lot about stuff like that."

"I know, sweetie. It's all good, and I wasn't put off by it. It was kinda sudden and shocking, I guess. But just so you know, it's not a typical thing to kiss each other on the lips."

"I thought so. I'm sorry."

"It's okay, Caroline. Don't ever be sorry for caring about someone. Even if they do something wrong or hurt you. Loving someone is never a bad thing. If someone doesn't understand or welcome that love, it's their own fault."

"We still talking about me, or us?" Caroline asked quietly, her eyes closed.

"I don't know. I've got issues myself I guess."

"There are different levels of crazy."

Evelyn stopped and looked down at Caroline, struck by the profoundness of her statement. It was so true, so genuinely spoken, and powerful. Evelyn tucked the notion away in her mind as a topic of her next paper and continued washing Caroline's hair, wondering how much time she'd spent on her own psychosis. She knew hearing the voices wasn't normal but was simply powerless to stop them.

"Wanna see?" Evelyn asked, holding a small mirror in her hand. She'd cleaned and doctored the wounds on her face, washed and dried her hair, putting it up in a ponytail. It was the best she could do under the circumstances, but Caroline looked much better than she had when she got here.

"I dunno. I probably don't, but I'll look." She took the mirror and raised it slowly in front of her face.

Evelyn watched carefully, noticing a slight tremble in Caroline's hand as she looked at her reflection. She turned her face slightly to one side then the other, looking at the scratches on her face for a long time.

"I really did a number on myself," she said quietly as her hand crept slowly upward, touching the wounds gingerly.

"It's nothing that won't heal," Evelyn told her. She's scarred because she's scared.

Finally, Caroline lowered the mirror and stared into the fire. "Tell me about this place."

"It seemed nice. There is a twenty-one-day voluntary commitment paper that you have to sign. It just means you'll have to stay for twenty-one days. After that, you pretty much come and go as you want. They said that a lot of girls come there and start to get nervous because it's a

257

new place and want to leave and go back to wherever they were, no matter how bad it was. But after a while, they get used to it and settle in.

"But it seemed really nice. You can have your own cabin or be with someone else. I think I mentioned that. But it's all women. There isn't a guy allowed on the place. They said almost all the women there had some sort of abuse. You know, sexually."

"Do I have to tell everyone what happened to me?"

Evelyn shook her head. "No. They do have counselors, and group meetings, but you don't have to go to them. I asked. From what I can tell, you pretty much just live there and do what you want, but there's people there if you need them or want to talk. I looked at one of the cabins. They're okay. A real bed, a bathroom."

"That'll be something," Caroline said with a wry smile.

"You'll be warm in the winter and cool in the summer. All the windows have glass in them. There's electricity."

"That will be nice," Caroline admitted. "I'm scared they'll look at me like I'm some freak. Especially now." She pointed to her face.

"I don't think you'll have to worry. I saw some of the women there. They seemed happy and healthy. Not all scars are on the outside, Caroline."

Caroline sighed heavily. "It'll be strange," she said looking around. "I've been in this old house my whole life, good or bad. I never got much schooling, but I tried to teach myself to read and write better. Prolly did a piss poor job of it though. I took care of myself when I got hurt or sick. It'll take some getting used to."

"Honey, if there's one thing that is easy to get used to it's a nice soft bed," Evelyn told her with a laugh. "And an indoor bathroom. Oh, and a tub to take a long, hot bubble baths in."

"I don't even have anything to take with me. No clothes, no money, nothing."

"You won't need any money, and we'll make sure you have whatever you need. Trust me. Mama's been talking to the women at church and you'll have more than you'll ever need."

"How can I ever repay you, Evie?"

"By getting yourself better and taking care of my friend, that's how."

Caroline smiled. "That'll be nice too.

Both women jumped and screamed as a sudden gust of wind blew open the back door, slamming it against the wall with a loud bang. One of the two remaining panes of glass fell on the kitchen floor and shattered.

"My God, that storm's getting rough," Evelyn said as she got up. "I'd better check and make sure we're not under a warning or something." She closed the back door and slid a chair in front of it. Outside, rain poured over the edge of the roof in a curtain of water. Another clap of thunder rumbled overhead, shaking the old house.

"I don't know how much more this old house can take," she continued as she walked into the living room, looking at her phone. "Be lucky to get a sig-" She froze mid-sentence as she looked up from her phone. A man was holding Caroline from behind, his hand over her mouth. The blade of the knife was covered in rust except for the edge. It had been filed to a sharp edge that shone in the low light.

He was a tall, rail thin white man with a scraggly beard and was soaking wet. Greasy-looking hair hung from beneath an even greasierlooking baseball cap, framing his small, narrow eyes. The back of the hand clapped over Caroline's mouth bore a home-made black ink tattoo that might have been a sun at some point in his life. The hand holding the knife had a moon, to balance things out, she thought.

Evelyn quickly assessed the situation as her heart raced within her chest. Forcing herself to breathe deeply, she first looked at her friend. Caroline's eyes were wide with fear and panic; she'd be of little help. Sizing up the man, she figured she could hold her own, and with the element of surprise, she could get the best of him long enough for them to get away. He looked sickly; malnourished. The tendons on his hands, protruding through the leathery skin, told her that they guy didn't eat regularly. He was probably homeless or living off the land back in the woods somewhere and had stumbled upon the house seeking shelter from the storm. The reason he was here wasn't important. All that mattered now was that he was here, and he'd somehow gotten the jump on Caroline.

Trying hard to remember what she'd been taught in the self-defense classes her father had forced her to take in high school, she slowly raised her hands to show she wasn't a threat and began negotiating with him.

"Look, man, just put the knife down and we can talk about this."

"You stop right thar," he growled, giving Evelyn a look at his teeth, the few he seemed to have left anyway. They protruded from his pale gums like rotten stumps. Coupled with sores on his sunken, hollow face, they told her he was probably a junkie. His drug of choice was more than likely home-made methamphetamine. That was good and bad. If he was high, his reactions would be slower, but it also meant he was unpredictable.

"Look, man. I don't know what you want, but we can talk about this," she said, making her way slowly around the room. Caroline hung limply in his grasp; her eyes locked on Evelyn.

"Tain't nothin' to talk about," he told her, matching her movements, pulling Caroline along with him. "You just stay put." He poked the knife in her direction, but quickly brought it back to Caroline's neck, just above the scratches she's given herself.

Evelyn stopped, staring into his sunken eyes. As each second passed, her fear began turning into anger. They were at the precipice of Caroline's decision to go into the retreat, and this would probably ruin everything.

"Look, mister, you look sick and probably hungry. If it's food you're wanting, we can help, but you gotta put the knife away before someone gets hurt."

"I ain't lookin' for no food," he spat with a filthy grin as he slid the hand holding the knife across Caroline breasts.

"You hurt her, and I'll kill you with your own knife," Evelyn told him, their eyes locked. "I swear I will." Employing one of the strategies she'd learned in class, Evelyn forced herself to breath in slow and deliberate breaths while she put up a brave front.

"You a feisty one, ain't 'cha?" came a voice from the kitchen.

Evelyn spun on a heel as another man hobble into the living room holding a shotgun in his hands at waist level. It was pointed straight at her stomach. Her heart dropped as she recognized him from the light blue truck that had passed her on the road the other day. This man, not as tall as the other, but equally as thin, was the one hanging out of the window to ogle her.

"What the hell took you so long?" the white man asked angrily.

"I tripped in a damned hole out there. Can't see shit. 'Bout near broke my damned knee." He limped over to the fireplace, favoring his left knee, and motioned with the shotgun for Evelyn to move back to the opposite wall.

"You probably the one who beat my truck all to hell, ain't you?" He asked Evelyn.

"I am," she said defiantly. "And if I had my bat now, I'd beat you all to hell too."

The black man smiled and wiped rain from his face with the back of his hand. "But you ain't got no bat now, do you? You ain't got nothing but a quivering mouse in yer pants. So scared you're about to piss yerself."

Evelyn watched the two men share a laugh. "You think I'm scared of you?" she asked and laughed herself as her mind struggled to formulate a plan. The one man with a knife would have been hard enough to disarm but adding another man with a gun complicated things exponentially. Whatever plan she came up with, she knew she'd have to count on Caroline.

"I'm sure you are," he laughed. "But it don't matter no way."

"Yeah," the white guy chimed in. "You two bitches."

Evelyn ignored him, identifying the black man as the leader; the stronger of the two personalities. He had the gun, that made him the boss. It had probably been his idea to come here. He'd probably planned the whole thing, and he was the one she had to take on first.

"What do you want?" she asked the black man.

"Nothing y'all ain't got plenty of," he sneered.

"I see," Evelyn said. "And just how did you think all this would go down? You think we'd be so scared we'd just lay down and let you two do what you wanted to us?"

"Might save ya both some beatin'."

"Yeah, or maybe save yuns from getting cut up too," the intruder restraining Caroline added, stabbing the knife at Evelyn again. A filthy grin slid across his leathery face.

Again, she ignored him, concentrating on the black man as their eyes remained locked. "You look sick, and thin. Maybe you're weak as a kitten. You already got a bum knee there. Be awfully hard for you to subdue me like that."

He grinned. "I like a little fight now and again. You don't worry about that, missy. I'm just fine. Besides, I could just blow yer guts out and we could take turns with that 'un. Or I could have you while you bleed out."

"And what about your friend?" she continued, working hard to keep her voice even. "He looks scared half to death. You do realize that any minute she chooses, my friend there could disarm him. She's strong. Stronger than your guy slim over there."

"Shut your mouth, you black bitch! I ain't scared!"

Watching the man's eyes, she saw a flash of concern that told her she was right.

"You just keep that knife tight to thatuns' throat. If she makes a move, cut her open like a pig." Turning back to Evelyn, he grinned. "This ain't the first time we done been here. Thatun never puts up much of a fight. Nothing a few slaps to the face won't quiten down."

The white guy let out a knowing laugh and jostled Caroline. "Ain't that right, sweetheart?" He laughed and kissed Caroline on the cheek.

Evelyn spared her a quick look and found only shame in her eyes.

"Don't worry about me. I got this one. You get that loudmouth under control."

Evelyn grinned despite the anger exploding within her chest. The first cracks in their bravado were showing. Her presence here was a surprise to them and they weren't sure what to do now. "There's still time for you to save yourself. You know the black man is gonna be the one to get the chair if this all goes to shit. Think about it? Is a little tail worth it?"

The man looked her up and down then grinned. "It might be. 'Specially if she put up a little tussle."

"Well, know this. If y'all make your move, our first aim is gonna be at your junk. Be hard to do much with a sore cock. Even if you got me down and got it up enough to penetrate, you'd drop your guard because you'd be enjoying it so much and then I'd have you. Maybe then we'd have some fun. Make you two suck each other's cocks or something."

She was taking a chance enticing them like this, but it felt like her only chance. One thing was for sure, she sure as hell wasn't going to let these two sick bastards get what they wanted. There was no way in hell that was going to happen, at least not as long as she was alive.

"You're a fucking liar!" the white man said. "That ain't gonna happen!"

The black man stared at Evelyn, considering what she said. He knew it was probably true, but he'd been thinking about having her since he'd seen her. She was a fancy bitch and he'd never had a fancy bitch before.

"What about I give you another pair of my panties?" she asked. "I've got a dirty pair right here. I been wearing them all day. They probably smell amazing, huh? You can smell them while your little friend over there sucks you off."

"I ain't sucking no dick!" he yelled. Evelyn spared a quick glance at Caroline and gave her a slight nod, raising one eyebrow questioningly.

In a look, she told her that things were about to happen, and she'd have to help.

"I got' em right here in my bag, see." She slowly bent as the men watched. "They been rubbing all over me, soaking up my scent." She unzipped the backpack, her eyes on the gun, and pulled a pair of pink and white flowered panties out teasingly.

"You like the way they look?" she asked seductively.

"Like little girl panties," the white guy honked with a goofy laugh.

The man with the gun was shaking slightly. She could tell his heart was racing with anticipation. There was a swell in his baggy work pants that said he was ready.

Evelyn dropped the panties back into the bag. "Oops, silly me," she said. "I'm just a silly little girl." Bending, she reached back into the bag, arching her back and pushing her butt out. "Is your boy gonna suck you off while you smell them, like he did the other day?"

"I ain't never sucked no dick!" he bellowed, loosening his grip on Caroline as he took a half step toward her, pointing his knife in her direction. "You shut your fucking mouth!"

"You the boss, ain't you?" she asked the black man.

"Shut that bitch up!" the tattooed man yelled. Distracted and angered by Evelyn he'd allowed his hand to slid to Caroline's shoulder.

"Calm down!" the black man yelled. "Everybody shut up!"

"You the boss and he's your little fuck boy?" Caroline asked, watching the man's frustration grow out of the corner of her eye. He was almost ready. "Does he like it? Or do you have to make him be your little bitch?"

"You shut the fuck up, you damned whore!" he screamed, pointing the knife at her, "before I cut your fucking tits off and shove 'em down your throat myself!"

In one motion, Evelyn grabbed the backpack, swinging it at the black man as hard as she could, and dove out of the way of the shotgun blast she knew would come. Out of the corner of her eye, she saw Caroline spin on her attacker and shove her knee into the white man's groin before leaping back, just clearing the arc of the knife as he swung it at her.

The backpack struck him alongside the head in a glancing blow and careened toward the mantle, knocking the camping light onto the floor and extinguishing it. The light from the fire kept some of the darkness at bay, but the room was considerable darker now. Above her, she saw the fire escape the gun barrel as the shotgun fired. It filled the room with a deafening report, ringing in her ears. Somewhere in the darkness on the other side of the room, she heard glass shatter and fall to the floor.

Caroline threw her weight onto the white man's back as he doubled over in pain, dropping the knife. He went to the floor beneath her in a crumpled mass of pain, and she began to pummel him with her fists.

Taking advantage of the moment of confusion, Evelyn leapt to her feet and grabbed the barrel of the gun just as the black man pumped another round into the chamber. Pushing the barrel toward the ceiling, she heard another blast and felt the recoil of the gun. It kicked the gun back into the man's collar bone, snapping it like a twig. As he howled in pain, she brought her knee up with all her strength. It sank into his baggy pants and struck his crotch, bringing forth another painful scream as he doubled over. The shotgun, now forgotten slipped out of his hands and fell to the floor. Lacing her fingers together, she raised both hands over her head in one fist and brought them down on the base of the man's skull, sending him sprawling on the floor at her feet.

Surveying the scene, the thought of collecting the men as prisoners and exacting revenge on them came to mind. It was what they deserved. She wanted to torture them; to make them pay for the abuse they'd inflicted on Caroline. She wanted them to die.

"Evie!"

Evelyn looked around at Caroline, then down at the shotgun in her hands, surprised to see it there. When had she picked it up? Following the length of the barrel with her eyes, she saw that it was pointed at the back of the black man at her feet.

"Let's go!" Caroline screamed, at her feet the white guy had curled into a fetal position, covering his now bloody face with his "sun" hand while the "moon" hand clutched his crotch.

Evelyn delivered a swift kick into the black man's ribs and joined her friend by the door. Pausing, shotgun in hand, she looked back at the two men.

"I told you not to ever come back." Turning, she joined her friend on the porch. "Let's get the hell away from this place."

The cold rain slapped them in the face as they ran down the steps, but they barely noticed. Caroline took Evelyn's hand as they quickly navigated the muddy front yard, expertly avoiding the holes she'd dug. Once they reached the tree line, Evelyn stopped to toss the gun into the woods and spared one last look at the old house, somehow knowing it would be the last time she'd ever see it.

As lightning flashed, she saw Caroline was looking back too. The look on her face told Evelyn that she'd never go back. It was a welcome sight. Better to leave the place on a victorious note.

"C'mon," Evelyn screamed and put a hand on Caroline's back as the rain poured down on them. "We gotta go. Now."

Turning to Evelyn, Caroline started to laugh loudly. They clasped hands and started running. "You one crazy ass black girl!" she screamed, loudly enough to be heard over the storm.

"I'm not crazy," Evelyn yelled as they ran together through the raging storm, laughing. "I just have issues."

FOURTEEN

Sparing Caroline one last look as she lay sleeping in her bed, covers drawn to her chin, Evelyn gently pulled the door to her bedroom closed behind her and tip-toed down the hallway. Like her, Caroline had showered and been fed a piping hot bowl of home-made beef stew. Unlike her, Caroline had passed out in bed as quickly as she laid down. Passing through the living room, she went to the kitchen to face the wrath of her parents.

Sitting down at the table, she steeled herself against the assault. Her father was sitting across the table, facing her in a plain white tee shirt and a pair of pajama pants. Her mother, wrapped in a lavender fleece robe, sat beside him. She shook her head as Evelyn joined them at the table, staring at her in disbelief.

"Girl," her father began, then lowered his voice some, "Are you out your god-danged mind?"

"No, daddy. I'm not."

"You're acting like it," Martha chimed in.

"You out here running around in a damned thunderstorm, a tornado warning, no damned less and scaring the hell out of your mother and me." As if to emphasize his point, a flash of lightning lit up the kitchen windows, followed by a clap of thunder.

"I'm sorry, daddy, mama. I am. I didn't have anywhere else to go."

"They's a girl laying in your bed right now," Freddy pointed his finger in her direction, "That two weeks ago was staggering around town mumbling to herself. That's what you just brought here in my house in the middle of the night. And soaking wet and muddy as a pig to boot," he added. "And telling us about how y'all were almost gangraped by a bunch of meth heads with knives and guns."

"Good Lord," Martha added, shaking her head.

"There were just two of them," Evelyn said, knowing it wouldn't make a difference. When her parents tag teamed her like this it was better to just let them get it out of their system. She'd scared them, and she knew it wouldn't go well, but it was the safest place she knew to go. With a heavy sigh, she slumped in her chair, resigning herself to the lecture.

"Oh, just two of them? Oh, then that's okay then." Turning to his wife he added, "Martha they were just two men, probably stoned and half-crazy trying to rape our only daughter."

"Just two? Oh, that's fine. Let's go to bed," she added, pretending not to care.

"What was I supposed to do?" Evelyn asked.

"I told you way back when that this was a bad idea," Freddy replied, ignoring her question. "I told you not to get involved, but you did."

"Jumped in with both feet," Martha added.

"You just had to help this girl. Why? Because you went to school with her twelve years ago? It just doesn't make any sense at all."

"I helped her because she's a human being and she needed help," Evelyn snapped, unable to hold her tongue.

"Don't get smart," her father told her, pointing his finger at her from across the table.

"I'm not getting smart, daddy."

"Let me tell you something, young lady, you our only child. You don't seem to remember that sometimes. Something happens to you and we childless from now on. You know what it'd do to your mother?"

"I'm sorry, mama," she said dryly, hearing that line for the hundred thousandth time in her life.

"Don't roll your eyes at me," Martha snapped, catching Evelyn's reaction.

"I'm sorry, mama."

"You should be sorry! Sorry you even put your poor mama through all this. ALL this. She done been down at the church asking for prayers, calling folks, doing all kinda stuff for that girl in there that she ain't even met 'till tonight."

"And you, all that mess with Trae and now this. What's gotten into you lately? You trying to kill us both?"

Evelyn sulked in her chair, chewing on a thumbnail in the corner of her mouth. "Look, as far as the matter with Trae and all that, I was just letting you know what was happening in my life, that's all. As far as tonight, I appreciate your concerns, and I appreciate all y'all have done, but I didn't know what else to do, so I came to the only people I knew who would."

"Don't even start in with that bull, Evie," her mother told her. "I ain't falling for it this time. You put yourself in danger all this time! More danger than you let on, I suspect. Do you realize you could have been raped and killed and dumped in the woods?"

"We'd be all on T.V. holding up a picture of you and asking folks if they seen you," Freddy said shaking her head.

Evelyn laughed, trying to hide it behind her hand. Sometimes when her father was angry or very upset his voice and tone reverted to a stereotype southern black comedian voice.

"You think all this is funny?" Martha asked. "Your daddy's gotta go to work in a few hours. Is that funny? After being up all hours of the night with this mess."

"No, Mama," Evelyn began, stifling her smile. "Look, I've said I'm sorry. What do you want me to do? You want me to go to a hotel? I'm a college student. I don't have any money."

"You ain't been bashful about using my credit card so far," Freddy told her.

"I'll pay you back, I promise."

"This ain't about the money!" her father declared. "Don't you understand why we're upset?"

"No, I don't, really. If you want to know the truth." She did, but she had no other argument to put forth in her defense.

"You could have been killed! How hard is that to understand?" Freddy told her, exasperated.

"I know, but I wasn't. It's not like we invited those freaks into the house," Evelyn said.

"House? House? That place is a shack, you said so yourself. Damned doors probably don't even lock. Are you outta your mind?"

"That's my whole point," Evelyn said, standing.

"Sit your butt back down," her mother ordered. Evelyn complied reluctantly.

Freddy drew in a deep breath. "You should have never been there. Don't you see our point. I told you, Eve. I told you and we almost lost you tonight."

"I'm sorry, Daddy. I really am. I'm sorry things went the way they did, but I had nothing to do with it. I was just trying to help someone who needed my help." She looked at her mother and added, "Like Jesus would do."

"Hell naw!" her mother said, pushing her chair back from the table. "Child gone start talking about, 'like Jesus would do'. No, that ain't what Jesus would do." Martha stood and leaned forward, putting her hands on the table. "How would you know what Jesus would do. Your skinny butt ain't been to church in forever."

"Well, I did recite the 23rd Psalm from memory the other day," Evelyn informed them curtly.

"23rd Psalm? Really? That's the Old Testament! See what I mean?" Martha went to the sink and got a drink of water. "It's late and my head hurts. I can't even deal with this child no more. I'm going to bed." She kissed her husband on the cheek and gave Evelyn a sideways look as she walked out of the kitchen and headed toward her bedroom.

"Really?" Freddy asked once the coast was clear. "Like Jesus would do? You going to throw the Lord up in this?"

Evelyn smiled, unable to contain the humor of the situation. "I'm sorry, Daddy. I know where y'all are coming from. I really do, but do you see my point at all?"

"Baby," Freddy reached across the table and took his daughters' hands in his. "I love you more than anything else in the world, and tonight I came close to losing you. I think I'd lay down and die if something happened to you. I really do. You scared the holy hell out of us."

"I know, but all that happened, it was pouring down rain, I was scared, it was dark. I didn't know where else to go."

"I know," Freddy said, calming down some as he rubbed his face with both hands and yawned. "But let me tell you, you gotta call that place and get her a spot tomorrow."

"I know. I am, Daddy."

"Am I gonna have to lock my bedroom door tonight? She ain't gonna go all nuts and kill us all is she?"

"Really? You need to ask that?"

"I'm just saying," Freddy answered defensively.

"I wouldn't have brought her here if I thought she would do anything like that. She's the one that's been hurt. She's never hurt a living soul, daddy." Evelyn thought for a minute. "Except for tonight," she said with a grin. "You should have seen us!"

Freddy looked at his daughter and shook his head. "Go ahead and tell me. I doubt I'll get any sleep anyway."

"I remembered all those self-defense class you made me do in high school."

"See! See, I told you. Didn't I tell you?"

"Truly, thank you." She told him. "Anyway, they had a knife on Caroline and the guy had a gun on me, but I wasn't scared. Well, I was, but I knew I couldn't let them see it. I was scared to death, but I knew we had to fight back. I couldn't just let them hurt us. Really, there was no other choice. I signaled to Caroline, and I threw that old backpack at him, the one I had from high school, and she kneed one guy in the balls and the gun went off, then I grabbed it and it went off again. But it came back and broke his collar bone, I think. Anyway, it broke something in his shoulder. That's when I grabbed him, kneed him in the balls. I did that thing with both hands and hit him on the back of the neck." Evelyn excitedly demonstrated the move. "When he went down, that's when I grabbed Caroline, who was beating the crap out of the white guy, and we ran like crazy. It was awesome! Like something out of a movie."

"Oh Lord," Freddy said, putting a hand to his chest. "I'mma have to go to church for a while on this one, baby, 'cause God himself was helping you out tonight." Freddy looked at his daughter with a mixture of pride and disbelief. He shook his head, rubbed his face with both hands and looked toward the ceiling. "Thank you, Jesus."

"Definitely," Evelyn agreed with a laugh. "I don't know what it was, but I was mad as hell at these guys. Something in me just took over. I'm not even sure it was a conscious decision to fight back, but I knew I had to do something. Daddy, it wasn't the first time they'd come after Caroline."

Freddy sighed, shaking his head. How much had the poor girl laying in his daughters' bed suffered? How many times had men done things like that to her? In his heart, he was proud of his daughter, but he wanted to wring her neck for putting herself in danger.

"I'll bet you didn't think you had a badass for a daughter, did ya?"

"You something I'm not sure what." He scratched his head and looked at her with a heavy sigh. "All that matters now is that you're safe and most of this storm is passing us by."

"It's been bad," Evelyn agreed, looking out the window as lightning flashed in the distance.

"Well, I'm going to try to lay down for a little before I gotta go to work. You taking the couch?" Freddy asked as he stood and yawned.

"I guess so," Evelyn yawned. "Now that everything is settling down, I'm getting tired." She yawned and rubbed her eyes with her fists.

"And a long one tomorrow," he told her as they walked together through the living room. Freddy stopped in the hallway and turned back to watch his daughter spread the sheets on the couch. "Love you, Eve." He shook his head and stared at her for a long time.

Evelyn dropped the sheet and ran to her father, throwing her arms around his neck. "I love you so much, daddy. You're the best."

"Thank you, sweetie. And for the record," he held her at arms' length and looked into her eyes. "I always knew my daughter was a badass."

He was a good father and she considered herself lucky to have had him as such. He'd always been there for her, always supported her, always loved her. "I love you, daddy," she said, smiling. "Thank you for being a great dad."

"I love you too. Good night, baby." He kissed her on the cheek and turned to walk down the hall. Pausing at his bedroom door, he looked back at his daughter as she dressed the couch for bed. A warm, loving smile broke out across his lips. She truly was amazing.

Freddy Jackson settled into bed again and could just feel the slight fingers of sleep beginning to tug at him when he heard a soft tap on his bedroom door. It opened slightly and his daughter poked her head inside.

"Can I sleep with y'all?" she asked quietly.

Freddy looked at his daughter and shook his head with a smile, "C'mon," he finally said, throwing his side of the covers back. Evelyn rushed to the bed and crawled between her parents, snuggling into the warmth of their covers.

"G'nite," Freddy told her.

"G'nite, daddy."

Freddy closed his eyes, doubting if he'd get much sleep. Even a king-sized bed was crowded with three adults in it. He edged himself to the side of the bed and gave his daughter and wife more room, admitting to himself that despite the commotion of the night and the strangeness of having another person in bed with he and his wife, it was good to have Eve so close. Here, within his reach, he could keep her safe.

Outside, a distant flash of lightning lit up the bedroom windows followed, seconds later, by a low rumble of thunder. The storm had passed and was receding. There would be more rain, but the danger was gone. All that was left now was to clean up the damage.

"Daddy?" came a small, quiet whisper out of the darkness.

"What, baby?"

"Are you scared of storms?"

"Leaving today. Can't take M&D another second!"

"What's wrong?" Evelyn asked, answering Aaron's text.

"Everything. 2 much 2 text."

"So sorry."

"Can U get away?" he asked.

"Today?"

"Yes, today??"

"I'm sorry, babe. Can U call?"

"OK. Gimme a min."

Evelyn sighed and took a sip of coffee. It had already been a busy morning. Awakened at nine a.m. by her mother, she called the retreat to reserve a spot for Caroline. The woman on the phone informed her that the storm knocked their power out for several hours and they wouldn't be prepared to take a new "friend" until tomorrow. Having no other choice, she accepted the conditions and broke the news to her mother, who didn't take it well. The ensuing complaint session sucked the little wind she had gathered out of her sails, leaving her deflated and tired.

Now, Aaron wanted her to meet him earlier than expected. That would surely lead to another argument. Leaning forward on the couch, she propped her elbows on her knees and buried her face in her hands, letting out a sigh and wondering how much more she could take. When her phone began to vibrate, she took it and her coffee outside.

"Hello," she said, answering her phone as she walked out onto the back deck.

"Hey, sweetie,"

"It's so good to hear a friendly voice," she told him, a smile sliding across her lips. "I feel like I've been through a meat grinder."

"What's wrong?" he asked.

"Oh my God, it's such a long story," she sighed, not wanting to go through her ordeal again. "I'll tell you later."

"Are you okay?"

"I'm fine. Just super tired. Big storm rolled through last night and I didn't sleep well."

"Speaking of storms, there was a huge blow here last night. My parents are driving me nuts!"

"I gathered. What's been going on?"

"It's not something I really want to talk about on the phone. I wish I could see you right now."

"Oh, baby," she moaned. "I so wish we could be together. I sure could use my man right about now."

"So, come up. Or we could meet in a hotel somewhere close."

"I really, really want to. But about that."

"No," he moaned. "Please don't tell me you're still at that old house with that girl."

"I'm not- at the old house, I mean. I'm at mom and dads. But she's here."

"What? She's in your house?"

"Yes. There was a situation, and we had to leave her house. She's pretty much been asleep since we got here. My parents aren't happy either. It's been a long night."

Aaron sighed heavily. "So, now what?"

"Well, we found a place she can go. It's a place for women. For, like, battered women."

"Okay, great. Dump her there and come on up with me."

"Aaron, really?" she asked.

"What? Am I wrong for wanting to be with you?"

"No, sweetie. I want to be with you too. I really do. But they can't take her 'till tomorrow and I can't just leave her here with mom and dad."

"Why not?"

"Because she needs me, and mom and dad can't deal with all this."

"All this?" Aaron asked. "What's there to deal with?"

It was Evelyn's turn to sigh. "She needs me."

"I need you," Aaron told her sharply.

"I know you do," Evelyn said, her heart torn. "I need you too, but I can't just leave her here. It's complicated."

"Fine then," Aaron snapped. "So, drop her off tomorrow then we'll meet up."

"Well," Evelyn said sheepishly. "That's the thing. I was planning to spend the night with her."

"At the nut house?"

"It's not a nut house."

"Whatever. Why do you have to spend the night with her?"

"Because she will need me to." Evelyn rubbed her forehead. "You do understand that she's been under a lot of stress lately?"

"Well, I haven't been on a leisurely vacation myself, Eve."

"I know, and neither have I. You have to believe me, baby, there's nothing I'd rather do than be with you."

"Okay then, that's what I want too. So, let's make it happen."

"I can't, baby. Not right now. I'm sorry."

"Is this a commitment thing?" He asked.

"What are you asking me? Am I committed to you?"

"Actually, I was asking if the girl was being committed, but since the question is out there, are you?"

"I can't believe you have to ask that," Evelyn told him, knowing in her heart he had every right to, considering what she'd done with Trae. Closing her eyes as a tear slipped down her cheek, she allowed her guilt to abate before answering. "You know I am."

"That's reassuring," he said sarcastically.

"It's the best I can offer right now." *What are you doing?* she asked herself. *Tell him that you need him; that you're tired, and scared, and worried, and that being in his arms would make everything better. Tell him your soul aches to be with him. Tell him something!* Her mind screamed, but all she could muster was a sad, "I'm sorry."

"Well," Aaron began with a sigh, "What are you going to do?"

"It will be good for her. It'll probably save her life. Aaron, look, I'm sorry. I truly am, but I just have to see this through. I can come back here Friday morning and pack up, then I'll be up."

"Yeah, unless some other hometown problem pops up."

"What's that supposed to mean?" she asked, taken aback.

"Nothing. Never mind."

"Aaron, what are you saying?" she asked as worry began to creep into the back of her mind.

"Nothing," he said flatly. "Look, I'm sick of fighting with my parents, and I'm tired of begging you to be with me."

"Why are you being like this? It's like a day and a half. You're getting all nutso about nothing."

"Nuts? I wish I was nuts, then you'd be all over me. I'll tell you what, Eve. You go and do your thang with your friends, and I'll be back at NC. If you wanna find me I'll be in my apartment, or maybe I won't.

But, hey, it's just a day and a half, so I'm sure your sucker boyfriend will wait patiently until you decide to grace me with your presence."

"Wait, what's the matter with you? You're acting like an ass."

"Well, I guess that makes your decision easier, don't it?"

"No, I love you Aaron, and I want to be with you. I don't understand what the big deal is."

"I guess not. Maybe that's part of the problem."

"Well, right now, you're part of the problem," she told him. The long silence on the other end of the line told her that her words had stung him. "Aaron, I'm sorry. I didn't mean it."

"That's fine," he told her. "I'm part of the problem? Really? You want to know what my parents are so pissed about? It's you. They want me to stop seeing you, Eve."

Stunned into silence, she closed her eyes and rubbed her forehead. She'd had her suspicions all along, but to hear it spat at her so vehemently shocked her.

"So, you see, you're not the only one who's been going through some shit, Eve. My whole future is on the line here. School, the apartment, everything."

"What? Really? They said that?" Her mind reeled as she tried to make sense of what he'd said. Were his parents really going to make him choose between her and their money?

"They told me I had to make a decision."

"Oh, Aaron, you should have told me. We could have talked about it."

"And what would that have accomplished?"

"I don't know, but we could have talked through it. Came up with a plan or something."

"Really? A plan?" Aaron laughed. "That's rich coming from you."

"What the hell does that mean?"

"Nothing, Eve. Nothing at all. I'm just mad and frustrated and tired and I want to be with my girlfriend, but that's too much to ask, apparently."

"Sweetie, I'm so sorry, I want to be with you. Don't you believe me?"

"You do what you feel like you need to do, Eve. You know where I'll be if you get some free time."

"That's just mean. Don't be assy. I'm doing everything I can." Evelyn quietly wiped a tear from her cheek, making sure he didn't know she was crying.

"What's that old saying? People do what they want to do, for everything else they make excuses. Yeah, that's close enough."

"That's just mean, Aaron."

"I've been through hell lately, Eve, and here I am still reaching out for you, begging to be with you, and yet you push me away for the sake of some headcase you found on the side of the road."

"That's not the way it is, Aaron. You know that's not how it is. I love you; I need you."

"Really? Because it hasn't felt like you love or need me lately, or even want to be with me. You've been so distant and stuff. Then you run off home. We didn't talk or plan then, did we? Now you've got excuses for not coming up. Maybe this girl isn't the only reason you're staying home?"

Evelyn's hand went to her mouth as she gasped. Did he know? Was that why he was so upset? Standing, she began pacing the deck, trying to gather the thoughts flying around her head.

"Aaron, I'll admit where I was wrong. I tried to explain that I had some stuff to deal with and I just needed a few days to think."

"And then you meet this girl and here we are."

"Look," Evelyn began with a heavy sigh. Was he just being insecure? Had he just thrown the comment about why she was staying home to hurt her, or did he know about Trae? Forcing a calmness into her voice, she continued, "I do love you so much, baby. I honestly do, but this could be a matter of life and death. I need to do this. As much for me as for her. I don't expect you to understand it, but I need you to believe me."

"I guess I don't have much choice. Look, I've got to go. I'm getting the hell out of this place and headed back up to school. I've got a lot to do."

"Don't go, sweetie. Please. Let's talk about this."

"I've been thinking and talking for a solid week nonstop, Eve. I'm tired of thinking and talking. I've been going out of my mind with all this crap. It's time to do something. Time to crap or get off the pot."

"What do you want me to do?" she asked, crying openly now. "What?"

"I want you to do what you want to do. Look, I gotta go, babe."

"Aaron? Aaron?" Evelyn looked at the screen of her phone and saw that the call had ended. She raised it above her head angrily, ready to slam it down on the deck, but decided against it. Instead, she grabbed it with both hands and shook it violently.

"Dammit!" she exclaimed. She sat down and began to sob. Everything was coming unraveled and there was nothing she could do to stop it.

Martha Jackson walked out of her house and went to her only child. Sitting down beside her, she pulled her close and held her, knowing there was nothing left to do but let her cry.

"Does it itch?" Evelyn asked, watching Caroline rub the bandages on her cheeks. She turned back to the road before as she drove toward "One Safe Place" for the second time.

"Some," she answered, taking her hands away like a child caught by their parent.

"That's a good sign. They're starting to heal." Evelyn had dressed the wounds in the wee hours of the morning after Caroline finally woke up.

"Evie are you okay?" she asked.

"I'm good," she answered, putting on a smile.

"You don't seem fine. Is there something wrong?"

"It's nothing. Aaron's being assy, but it's no big deal."

Caroline cleared her throat. "You know, the odd thing about being crazy is hearing voices. And when you do, your brain kinda picks up on them. Sometimes you hear voices in your head, sometimes you hear voices through the window."

"So, I guess you heard my conversation with Aaron?" Evelyn asked.

"Well, just your end. I'm crazy, I don't have super hearing."

Evelyn smiled. "It'll be okay. He's just being a jerk. I'll talk to him tomorrow and we'll straighten it out."

"Are you sure?"

Evelyn thought for a minute then said, "No. I'm not sure at all." She took in a deep breath and released it slowly, composing herself. If she let her emotions out, she knew they'd bury her in an avalanche.

"I'm sorry. It's all my fault."

"No, actually it's not. I mean, he'd be all pissy if it was just that I was going to wait to see him, but we'd make up and he'd get over it. I'm fairly sure he knows about what I did."

Caroline nodded. "It's a pretty big thing."

"I know. Believe me, I know."

"Maybe you should tell him how you feel."

"That's easier said than done. I don't even know how I feel lately. My head is all over the place. Anyway, he won't even take my calls. I've left him like a hundred messages. It's complicated."

"I don't know," Caroline said with a shrug. "Where is your heart? You love him and want to be with him?"

"With everything I am."

"Does he love you and want to be with you?"

"He did. I hope he still does."

"Then go to him and convince him of that. Tell him."

"What am I going to say? That cheating on him was the stupidest thing I've ever done; some convoluted surrender to nostalgia. That I'd give my right arm to make it never have happened?"

"That might be a good start," Caroline said softly.

Evelyn rubbed her forehead and sighed. She was beyond tired. Mentally and emotionally, she was exhausted. Physically, there wasn't an inch of her body that didn't ache. She was tired and worried down to her very soul and her heart was broken. She just wanted to crawl into her own bed and sleep until everything was okay again.

"You know, people act like I just made a flippant decision to not have a baby and move on with my life, but that couldn't be further from the truth. Afterwards, I cried myself to sleep for a week. Every time I saw a baby I would have to run to the bathroom and cry. I think it's something that I'll think about my whole life. Every time someone asks me if I have kids and I say no, I know it'll be a lie. When I do have kids, I'll wonder if this one would have been like them. Every September 27th will be an unrealized birthday. Every Mother's Day, I'll feel guilty."

"Evie," she began, watching her friend wipe tears from her face. "That is your cross to bear. Nobody will ever be able to take it from you. It's happened. You can't undo any of it."

"Thanks," Evelyn said sarcastically.

"I'm not good at this stuff. Give me a break." Caroline thumbed a tear from her own cheek and continued, "If you had a set of those fancy dishes"

"China?" Evelyn interrupted.

"Okay, whatever. If you had a set of China and broke one piece, would you throw it all out? No. You'd keep using it, but you'd remember that one piece is missing. You could still eat off them, have a lot of good meals off them, just with one piece missing."

Evelyn shrugged. "I guess so," she finally agreed. "One word of advice though, don't take a job writing greeting cards. I don't think it'll work out," she added with a laugh.

"Whatever. You know what I mean. I told you I wasn't good at that stuff."

"I'm playing. Thank you. It makes a lot of sense. I'm just sad. I feel like I disappointed everyone; that I've hurt everyone I love with one stupid mistake and I thought that without the constant reminder of a baby everyone would forgive me and we all could just pretend it never happened."

"You're a good person, Evie. You're a beautiful, smart, wonderful woman. Don't ever forget that."

Evelyn smiled as she slowed the car. "Thank you. You ain't going to kiss me again, are you?"

Caroline laughed sarcastically. "Probably not."

"Here we are. You ready for this?" Evelyn asked as she pulled off the road and stopped by the gate.

"I think I am," Caroline answered, leaning forward as she eyed the gate.

"Okay, get out and push the button," Evelyn said.

"I can't do that. I wouldn't know what to say," Caroline told her nervously. "I've never talked on one of those things."

"Really? I gotta do it again?" Evelyn opened the door and walked around the car. "Hello, it's Evelyn Jackson with Caroline LeBeau." In her mind, she heard a child-like voice add, "and she's my best friend," and smiled. Looking back at the car, she gave Caroline a thumbs up.

"We will be right there. Park by the gate please," instructed the voice over the intercom as the gate began to open.

Evelyn pulled into the small lot and popped the trunk. "It'll be a minute. It's about a five-mile ride on a golf cart."

"Great," Caroline said. "That'll give us a chance to say our goodbyes."

"What? No. I was going to spend the night," Evelyn replied, her eyes welling with tears.

"You was, now you're not. Go find that fella that makes you happy and you win him back, no matter what it takes."

"I can do that, but I don't want to just leave you."

Caroline took Evelyn's arms in her hands and squeezed. "Evie, what you have done for me is better than any living soul on the world ever did for me." Tears began to roll down her cheek. "You saw the worst of me and didn't leave. Just being my friend has made so much difference in my life."

"I wasn't prepared for this," Evelyn said, crying.

"You are my best friend," Caroline told her, "Mostly because you're my only friend so it's no big prize, but you have been my best friend all my life, whether you knew it or not." The two shared a tearful laugh and embraced.

"You deserve to be better, Caroline. You are stronger than you give yourself credit for, remember that. You need to learn to value yourself because you're an amazing person."

"The strength and courage you showed me means more than I can even describe, not to mention a little scary. Does that guy of yours know how you swing a bat?"

"I told you, I don't like it when people mess with my friends." Evelyn looked at Caroline and smiled. "I need to thank you too. You've taught me a lot."

"That sounds like a lie, but I'll take it. Evie, you showed me what strong looks like, what beauty looks like, what courage looks like, what love looks like, and I can never thank you enough."

"There they come," Evelyn said as the golf cart climbed the gentle hill and stopped behind them. "Are you sure you'll be okay?"

"After everything we've gone through lately, do you have to ask?"

"True, but I could stay one night."

"Ladies," the short brunette got out of the cart and joined them. "I hate goodbyes," she said, fanning her eyes with her fingers. "I'm Joan."

"Evelyn, we've met," she said, shaking hands.

"Caroline LeBeau." She extended her hand to the woman.

Bypassing the hand, Joan wrapped Caroline in a full embrace and squeezed her tightly. "I don't do handshakes. Welcome to the rest of your life. You're safe now,"

Caroline looked over the woman's shoulder and mouthed, "Help me," with a wide grin.

Releasing Caroline, Joan looked at the trunk. "Let's start getting you settled in. Miss Jackson, you'll be staying with us for the night, right?"

"Actually, no," Caroline said. "I've decided to try it alone."

"You'll do fine, sweetie. You'll love it here. There's so many women who will love you that it won't be long before you learn to love yourself as much as we do."

After unpacking the trunk and loading the gold cart, Joan went to secure the luggage, giving the two women a moment of privacy.

"You know I'll come visit," Evelyn told her. "This isn't goodbye."

"I hope not," Caroline said as she hugged her friend. "I love you, Evie."

"I love you too, Caroline. You go and get better."

"You go and get that man back," Caroline told her.

Locked in the embrace, Evelyn whispered in Caroline's ear, "No kissing on the lips."

"Only you," Caroline said as they shared a laugh.

Releasing from the hug, Caroline smiled and touched Evelyn's face gently. "Go get him," she said. "You deserve to be happy too. Mistakes don't make us weaker; they make us stronger."

Evelyn looked at her friend, impressed. "That's very profound. Thank you."

"It was in the booklet," Caroline admitted with a shrug, offering a sad smile.

"Well, it's true." Evelyn smiled.

"Okay, you have things to do and you'd probably stand here all day if I didn't just walk away," Caroline told her as she slowly backed away. "I'm fine, mom," she added with a smile.

"I'll see you in a couple weeks. Be safe."

"Go." Caroline waved her away. "I'm good." She mounted the golf cart and waved to her friend.

Evelyn watched them turn around and waved to her friend before getting into her car. She pulled through the open gate and stopped, watching in the rear-view mirror as the golf cart disappeared over the hill. She watched until the gate closed, then grabbed the fresh box of tissue as the avalanche she'd been holding back finally broke through and swept over her weary mind and body.

FIFTEEN

"Everything happens for a reason," Evelyn told herself as she entered her parent's neighborhood. Taking her time driving back from dropping Caroline off, she'd run the gamut of emotions. Now, sure that her friend was safe, she'd turned her full attention to her own problems, realizing she'd been delaying the inevitable. She'd have to tell Aaron about everything. She couldn't spend the rest of her life with this secret. It would destroy them both eventually.

She'd also forced herself to face some cold hard facts: She both regretted doing what she had done about the baby, and she didn't at the same time. It was part of the complexity of the decision. It was something she'd have to wrestle with for a very long time, maybe the rest of her life.

She had made a mistake in sleeping with Trae. That was undeniable. It was a mistake she would always know that she'd made it. Innocent lives were affected. It wasn't just about her. She'd hurt the people she loved, but she loved the people she'd hurt and would do her best to make sure they knew that. On the days when they didn't think about what she'd done, she would. She would take the mantle of her father and bear the weight of what she did and try to use it to remember what she could have lost and be grateful for the forgiveness of others.

She loved Aaron Devours with all her heart. She always would. If he wanted to be with her, she would make it a point to show him how much she loved him every day. If he didn't, she would love him in her heart and let him go without causing him further pain. He deserved that much.

Turning onto her street, the weight of the world settled on her. A heaviness hung on her like a blanket. As a ship tossed about on the ocean, she'd come a long way and had a long way to go yet before she could rest.

Drawing near her parents' house, her heart leapt into his throat as she saw a familiar truck sitting in the driveway. Turning in, she threw the car in gear and jumped out. Running around the car and stopped suddenly, absorbing the sight of Aaron and her father sitting on the porch, staring back at her.

Her mind groped for an explanation but was too confused to find one. The sight of the man she loved filled her heart with equal parts love and dread, leaving her frozen with indecision. Why was he here? Had he come to out her to her parents? Was he so angry that he wanted to hurt her by revealing her secret? Did he want to break up with her? Did he want to tell her not to bother coming back to his apartment, that he didn't love her anymore?

Standing, Aaron walked down the front steps of her childhood home, his hands in the pockets of his tan cargo shorts. He looked at her, his eyes searching hers for the answer to some unasked questions, then he started towards her, his arms spread wide.

Snapped from her paralysis, Evelyn ran to him and jumped into his strong arms as her tears began to flow. He wrapped her in a strong embrace and lifted her from the ground, spinning her a half turn as his lips met hers.

"I love you," he whispered into her ear.

"I love you so much," she told him. "So, so much!"

"I can't live without you, Eve. I'm sorry."

"I'm sorry," she told him, holding him tightly to her as he put her down. "I can't live without you either." She kissed him all over his face. "I never want to be away from you again."

"Me either," he agreed, giving her another tight squeeze before taking her shoulders and separating himself from her.

Evelyn wiped tears from her face as she spared a glance to her parents, standing on the porch, watching the scene with uncertain smiles.

"We don't ever have to be apart," Aaron said, taking her face in his hands. "You are the most beautiful woman I've ever seen, and my heart would die without you in it. I know that now. I've been here for a while. I guess I just missed you." His thumb gently wiped a tear from her cheek. "And we've been talking."

Evelyn looked at her father questioningly, confused. Had he told Aaron about Trae? Had he betrayed her? What could they possibly have to talk about if not her?

"He told me what a strong-willed, head-strong woman you could be, but I already knew that. That's part of what I love about you."

Evelyn looked at Aaron, sniffling as she fought back tears. "I guess we need to talk." She swallowed hard, never taking her eyes off the man she loved.

"Eve," Aaron began. As he stared into her eyes a tear welled in his eye and rolled across the stubble on his cheek. "There's nothing left to talk about."

"Baby," Evelyn said pleadingly as her tears began to flow again. "I'm so sorry."

"Don't," Aaron began, wiping the tear from his cheek with the back of his hand. "I just have to ask you something, and I want an honest answer."

Evelyn's hand covered her mouth in an effort to contain her sorrow. Nodding to let him know that she'd answer any question he asked, no matter how much it hurt. He deserved that much.

"Eve," he began, taking her hand as he knelt before her. "Will you marry me?" He produced a ring from the pocket of his shorts and held it out to her.

Evelyn stared at him, dumbfounded. She felt herself falling slowly as blackness closed around the edges of her vision. A sense of nothingness closed in around her as the world went black.

The sense of falling stopped suddenly, and two strong arms lifted her back to reality. From a distant place she could hear someone calling her name. "Eve. Eve."

She opened her eyes and saw Aaron's smiling face peering down at her. "Are you okay?" he asked.

"Yeah, yes," she said, shaking off the fig.

"Is that a yes you're all right, or a yes to my question?" he asked with a smile.

"It's the biggest yes in the world," she told him and pressed her lips to his. "Yes, yes, yes! Oh my God, baby. It's a thousand yeses!"

"I love you, Eve. I've loved you since the first time I saw you and I'll love you till the day I die." Pulling back so that he could see her face, Aaron held the ring up. "There's a little detail you may want to take care of."

Evelyn took the ring and looked at it. Sparkling in the sunlight, it represented the best outcome that she could have ever hoped for; an outcome she hadn't dared to dream of.

"Before I put this on," she told him. "We have to talk, baby. I've got to tell you something." She wiped her eyes and nose on the sleeve of her shirt and looked at him.

Aaron shook his head. "There's nothing we need to talk about, Eve. There's no secrets to tell."

"What?" she asked, sniffling as she wiped her nose again.

"Baby, I know."

Evelyn's heart sank and her eyes fell to the ground at her feet. Shame shrouded her face as she looked back up at him. "I'm so sorry."

"I know you are, baby. So am I. We'll get past this, I promise. All I know is that I love you and I want to be with you. That never changed when Kevin told me. It hurt, it really did, but I never stopped loving you. It hurt because I thought you didn't love me anymore."

"Oh my God," she said, her tears flowing openly again. "I was just stupid, and I messed up, but it wasn't because I didn't love you, baby. I'm going to love you for the rest of my life and the rest of yours if you'll let me."

Aaron cleared his throat and put his hand over hers, lifting the ring in front of her face. "I think that's what I'm trying to do here."

Evelyn slid the ring on her finger and threw her arms around his neck. "Yes."

Thanksgiving Day

"Here you go, sweetie." Evelyn handed Aaron a glass of sweet tea as he sat on the couch, watching the parade with her father.

"Thanks, babe," he said, accepting the glass. Grabbing her hand as she turned to leave, he pulled her closer and planted a kiss on her cheek. "Love you," he whispered.

Smiling, she kissed him on the lips. "Love you too."

"Okay, y'all ain't gotta do all that. I'm sitting right here," her father told them with a grimace.

"Oh, let us alone, Daddy. We're young and in love. Surely you remember what it was like," Evelyn told him with a laugh.

"I'm trying not to," he replied, his eyebrows raised. "And I don't get no drink?"

"You've got coffee." Evelyn gave Aaron's neck a quick caress and headed back into the kitchen.

"What can I do?" she asked, joining her mother at the sink.

"You can peel these potatoes," Martha told her, offering the peeler.

"Anything else?" Evelyn asked. "I hate peeling potatoes."

"You think I live for it, but they ain't gonna peel themselves," Martha told her as the doorbell rang.

"Saved by the bell," Evelyn laughed. "I'll get it." Evelyn rushed to the door, knowing who was there.

"Hey, girl!" she exclaimed, opening the door to Caroline. "You look great!" she told her as they embraced.

Caroline did look great. The wounds on her face had healed better than expected, leaving only a few very small, pink scars, which she hid with a light coat of base. Her hair was healthy and vibrant, and her eyes were bright and happy. The retreat was definitely good for her. Dressed in black leggings and a light sweater, she looked well put together.

"It's so good to see you again," Caroline told her friend. "You look good. Happy even."

"You better believe it," Evelyn laughed, drumming her fingers on her chest to bring attention to the ring. She'd visited Caroline twice at the woman's retreat and told her all about the upcoming wedding, but she was so proud that she liked to remind people.

"So good to know. I'm so happy for you." She paused for a moment, looking at Evelyn. "I've missed you."

"I've missed you too," Evelyn said, taking her hand. "You've gotta get a phone so we can text every day!"

"Well." Caroline shrugged. Phones cost money and she had none.

"Glad you could come," Martha told her, wiping her hands on her apron as she joined them at the door. She gave Caroline a one-armed hug. "Bring the girl in the house and close the door for goodness sake."

Freddy gave her a wave from his perch on the couch, obeying Eve's warnings about he and Aaron being too "in your face". Whatever that meant. It was Caroline's first adventure out by herself and she was being extra cautious.

"You must be Aaron," Caroline asked as he stood and joined them.

"Aaron? What? My name is James." He asked then turned to Eve. "Who is this Aaron guy?"

"Stop it," she told him as her arm snaked around his waist, giving him a slight pinch on the side as her other hand slapped him playfully on the chest. "He's just being a goofball."

"Guilty as charged," Aaron relented. "Nice to meet you. I've heard a lot about you."

"Me too. I mean, I've heard a lot about you," Caroline said with a nervous laugh. She looked at his hand then decided to give him a quick hug. "Anyone that can steal this girl's heart must be something special."

"He is," Evelyn agreed, taking his hand. "He's the best."

"Well, come on in." Martha ushered them into the kitchen. "You go and tell Freddy some jokes, funny man," she told Aaron as she shooed him toward her husband.

"What?" Aaron asked, slumping back toward the couch.

Evelyn patted him on the back gently. "It's okay. Just hang out with dad." She planted a kiss on his cheek and hurried into the kitchen.

"Really, mom?" she asked. She joined Caroline at the sink where she was already peeling potatoes. "She's here, literally two minutes, and you got her peeling potatoes?"

"She asked," Martha replied with a shrug. "And you won't do it. I'm busy."

"It's fine. Really. I'm glad to help." Caroline nudged Evelyn with her shoulder and smiled.

"Okay, I'm good with that," Evelyn laughed. There was a festive air in the kitchen that Evelyn reminded her of her youth. Warmed by the oven, the air filled with the rich aromas of her mother's cooking, and the fact that everyone she really cared about was around her made the scene perfect.

Standing with her back to the counter next to Caroline while she peeled potatoes in the sink, Evelyn nudged her friend back with her shoulder and smiled. "You ever think you'd be in a black woman's kitchen preparing Thanksgiving dinner?"

"I do have to admit that I didn't, but then again I don't think I even really knew what Thanksgiving was."

"You poor child. I don't know how you do it," Martha said, shaking her head as she checked the pot of turnip greens cooking on the stove. "I guess this'll be your first real Thanksgiving meal."

"I guess so," Caroline said with a shrug as she went back to her task.

"Well, pilgrim, you're in for a treat," Evelyn said, using a very poor John Wayne voice.

"That was just terrible," Martha told her flatly, pronouncing it "Turrable". "You better not quit your day job."

"What? It wasn't that bad." Evelyn looked to Caroline for help, but she shook her head and shrugged. Growing up isolated the way she did, it was a common occurrence to not know what people were talking about when they referenced music, movies, or other current happenings. She was taking a class to catch up but had a long way to go.

"I don't even know what y'all are talking about," she said. "Sorry."

"It wouldn't matter if you did, sweetie. It was so bad you wouldn't have recognized it anyway." Martha laughed and shook her head. She crossed the room and checked the potatoes. "That'll be plenty, sweetie."

Wiping her hands on a dish cloth Caroline motioned for Evelyn to go outside with her.

"Lord, it's hot in this kitchen," Evelyn lied, fanning herself with her hand. "Mama, we're going on the deck for a minute. Do you need us?"

"I been cooking this meal for twenty-five years now. I think I can muddle through for a few minutes." Martha looked at the two girls and smiled. She knew they wanted to talk in private and that was fine by her. She'd visited the retreat several times and had spent her time with Caroline and some of the other girls, but Evelyn was busy with school again and with her fella. They didn't get as much time as they both probably needed.

"Everything okay?" Evelyn asked as she closed the door behind her.

"It's good," Caroline said. "Just a lot happening at once."

Motioning for Caroline to join her, Evelyn sat on a sunny bench. There was a crispness in the air that signaled the end of a long, hot summer.

"How are things at the retreat?" she asked casually, closing her eyes as she stretched her face to the sunshine.

"Good." Caroline sat beside her friend. "Really good. They suggested a couple medicines. I've been on them a few months now. It really helps."

"That's good," Evelyn said, her eyes closed to the bright noon sun. "Have you made friends yet?"

"A couple, I guess, but everybody is pretty relaxed about that. Women come and go, you know."

"I guess so. I'm glad you like it." Evelyn shielded her eyes and looked at Caroline. "How long do you think you'll stay?"

Caroline shrugged. "A long time probably. I got nowhere else to go. We haven't really discussed that."

"As long as you're happy." Evelyn closed her eyes again, resuming her sunbathing. "Any problems?"

"A few minor incidents."

Evelyn sat forward and looked at Caroline. "Incidents?"

"Nothing major. Things are calm there. I've had some issues now and again, but we've worked through them." Caroline picked up a leaf from the porch and began shredding it with her fingernails. "Sometimes the voices break through."

Evelyn rubbed her back. "That's to be expected. Stress can cause all sorts of problems. It'll work out. Give it time."

"I am. It's so much better. Sometimes I just miss the old place. My babies and all."

"I know you do. Anyone would. Have you been back?"

Caroline shook her head and dropped what was left of the leaf. "It's just hard sometimes when you feel like people expect things from you."

Evelyn smiled. "I could write a book about that, sister. But you do what you can, and the rest will sort itself out. No more kissing?" she asked with a laugh.

"Didn't you get the memo?" Caroline asked.

"What memo?" Evelyn asked, her brow furrowed with confusion.

"I think I got it right here," Caroline dug in the pocket of her leggings, brought her hand forth and held her hand in front of her, as if to read a note in the palm of her hand. "It's was an emotional outpouring, not an unwanted sexual advance. P.S. It's been six months, let it go."

Both women burst out laughing at the joke as Caroline sat back down.

"You got me, you got me good," Evelyn admitted, putting an arm around Caroline's shoulder.

"There's a girl, Madison, who does that stuff all the time. She's pretty funny when you get to know her. She's in my cabin."

"Sounds like someone I'd like." Evelyn gave her friend a quick hug and released her. "It does my heart good to see you like this; happy and healthy. You're practically glowing."

Caroline smiled. "You're the one glowing. How have you two loving birds been?"

"Love birds," Evelyn corrected. "And it's been amazing," Evelyn said with a happy sigh. "We talked about everything that happened once. It broke his heart, I know it did, but he never held it against me, you know. He never brought it up again, but I've been doing everything that I can to make it up to him."

"Penance?"

Evelyn looked at her friend, one eyebrow arched questioningly.

"There's a preacher who comes every Sunday. A woman preacher. We've talked a few times."

Evelyn shrugged. "Maybe it is some kinds penance, but it doesn't feel like it. I've talked to a counselor a few times myself. But things are good. We're planning the wedding and our future. We're young and in love and doing it all the time. Between that and school we stay pretty busy."

"Sounds like a full plate," Caroline told her. She took in a deep breath and let it out slowly as she looked toward the house. "Did his parents get over not liking you?

"I don't know. It wasn't as much as them not liking me as not wanting Aaron to propose. He said he'd been thinking about it a while.

304